PRAISE FOR
MOTIVE FOR MURDER

"*Motive for Murder* will draw you into the exciting chase for a serial killer. Political and international intrigue are woven together to form a tapestry of deception. The nonstop action is an adrenaline roller coaster that will keep you guessing."

—Les Lo Baugh, Author of *Synergy*

Motive for Murder
by Ray Collins

© Copyright 2023 Ray Collins

ISBN 979-8-88824-165-3

Published by

 köehlerbooks™

3705 Shore Drive
Virginia Beach, VA 23455
800-435-4811
www.koehlerbooks.com

MOTIVE FOR MURDER

RAY COLLINS

VIRGINIA BEACH
CAPE CHARLES

To my wife, Betty Ann, and our children,
Jim, Ann, Nori, and Susan.

CHAPTER 1

Her diary was missing. Deborah Chu stared at the empty bottom drawer of her bedside table. At first, she considered the possibility she might have mislaid the journal, but then she realized the lock on the drawer had been forced. There was no doubt the diary had been stolen.

Her unfailing routine—even when arriving home near midnight, tired from teaching an economics seminar at Georgetown University—was to climb into bed, pick up a Mont Blanc fountain pen, and watch blue ink flow onto the page. She would inscribe each entry, then secure the diary in the drawer.

The diary recorded her innermost feelings and a brief synopsis of the day's events. But what terrified her was the fact that the diary documented her most shameful act.

Deborah's thoughts focused on the faceless tormentor who'd made her life miserable for the past week. Objects were missing from the condo. The diary was the latest to disappear. The thought of anyone plundering her private memories and secrets was more upsetting than having her home sanctuary violated.

The following day she had new locks installed on her condo door.

Confirmation the thief wasn't finished came the next day. She discovered an eye-catching Michael Kors red stretch wool dress was gone from her bedroom closet. Friends always assured her the dress complemented her petite figure to perfection. It cost two thousand dollars and was her go-to ensemble for those all-too-rare special dates.

The thefts aside, the intrusions heightened fears a thief could so easily access her home. This burglary forced her to realize there was no point in changing the locks. She was unable to decide whether her nagging fears were overblown or if she should notify the Fairfax County police. In the end, the mistrust of law enforcement instilled by stories told by parents and grandparents caused her to hesitate.

Deborah knew if she wasn't safe here in the gated community at the Rotonda—in the heart of Tysons, Virginia, the pride of Fairfax County, one of the wealthiest communities in the United States—there was no place she would be.

Determined to overcome her fears, she thought about working out at the rec center. Impatient with that idea, she decided instead to head for the library and continue researching her book about China's economy. Returning for lunch after a largely unproductive work session, she gaped at her home computer. An ominous appointment, *Rendezvous on the River Styx*, was entered into Thursday evening's ten o'clock slot—just after her seminar would end. This latest was no prank. Was it a death threat?

She wandered aimlessly into the living room and collapsed in her favorite chair, holding her head in her hands. Tears trickled down her cheeks. She angrily brushed them away, struggling to face up to whatever these events foreshadowed.

Who would want to harm her or, worse yet, want her dead? Her romances were uneventful, except for a stupid affair with Congressman Blackwell, which was a thing of the past. She believed her life was ordinary, even praiseworthy. A habit of honest self-appraisal forced her to admit there was one screaming exception, but no one could possibly know about that.

But, she now realized, with the diary missing, the thief knows.

Deborah forced herself to review her notes for the evening seminar, but the crisis of the thief's intrusions kept invading her thoughts. Glancing at her watch, she rationalized it was too late to notify the police or do anything without risking being late for her seminar.

On her evening drive from the condo to the university, she

glimpsed the image of a white vehicle several cars to her rear. The halo around headlights in the traffic on Key Bridge made it impossible to be certain, but Deborah worried she was being shadowed.

Once in her classroom, she felt safe. This was her domain, and, despite her diminutive figure, she reigned supreme, regal in a dark gray Alexander McQueen pantsuit. She concentrated on presenting a meaningful seminar for her students.

At the close of the discussion period, she wrapped up the session. "Work on your term paper forecasting China's economic development over the next five years. Pay particular attention to the impact on US-China relations if growth continues to taper off. That's it for tonight. See you next week."

She packed up her seminar materials and laptop in her well-worn leather briefcase and headed out to the parking garage. The hairs on the back of her neck stood to attention as she scurried through the dark valleys between buildings, quiet in the aftermath of students escaping at the end of classes. Instinct made her worry someone was following her. She longed for a full moon to dispel her anxiety, but only a quarter moon peeking through a cloudy sky served to dimly illuminate her path.

Deborah walked by the football field and tennis courts, noting the contrast between the eerie quiet of the nighttime campus and the frenetic activity during the day and on weekends. Not recognizing anyone, she exchanged nods with a few students whose carefree laughter raised her spirits, however briefly.

The April air was damp and foggy, fragrant with the odor of spring mulch. She shivered from the chill and vowed to wear something warmer to next week's seminar.

She crept cautiously through the parking lot, closing the distance to the faculty garage. Imagining she heard footsteps, she jerked her head to the rear, but there was no one in sight.

Walking alone in the deserted garage always made her feel threatened. Tonight, the feeling was worse due to her lingering apprehension. She saw the ceiling lights were out at the far end where she'd parked her Benz, which added to the feeling of impending menace.

She remembered a recent course on women's self-defense and recited to herself the instructor's guidance: Keep to the center of the garage. Remain vigilant. Move with a purposeful stride.

Deborah added an old-fashioned metal key to the keyless entry electronic system when she learned from the demonstration how keys became a serious weapon if stabbed at an assailant's face. She removed the fob from her purse and clasped it with the condo key thrust out through her middle fingers like a knife blade.

She pulled the door handle to initiate the Smart Key system. She heard the Benz unlock with a welcome beep. She relaxed as she opened the door. Deborah had done this a hundred times. Why should tonight be any different?

When she was part way into her car, she felt something brush her hair as it circled her head. She choked from the pressure on her throat.

Desperate for air, she dropped key fob, purse, and briefcase.

Deborah regained consciousness, aware the attacker was dragging her to a white van. She was forced through the vehicle's rear double doors. When she fought to get free, her assailant slammed her head against the unyielding metal of the van's side. The attacker threw her onto the vehicle's floor, where she landed with an audible thud.

She could feel the plastic that covered the floor touching her bare thighs and knew her pants were being removed.

Her body convulsed as the lace thong ripped past her ankles.

The fear she experienced in her condo at the imagined threat was nothing compared to the trauma of the actual attack. She trembled violently.

"Don't rape me."

Deborah struggled to escape the predator's iron grasp.

"Who are you?"

A terrifying silence was the only response.

With a burst of strength, she made a desperate effort to flee. She flipped onto her stomach and crabbed toward the van's doors.

"HELP!" she screamed, but knew it was futile. There was no one to hear.

Fingers grabbed her hair and yanked her violently away from any possibility of breaking free. The attacker flipped her onto her back. Her eyes widened at the knife blade poised over her exposed neck.

She glimpsed her attacker's face and gasped, "But, you're . . ."

CHAPTER 2

Hana Brown stood in the exact center of the giant blue exercise mat, her preparations complete for her Thursday afternoon unarmed combat class. Having bowed before countless sensei in countless dojos, she knew the importance of projecting dominance, strength, and leadership. She'd dressed for it in a white quilted *judogi*. A black belt girdled her slim waist. Her bare feet were anchored to the mat.

She knew she looked the part, broad-shouldered and nearly six feet tall. A jagged scar above her left eyebrow added character to her face.

Turning to scan those standing around the perimeter of the mat, she sized up a class of police cadets—mostly men, but a scattering of women. Fourteen faces stared back in silent anticipation.

In the moments before the class began, she sought to gauge each trainee's strength and weakness. Did the nervous tension displayed by most participants betray inner fears, or did it portray the pre-event performance anxiety of the natural athlete? Her role was to reassure the one and unleash the pent-up energy of the other. Compensate for weakness, build on strength.

"My name is Hana Brown." No visible reaction. Those cadets who cared to know about their instructor would have already looked her up.

"What is unarmed combat?" She always started classes with this question. The blank looks the query elicited never failed to amaze her.

The assembled cadets, for whom the course was required training, hadn't given thought to a matter on which their lives could depend. The instructor knew they came expecting to see the acrobatics showcased in the movies and on TV. Some version of police kung fu.

A female cadet took a tentative step forward and coughed theatrically. Impishly cute and petite, she must have exceeded the department's height requirements by barely a half inch.

Hana's look invited a response.

"Unarmed combat is how we defend ourselves if we're attacked," the cadet said.

"Half-right. Focusing on defense is a risky strategy. Besides, how are we going to arrest the bad guys if we don't go on offense?"

A hulk stepped forward, attracting the instructor's full attention. He was a few years older than the other cadets. Blond, with a military-type buzz cut, his craggy face was guaranteed to intimidate the bad guys. Six-four, 240 pounds. A mountain of a man whose athletic shorts and sweatshirt with the sleeves cut off at the shoulders left little doubt his bulk was all muscle.

His authoritative voice resonated in the large gym. "Unarmed combat is how we beat up on the bad guys before we arrest them. It's self-defense with an attitude—'us or them.'"

"Close enough for government work. What's your name? And where are you from?"

"I'm Rambo." The challenge in his voice was unmistakable. "I moved here from Philadelphia where I was a police officer."

Hana wondered what Rambo did to fuck up so bad he'd been required to take classes at the Academy to join the Fairfax County Police Department.

Her custom was to select from each class the toughest looking, biggest man as an opponent to dramatize how anyone, even a woman who weighed 140 pounds soaking wet, could win in unarmed combat using the proper technique.

"Where'd you get a name like Rambo? The fictional Rambo was defiantly anti-cop."

"They call me Rambo 'cause I'm the baddest mother around. If Hana Brown is a good name for a cop, Rambo can't be too weird." The hulk smirked at his riposte.

"You've got a point there, Rambo. Suppose we show the class how it's done."

"How do you want to play it?"

"For starters, you attack me."

The hulk charged without warning. Incredibly quick. One instant he was standing still. The next he was on her. His fists hammered like pistons.

He anticipated her defensive maneuver and struck where she was moving rather than where she'd been. His ruthlessness caught her off guard.

Two blows landed—one on her stomach, the other on her left shoulder. He hit like a pile driver. Without her superb conditioning, the contest would have been over in an instant. Her gut pained. She gasped for air.

She evaded the brunt of the shoulder strike, but her left side was partially paralyzed. She spun away to give herself a few seconds to recover, knowing the former cop was not only big, strong, and fast, but cunning as well.

Aware Rambo would pursue his advantage, Hana drew on her years in the dojo facing world-class judo opponents in Japan and in tryouts for the US Olympic Team. Rather than continue to retreat, she spun back and executed a leg sweep. He fell for the trap. Her right leg caught the hulk behind his legs like a scythe as he pressed to finish her off.

Rambo flew into the air and crashed down on the back of his neck. A lesser man would have been knocked out from the force of the fall. Not the hulk. He vaulted to his feet and shook himself like a wet dog coming out of the lake.

He hesitated, circling the mat and eyeing her warily. He'd underestimated Hana, just as she'd earlier misjudged him.

11

The momentary pause was all it took for her to formulate a strategy.

She assessed Rambo as a boxer who knew the basics of judo and karate, but who was no expert. She determined to show him and the class what it meant to be ruthless.

Hana waited for the anticipated charge and let the overeager boxer get close enough to land another frontal blow. The blow's force was weakened as she fell away from him. Executing a backward somersault, she grasped the hulk's sweatshirt and pulled him forward over the top of her prone body. She kicked him sharply in the stomach, using his momentum to catapult him into the air like a circus performer. Two hundred forty pounds hit the mat with an audible thump.

Rambo started to repeat the maneuver of leaping to his feet, but he was stunned by crushing strikes to his neck and kidney. When he pivoted to protect his back, she smashed him in the solar plexus. The blows left the cocky challenger gasping for breath and unable to push himself up from the blue mat.

The victor stood erect, hiding her pain. Hana eyed her opponent carefully to make sure he was beginning to recover. More than a year had passed since she'd faced a student as determined as he was to be a badass. With a resigned sigh, she turned to the class.

"What you've witnessed, ladies and gentlemen, is unarmed combat with an attitude. Who's ready to learn how it's done?"

CHAPTER 3

Hana and her dad walked under the bright red and gold Chinatown Friendship Archway and entered the five-block neighborhood that comprised the heart of the District of Columbia's Chinese district.

They crossed the virtually deserted street, headed toward the Three Dragons Restaurant. The twilight sky shaded from azure blue to steel gray as an oppressive summer smog crept across the dingy buildings.

A black Expedition, lights turned off, appeared out of the haze, and sped toward them. The driver slammed on his brakes and spun the SUV so the right side faced them on the sidewalk. The windows were down. Automatic weapons poked out. Shots exploded.

Hana screamed "GUN!"

Her dad jumped in front of Hana, pushing her away from the line of fire. He was already turning as he reached for the .38 Smith and Wesson in the holster at the small of his back. A volley caught him in the head and chest. Spinning, he pitched into the gutter and landed face down. Red flowers bloomed on his back.

Hana's world geared down to slow motion. The sensation of swimming in quicksand came with sensory overload. Her arms stretched futilely toward her dad. Projectiles punctured her left arm and side. Adrenaline brought immunity to pain from the graze that creased her forehead. Blood blinded her left eye. Falling to her knees, she inched toward the .38 snub nose revolver that had slipped from her dad's lifeless fingers.

When she grasped the revolver, it turned into a tiny red dragon and bit her hand. Tears cascaded down an anguished face. She shrieked, but no sound came out. Repeated tries failed to shake off the red dragon. A gold dragon leaped from the sidewalk and sank its fangs into her chest. She flailed at the creature. A temple gong sounded. The dragons disappeared.

Hana writhed in the damp sheets. A hard chop with her hand knocked the clock radio to the floor. The ringing reverberated. But the haunting nightmare refused to dissipate. The finale of the dream was always the same. The temple gong brought an end to the scene of her dad's assassination, which had transformed her life as it ended his. Most often, the ringing was the wake-up alarm on the clock radio. Tonight, she continued to hear the ringing.

She sat up in bed and saw Othello, paws on the mattress, staring with a look that, on a human, would have passed for concern. Distracted, she scratched behind the Lab's ears.

The lethargy refused to go away.

At the last ring, Hana fumbled the phone to her ear. "Brown here."

The face of the clock radio recording the time stared up from the floor.

Hazy thoughts wondered why dispatch was calling past midnight. "What's up?"

"A gangbanger was killed in Bailey's Crossroads. McNab named you lead detective. He says for you to get to Culmore Park on the double."

Synapses fired, shocking Hana wide awake.

She couldn't believe it—her first homicide since making detective.

Captain Brian McNab had granted her unspoken wish to be assigned something more exciting than the routine tasks she'd been receiving from Lieutenant Walter Krause, her immediate supervisor in Major Crimes.

Dispatch echoed the few details called in by the officer on the scene. A Vietnamese female was reported dead of a knife wound. The victim was found in Culmore Park by a nurse walking her dog after the evening shift at Fairfax Hospital.

Hana, the reigning expert on Asian gangs in the Fairfax County Police Department, was assigned most cases in Bailey's Crossroads calling for a detective from Major Crimes. Washington still had Chinatown, but, since commercial development mushroomed from the Verizon Center sports complex, forcing up real estate prices, the Chinese community was being displaced by gentrification. Fairfax, starting with Bailey's Crossroads, had become the residence of choice for Chinese, Koreans, and other Asians. One out of five of the million-plus Fairfax residents was Asian.

The medicine of a quick hot shower with an ice-cold finish shocked her awake. Now fully alert, she strode out of the bathroom, rubbing her towel vigorously through ebony hair.

Sitting on the edge of the bed, Hana tugged on wide-leg pants. The pants were designed for practicality more than fashion. Grabbing her ankle holster from the bedside table she pulled it tight over her shin, adjusting the Velcro for a snug fit. She nestled Mike's snub nose revolver into the holster, fighting a flashback to the evening in Chinatown. Her SIG SAUER P226 9mm was holstered on the right side of her belt, facilitating a strong-side quick draw.

She bent down and gave the Lab a quick hug.

"This is the big time, Othello. What I've been waiting for since Chinatown. A chance to show what I can do to honor Dad's memory."

Anticipating the chilly April night ahead, she opened the hall closet and pulled on a blue wool blazer, aware of the need to look professional to impress the media, who was sure to swarm the crime scene.

She raced outside, headed for her Toyota Camry. Hana jerked

open the gray sedan's door.

She was stopped cold by a note on the driver's seat. Puzzled, she picked it up and read the message written in red ink.

Good luck! You'll need it.

Deciding her priority was to get to the crime scene, she tucked the note into her blazer pocket. The mystery of how an intruder had bypassed the Toyota's security system to leave the cryptic message baffled her but would have to wait.

She texted her next-door neighbor that she'd been called away on a homicide, asking him to look after Othello in the usual fashion starting in the morning.

CHAPTER 4

Hana made a quick drive-thru at the twenty-four-hour McDonald's on the outskirts of Vienna and picked up a to-go coffee. Taking a gulp—a burned tongue the price for impatience—she rested the large cup in the holder. The imperative to get to the crime scene put her system in overdrive faster than the caffeine.

Blue police lights winked behind the grill. She muted the siren out of deference to the midnight hour, veered right past Tysons, and sped east on Route 7. Crowded during rush hour, often bumper-to-bumper in a sleepy conga line, tonight, the detective was one of few motorists on the road.

She thought about the murder, and tried, but failed, to ignore signs of the diversity visited upon Fairfax County in her lifetime—Asian, Hispanic, and Muslim presence in the heartland of last-ditch resistance to desegregation that marked Virginia's legacy little more than a generation earlier. Heading toward Bailey's Crossroads, on her left, she glimpsed a mosque, cited in media speculation about sources of Muslim terrorism. She remembered dreary hours spent in front of the mosque on routine traffic duty while she was still a policewoman. A few weeks ago, she'd been pleasantly surprised at the friendly welcome beamed at her during an interfaith event there.

The mosque was located across from a century-old church, another reminder of the extent to which the cultural mixing bowl had been stirred in recent years. Vietnamese, Chinese, and Thai restaurants commingled with Hispanic and Middle Eastern boutiques. Signs on shops hinted at a mini-United Nations and signaled she was approaching Culmore Park at Bailey's Crossroads.

Arriving at the crime scene, she pulled in behind two police cruisers positioned to block off the park road. The crime scene investigators and the media had yet to appear.

This was her crime scene. She was the one responsible for the outcome of the case. A hot glow of satisfaction set her pulse racing.

Pacing back and forth, the nearest police officer guarding the scene was young and fair-haired with a medium build. When she glimpsed his profile's distinctive hooknose and jug ears, she recognized him from her unarmed combat classes at the Academy.

"Officer Yardley?"

"Hi, Detective Brown. Call me Pete. Dispatch said you caught the squeal. This is a bad one. Are you ready to see the victim?"

"I am, Pete. Who else is here?"

"Officer Manley," he said, gesturing toward an African American giant in his midthirties who somewhat resembled the former Redskins star defensive end of the same name.

Pete guided her in the direction of the victim and pointed to a woman sitting on a bench. "Over there is Stella Houston, a nurse from Fairfax Hospital. She found the body when she was walking her dog, Wolf."

Hana's eyes bugged at the biggest German Shepherd she'd ever seen lying on the ground by the nurse's feet. No wonder Stella would feel safe in the park at midnight with Wolf as a protector.

"What's the story with the victim? Dispatch said you described her as a Vietnamese gangbanger."

Pete looked embarrassed. "Yeah. That's what I told dispatch. It seemed like a no-brainer. We've been having these attacks involving gangs. In the past, the gangs were mostly Vietnamese. Lately, growing numbers of gang members are MS-13 or other Spiks . . ."

The officer blushed. It was as if a light bulb flashed over his head when it dawned on him a Japanese American might not appreciate ethnic slurs.

"I mean Hispanics. But she looks Vietnamese, well, Oriental anyway. And she was killed with a knife, their favorite MO."

"Asian," Hana said absently, as she continued walking toward the victim.

"Asian?" Pete echoed.

"Yes. The preferred term is Asian, not Oriental."

"Gotcha." He nodded, plainly not caring about political correctness, but eager to please.

"Apart from knowing a lot of violence in Bailey's Crossroads involves gangs, did you have any reason to think the victim was a gang member?"

"No."

The young cop's expression communicated he was aware he'd stepped in it by speculating beyond the evidence in his eagerness to report the homicide.

"Forget it, Pete. Any officer might have assumed the same thing." She didn't believe what she told the young cop but saw no harm in letting him off the hook.

CHAPTER 5

Hana followed Pete into the park's dense woods. He stopped and focused his Maglite on the petite body lying at the edge of the path.

"Stella said Wolf went crazy, probably from the smell, and practically dragged her over here. She freaked out when she spotted the corpse—a lot to stomach, even for a nurse. She called 911 from her cell. I was here within three minutes. It was all I could do to keep it together."

"Did Stella say anything else?"

"She thought she heard a car drive off just before finding the victim."

Catching a glimpse of the mutilated body, Hana froze, forcing herself to remain professional and refrain from touching the victim. She thumbed on her tactical light to enhance the view Pete's Maglite provided.

The Asian woman was lying face up. Nude. Maybe five-three, 110 pounds. Possibly midthirties, although she could have been anything from twenty-five to forty. Hana identified red spots in the eyes as petechiae, telltale signs of burst blood vessels due to strangulation. Throat cut ear to ear. Both breasts slashed in the form of a cross. Hana was unable to see the genital area clearly because of the strange way the legs were positioned.

Viewing the victim made her understand why Stella and Pete freaked out. Hana was conscious of the need to go by the book in order not to lose it.

After examining the horrific sight nearly a minute, she turned to Pete.

"Wait here. Don't move. Not one step. I'll be right back."

Hana hustled over to the cop guarding the scene.

"Officer Manley, I'm Detective Brown. Call in additional officers to help secure the scene. Tell them to tape fifty feet on all sides of the stand of trees surrounding the body. No one is to go inside that perimeter except CSI and the ME Absolutely no one. Especially the media. And no other cops."

Hana worried what Manley would do if the chief of police showed up. She conjured up a vision of Chief Erin Mahoney, nicknamed "Fire Engine Red Mahoney," calling to mind both her flaming shock of scarlet hair and tendency to appear at all major fires and crime scenes covered by the media.

Manley, big, solid, dependable—clearly a veteran of many grisly crime scenes—was not the type to rattle easily. But, he blinked in amazement and started to open his mouth, quickly clamping it shut.

She caught the reaction. "What's on your mind, officer?"

"Detective Brown, not my job to comment."

"Look Manley, level with me. Call me Hana."

"Call me George. Okay. If you want my opinion."

"Let's have it straight, George."

George gestured to encompass the perimeter Hana had identified.

"Hana, you could be in deep shit if you keep this up. Your first homicide, right?"

She nodded.

"Everyone'll think you've overreacted to a gangbanger getting killed. It's not routine in Fairfax County. But it's not the Saturday Night Massacre either."

"If it were a gang killing of a Vietnamese female, you'd be right. But let me tell you what I saw in the few seconds I viewed the body."

Hana took a deep breath and paused to collect her thoughts, before describing what she'd witnessed.

"The victim is female, although her condition might make the ME look twice. A cross was carved on each breast. Probably strangled, but her throat was cut, which may have been the cause of death. My bet is she's upper-class Chinese, not Vietnamese, and certainly not a gang member."

"Not a gang killing? What about Yardley's report?"

"Pete's a newbie. He jumped to conclusions. Cut him a little slack. Now make that call for more officers." She turned and headed back into the woods, feeling guilty for not telling Manley how to handle Mahoney if she showed up. She shrugged and decided to focus on the things she could control.

The detective crouched by the victim, attempting to take in every detail. Her hands were shrouded in surgical gloves, even though she had no intention of touching the deceased. She mentally reviewed her earlier impressions and validated them.

She wanted to turn the corpse over in the worst way, but resisted the impulse, knowing the ME must be first to examine the victim. The face was attractive, with a fine bone structure, and remarkably peaceful, except for clouded, haunted eyes. She took in the stylish hairdo and well-manicured fingers. The pear-shaped diamond on a platinum chain around the victim's neck looked like the real McCoy.

The victim's right arm was tucked coquettishly behind her neck. The right leg, bent at a slight angle, almost, but not quite, obscured the genital area.

The body seemed posed for a painting. Paintings—*The Blue Nude* and *The Pink Nude* by Henri Matisse—came to mind. The two paintings morphed together while she struggled unsuccessfully to bring her recollection of them into focus. She supposed she'd seen the paintings either in the many art books that cluttered her childhood home or during a museum visit with her mom in the days before Chinatown when they did things together.

Blue and pink nude females morphed into a gauzy faded purple and darkened as the wounds appeared on breasts and loins.

Her tactical light scanned the crime scene, revealing surprisingly little blood and no obvious signs of blood spatter in the surrounding grassy area.

She concluded it was a mystifying crime scene and decided that was what the killer wanted her to think. The realization she was being manipulated triggered thoughts of the mysterious note left in her Camry.

CHAPTER 6

S iren wailing and light-bar flashing on her Ford Police Interceptor, Erin Mahoney sped into Culmore Park. As she arrived at the crime scene, she skidded to a fast stop, inches from the rear bumper of the CSI van.

Agile despite her impressive size, Mahoney leaped out of her vehicle, fully decked out in the uniform signaling her rank as chief of police. She strode toward the yellow *CRIME SCENE—DO NOT CROSS* police tape. The herd of reporters surging forward to demand a statement were hardly worthy of a sideways glance.

Shouted questions assailed her like hail in a thunderstorm. She ignored the media. They'd expect her to check out the crime scene before meeting with them, however much they competed for an early comment.

Officer Rickey Watson, scrambling to keep up, followed on the chief's heels. Although he was Mahoney's assigned driver, he rarely got to man the wheel, and was never given the opportunity to drive her to a crime scene or fire.

Mahoney approached the yellow tape with the intent to pull it aside. A formidable-looking officer stepped forward from the human fence of police manning the barricade. His bulk loomed in front of the chief. She eyed his name badge: George Manley.

"Pardon me, Chief." George hesitated and cleared his throat. "Detective Brown told me to keep everyone outside the crime perimeter except for CSI and the ME"

Mahoney halted. Mouth agape, her face turned white with

astonishment at being spoken to in such a way by a street cop. She could feel her cheeks start to burn as her complexion morphed from white to mottled pink to a vivid scarlet. "I beg your pardon!"

The burly cop backed up. "That's what Detective Brown said."

"I'm the goddamn chief of police. I don't need some rookie detective's permission to do anything. Now, get the hell out of my way, or you'll be walking a beat with the ducks in Occoquan."

With that, she charged forward, determined to barrel through the two hundred pound obstacle blocking her path.

George moved aside and graciously lifted the yellow tape to ease the big woman's passage.

Partially mollified by George's gallantry, Mahoney nodded curtly and strode up the path in the direction of the CSI lights.

By the time she reached the head of the path, Mahoney had calmed down and appraised the situation. The chief recalled Hana had been shot beside her dad Mike Brown when he was assassinated in the Chinatown drive-by six years earlier. Moreover, Hana had been responsible for the rescue of Lizzie Jackson. The kidnapping of Hazel Jackson's daughter was a high profile media event during ex-Chief Field's tenure, shortly before she had taken over.

Mahoney's scarlet locks cloaked a brain as calculating as a Las Vegas bookmaker's. The odds were easy to figure.

On one side, little was at stake for the media in the murder of an unknown Asian gangbanger—inside coverage in the Metro section of the *Washington Post*. On the other, assigning a young Japanese American detective to the case would make the department look good, visible testimony to the cultural sensitivity so prized by the *Post*. Hana was a strikingly photogenic female, the offspring of Fairfax's hero cop and a professor at a local university. In addition to being wounded when her dad had been killed, Hana was famous for rescuing the Fairfax County Board chairwoman's daughter. Her profile could lead to a bigger headline, on the front page of Metro, maybe even page one of the goddamn *Post*.

The chief had decided to back Hana and dramatize support to the assembled news hounds. A strategy certain to enhance the department's image and her own. She rationalized, with any luck, Hana might even solve the murder.

Glancing up from her scrutiny of CSI's operations, in the glow from the portable lighting systems, Hana saw Chief Mahoney approaching.

She had a sudden *aw shit* moment. Fairfax's top cop must be on the warpath.

"Detective Brown, you did an outstanding job taking control of the crime scene." Mahoney strode up to Hana and firmly shook her hand. The chief ignored the filmy gloves the detective still wore.

Hana was astounded. Not only did the chief recognize her, the two having met only once during a large reception, Mahoney was giving kudos rather than reprimands. She struggled to maintain her composure. "Thanks, Chief. I'm only trying to go by the book."

"Of course. But the way we interpret and act on the manual is what separates the great cops from the rest."

Mahoney took a hurried look at the victim's body, partially obscured by the CSI team. "Everything appears to be under control here. Can I pull you away long enough to talk with the media?"

Although bewildered by Mahoney's apparent indifference to being briefed on the details of the crime, apprehensive about meeting the press, and reluctant to leave her crime scene, she dutifully followed the chief toward the forest of arcane technology on the TV trucks assembled in the parking area. Blow-dried reporters and their sidekick photographers, aiming heavy cameras on their shoulders, swarmed forward.

"Good evening, ladies and gentlemen. I'm the new chief of police, Erin Mahoney."

Hana was favorably impressed by how adroitly Mahoney quieted the assemblage.

"A brutal killing in Culmore Park was reported around midnight. The victim is an unidentified Asian woman. We've assigned this case to one of Fairfax's finest, Detective Hana Brown."

Mahoney indicated Hana should join her as she faced the assembled reporters and technicians. The older woman exuded an air of total calm and control. The two stood, shoulder to shoulder, projecting strength and competence. The chief allowed a moment for the image to sink in and the glare of flashes to dim.

"Detective Brown carries on a proud family tradition. Her father, Detective Lieutenant Mike Brown, exposed the biggest drug ring in the metropolitan area. In retaliation, six years ago, Lieutenant Brown was gunned down in a savage drive-by shooting in Chinatown. Hana Brown was wounded so severely in the attack, she lost her chance to compete in the Olympics. She made a full recovery, earned a bachelor's degree in criminology at our own George Mason University, and joined the Fairfax County Police Department immediately upon graduation. She recently distinguished herself by solving the kidnapping of Lizzie Jackson, the Fairfax County Board chairwoman's daughter. I have every confidence Detective Brown will bring to justice the person or persons who shattered the peace and tranquility of our community. We'll keep you updated on further developments."

The chief ignored the shouted questions, turned her back on the crowd, and signaled for Hana to accompany her to the police cruiser.

CHAPTER 7

Hana was embarrassed by the public exposure of her private life. The memory of the incident in Chinatown was still too painful to share. She simply didn't discuss it, not even with her own mother, especially not with Eriko Shikibu Brown.

Despite her chagrin, she marveled at Mahoney's performance. Notwithstanding a reputation for being self-centered, Mahoney did her homework.

The chief knew the salient facts of my life long before today. How? More importantly, why?

"Hana . . . may I call you Hana?" Without waiting for a reply, Mahoney went on. "Give your car keys to Officer Watson. He'll drive your vehicle and follow us. During the trip to my office at FCPD headquarters, you can fill me in on your crime scene observations. After the briefing, you can return to Culmore Park to continue your investigation."

Hana handed her Camry's keys to Watson and pointed to where her vehicle was parked.

She wondered why the chief had ignored the information at the crime scene prior to talking to the press. And even more why Mahoney now insisted upon being briefed on the details of the murder. The media event was over. Everyone in the department believed the media was all the chief cared about. But her behavior proved it wasn't all.

She concluded there was more to Fire Engine Red Mahoney than met the camera's eye.

Sitting in the cruiser's shotgun seat, Hana mentally prepared for briefing the chief. Should she mention the note left in her Camry? The note demonstrated a terrifying foreknowledge of her assignment to the horrific murder. She couldn't imagine how it would be possible for the assassin to get from the crime scene to her home after the killing and before she received the call from dispatch and ran out to climb into the Camry. Even more unbelievable: what if the note had been planted before the killing. The assassin would have had to predict she would be named lead investigator, despite no prior history of having the lead on a homicide.

She wondered if the note had been left by someone in the department. Considering that possibility, she decided there was no way to assess the pros and cons of revealing she'd received it.

She knew she'd really be in the shit if Mahoney ever found out she had been kept in the dark concerning salient facts about the case. In spite of that, Hana resolved to keep the information concerning the note to herself.

CHAPTER 8

The express elevator to the morgue complex whispered open and Hana entered directly into a secure anteroom with thick glasslike walls on three sides. She placed her ID on the marked computer panel.

Dominga Gomez viewed a magnified image of the ID and, with a friendly nod, acknowledged the detective. "Morning, Detective Brown. Lieutenant Krause notified us you were coming. Dr. Williams is ready to begin the autopsy."

"Good morning. Call me Hana, Dominga."

Hana had heard tales from her fellow cops about Dominga. A combination administrative assistant, receptionist, and guard dog, she ran morgue operations on behalf of the medical examiner, Wilhelmina Williams, MD, with brutal efficiency. Dominga resembled a petite Jennifer Lopez, with an olive complexion, flowing brown hair, and a well-endowed figure.

Dominga's responsibilities extended beyond Fairfax County. She was the major liaison with Virginia's unique statewide medical examiner system, which oversaw homicide investigations through four district offices throughout the commonwealth. With a big-city population, the county was among the jurisdictions that accounted for the highest number of homicide deaths.

Pointing to a doorway marked *Women's Lockers*, Dominga said, "You'll find personal protective gear on the bench. I took a guess at your size."

"George Manley will be joining me shortly to observe the

autopsy." Hana still chafed at being left out when she was a beat cop, and she took pride in having persuaded her boss, Lieutenant Walter Krause, to authorize an officer familiar with the crime scene to add his perspective to the examination.

"Manley's on the list. I picked out our largest size outfit for him. Let's hope everything fits . . . here he is now," Dominga said as the two women observed the elevator doors slide open and the rugged cop stride into the anteroom.

Properly outfitted, the tall lean Asian detective and the husky Black patrolman joined up as they entered the autopsy room.

"Hi, Hook." Hana called to the white-gowned medical examiner standing beside a stainless-steel examining table.

Wilhelmina owed her nickname to her skills on the basketball court, rather than to her prowess with curved weapons or surgical tools. A majestic six-two, the dynamic Black athlete had won many close games with a deadly hook shot from the key. She was a stalwart on the quintet that had led the Maryland Terrapins to the NCAA Final Four.

"Hi yourself, Hana. Welcome to my world." The ME acknowledged George with a friendly grin.

In a commanding surgeon-takes-charge voice—gesturing at a microphone hanging from the ceiling—Wilhelmina said, "I dictate my observations. The mic is linked to a voice-activated computer. If you want to add a comment at any time, let me know."

Leaning over the naked figure of Jane Doe, the ME proceeded to wield her scalpel to make the Y incision. "Computer, start. Beginning the autopsy of unidentified victim, an Asian woman, approximately forty years of age."

After a few minutes of routine autopsy activities, Wilhelmina stopped what she was doing and looked directly at the two cops. "Crosses were incised with an extremely sharp instrument on the victim's breasts. Judging by the precision of the cuts and the absence of hesitation marks, whoever did this was highly skilled in wielding knives or other edged tools. The perpetrator or perpetrators acted with apparent control. Incidentally, our murderer is probably right-handed."

Hana, feeling queasy and generally overwhelmed with the sights, sounds, and especially the smells of her first autopsy, was nevertheless captivated by the process.

She glanced at George to see how he was bearing up and was surprised at the star-struck attitude in his expression. The big guy was mesmerized by Hook.

Wilhelmina looked up from time to time to confirm her audience was still with her. "In the vaginal region, the wounds show an absence of control, which we tend to see when the perpetrator is exhibiting extreme rage. In contrast, the way the body was posed, taken together with the meticulous wounds to the breasts, suggest the perp was in control and making an artistic statement."

Hana explained why she believed the body at Culmore Park had been posed to resemble Henri Matisse's paintings *The Blue Nude* and *The Pink Nude.*

Wilhelmina nodded to acknowledge the contribution.

"She wasn't murdered in Culmore Park. She was killed elsewhere and brought to the site. The lividity or postmortem staining confirms she was not initially lying on her back. There are unmistakable signs of ligature strangulation, which doesn't require as much brute strength as manual strangulation. A few seconds of pressure would have been enough to render her unconscious, a minute enough to kill. Testing suggests a rawhide garrote was used to strangle her. But, the cause of death was severing the throat, probably from a knife wound, causing her to bleed out from the carotid arteries."

Wilhelmina described a similar murder in Philadelphia. "Hana, in addition to reading the file, you might want to go to Philly and talk with the medical examiner and the detective who worked the case."

Hana grimaced. "Assuming the loo will sign off on a travel voucher for what he will doubtless label a fishing expedition." Her shaky relationship with Lieutenant Krause was proving to be the only downside in an assignment that otherwise exceeded her expectations.

Wilhelmina turned back to the corpse. She examined the mutilated genital area with care.

The ME flushed. "What the hell . . .?"

She picked up a pair of long tweezers and inserted them into the vagina. With intense concentration, she manipulated the prongs to remove a folded piece of paper or cloth.

"Foreign object found in vagina. Computer record off."

"Let's head up to CSI," Wilhelmina said. "Dr. Edison can help us determine what we've found."

Before she left the morgue, the ME said to Dominga, "Tell Dr. Chan I've gone to CSI. Ask him to take over the autopsy of Jane Doe."

Wilhelmina headed for the elevator with Hana and George close on her tail.

She handed Hana the plastic envelope containing the unusual discovery, then scribbled the paperwork to ensure a clear chain of custody.

Holding the autopsy evidence gave the detective a creepy feeling.

Entering the CSI lab, the ME approached a tall thin figure hunched over a forensic microscope. Wilhelmina said, "Ed, I need your help. Urgently."

The nameplate on her desk read Edwina Edison, PhD.

The CSI tech looked up with a blank stare, disentangled her eyeglasses, which were stuck in thick blond hair, and pulled them in place. "Oh, there you are, Hook. I see you've brought company, including Detective Brown."

Wilhelmina took charge. "Meet Officer Manley. He and Detective Brown are observers during the autopsy of Jane Doe. I found an object in the corpse's vagina."

The CSI tech took the envelope from Hana and opened it. She started speaking to the evidence as though the others were no longer present. "Let's clean you up so we can talk. You're a bloody mess. A good solvent bath will make you feel better."

Manipulating small forceps, she swished the evidence in the solvent tray and, with great care, unfolded it. "Let's spread you out on this x-ray reader for a better look. Yes. Just as I thought. You've written us a message from the grave. Well, not quite the grave, but Hook's morgue is only one slippery step away."

Tall and thin, she stood in front of the small screen, obscuring the view of the others. After a few moments of silence, Edwina turned to them, smiling sardonically. "I'll summarize my discoveries. First, this is not paper, it's parchment. Second, I know who the killer is."

"You know?"

"Yes." With a dramatic flourish, she pointed to the screen, "Look for yourselves."

Written in red, Hana saw:

Catch me when you can.

Jack

"Who's Jack?" George asked.

"Jack the Ripper, of course," Edwina said.

"Now we know who did it," Hana said. "Our only problem is catching a suspect who's more than a hundred and fifty years old."

George said, "I thought Jack the Ripper's famous phrase was, 'Catch me if you can.'"

"No," Wilhelmina said, "That's a common misconception based upon the movie by the same title starring Tom Hanks and what's-his-name."

"Leonardo DiCaprio," Hana said.

Edwina grinned. "I bet our perpetrator is saying right now, 'Fuck 'em if they can't take a joke.'"

CHAPTER 9

Wilhelmina Williams and George Manley left the CSI lab. Hana lingered behind to meet privately with CSI tech Edwina Edison.

"Ed, could I have a word with you?"

Although the two women were not close, they shared a common bond of sorts—a reputation as loners. Neither socialized with the other or with colleagues in the department. Each kept her private life strictly private; the CSI tech in her quirky way, and the detective in hers.

Edwina raised her eyebrows but nodded affirmatively.

The detective reached into her blazer pocket, pulled out the note she'd found in her Camry the previous night, and handed it to the CSI tech.

Edwina's eyes widened when she saw the red ink on the parchment.

"I found this note on the front seat of my locked Camry when I was about to drive to the scene of the crime. The message has to be connected in some way to the murder in Culmore Park. My guess is the note was left there by the killer, probably before the murder. How he'd know I'd be named lead investigator is beyond me."

The CSI tech lined up the note on the x-ray reader next to the message signed by Jack.

"Superficially, they look identical—parchment, ink, and handwriting. I'll have to do some tests to confirm the match."

A mischievous grin twisted the corners of Edwina's mouth. "You don't want this to be part of the official record, do you?"

"Is that a problem?"

Edwina leveled an indignant look at Hana. "Of course it is. I could lose my job for violating departmental rules and professional ethics."

"But will you do it?" The detective knew her career would be in jeopardy if her attempt to conceal evidence came to light. She could expect no support from her supervisor Walter Krause.

Edwina beamed. "Yeah. But you owe me one."

CHAPTER 10

Thirty Years Earlier

The thickset man stalked through the dwelling, the largest mansion in the seaside village. Considering his status as the richest foreign merchant in Southern Taiwan, the scale of the dwelling was fitting.

He'd reluctantly agreed to entreaties by the village elders to grant the Chinese servant girls an unaccustomed night out to attend the holiday festival by the sea. With them out of the house, he was denied his customary outlets for amusement and sexual release.

He was drunk, but no more than usual for that time of night.

Lurching forward, he climbed the stairs to the second floor and moved unsteadily down the gloomy hall. Bumping into the wall, he knocked against a table upon which sat a large silver candelabra. He attempted to right it, splashing hot wax on his hand.

Cursing and staggering, he stumbled to the other side of the hallway, headed toward his daughter's room.

Since her thirteenth birthday, he'd grown more and more conscious of the changes in her body. The curve of hips and breasts swelling to womanly dimensions caused his loins to burn with desire. Tonight, he intended to give rein to his baser impulses.

He heard the sound of steady breathing coming from the room. He leaned on the jamb of the partially open door and gazed at his daughter Victoria lying on her bed. She was asleep; the sheet thrown back on a warm night. Her shapely form attracted him like a magnet. He sat down on the edge of the mattress and began stroking her thigh, edging closer to her maidenly core.

The girl woke screaming and attempted to leap from the bed.

"Stop. Go back to your concubines. Leave me alone."

Exerting superior strength, he seized her by the shoulders and threw her down on the bed, pulling the filmy nightgown above her waist.

She struggled to escape the prelude to rape. Muscular beyond her years, she struck him with her fist. Blood spewed from his split nose.

Enraged, he began to beat her. His blows hammered her head and upper body. He was determined to show her who ruled this domain, the same way he'd had shown her English mother before she died of heart failure three winters ago. Two hands circled her soft throat. His aim was to force her to submit. He had no thought of strangling his offspring.

Muffled croaks came from her imperiled voice box. Her movements grew feeble. Hands that clawed at his wrists fluttered and fell limp.

CRACK.

Shocked and surprised, he knew the terrible pain in his left side stemmed from a broken rib. Releasing his daughter, he spun around to see her twin brother, face contorted, swinging the baseball bat with which he'd hit home runs in a Little League tournament in Taipei the prior year. He had been proud of Conrad on those occasions. Now he was furious.

The ash wood connected a second time, fracturing his left shoulder. He struck back, punching the youth in the face. Confident his greater size would give him an edge, he ripped the bat from the youth's grasp, and flung it across the room.

The burly man pulled Conrad close to his chest and began choking his son, compressing his carotid arteries.

He let out a piercing scream when he sensed he'd been stabbed in the back. But he continued to squeeze his son's neck, thumbs pressing life away. The agony was excruciating; each stab wound more painful than the last.

The man tried, but failed, to increase the pressure of his thumbs on his son's throat.

His eyes began to flutter, then close. He imagined he saw the Spectre of Death invade the room.

A figure slipped from the bedroom, seized the candelabra, and crept back to the room. The bedroom curtains were the first to be torched. The seasoned wood of the wall quickly caught fire. Flames leaped around the room and across the ceiling. Oppressive smoke engulfed the second floor. The roof blazed. An explosion consumed the mansion.

A lone figure strode into the night, up the path toward the village, silhouetted against the false crimson sunset.

CHAPTER 11

B one tired, but still exhilarated from the excitement of heading her own crime scene investigation, Hana opened the door to her town house to the welcoming bark of a frolicking seventy-five-pound black Labrador retriever. Laughing, she dropped the bag of sandwiches from the local bakery.

"Othello, sit."

The Lab obediently plunked his bum on the entryway tiles and looked attentively at his mistress. His friendly brown eyes denoted intelligence and an even temperament. The wide-open pupils, designed to let in as much light as possible, were the only clues the dog was almost blind in the right eye and visually impaired in the left.

Hana stooped and hugged Othello, who lavished her face with affection. She rubbed her hands over the dog's short, dense coat. Grabbing the Lab playfully by the ears, she looked into his eyes with mock sternness.

"If we keep horsing around, we'll be late for Sam's."

Othello wagged his tail enthusiastically upon hearing Sam's name.

"Gimme a minute to change, and we'll head over."

Moving into her bedroom, Hana took the SIG SAUER P226 from its holster and slipped the weapon into the oversized Kate Spade shoulder purse on the dresser. Despite its greater bulk, she preferred the P226 to the smaller SIG SAUER P229 favored by many females.

She unfastened her ankle holster and put the holster and her .38 snub-nose revolver in the drawer of her bedside table. She shed the clothes she'd been wearing throughout the day and stood nude in front of her dresser. Curious if being named lead detective in a murder investigation led to any visible changes in her appearance, she was mildly surprised as she locked eyes with the familiar image staring back at her.

The mirror above the dresser revealed a well-healed scar, starting at the elbow and ending several inches up her left arm. Another scar traversed her left side, beginning just below her rib cage. These vestiges of the Chinatown drive-by shooting always jarred more than the scar above her left eyebrow, probably because she was more accustomed to seeing the reflection of her face. She'd long since forgotten the pain caused by the wounds. But she could never forget the way Chinatown changed her life.

Hana selected blue jeans and a red turtleneck from her closet and threw them onto the bed. Othello sat at attention, a silent audience as she donned fresh lingerie and changed into the casual outfit.

She headed to the kitchen, followed by the pitter-patter of dog paws. Opening the bakery bag, she took out the sandwiches and arranged them on a platter. Her role was to bring the sandwiches. Sam's was to furnish the Earl Grey tea.

Preparations complete, she gave the command, "Othello, forward."

Whenever possible, she used commands the Lab had learned during his training to be a guide dog for the blind.

Othello led the way down the familiar path to Sam's.

Rudolph Warrenton Samuelson, known to his many friends as "Sam," greeted them at the door. He bent down to pat Othello, unobtrusively slipping him an eagerly expected dog biscuit. He kissed Hana on the cheek and took the platter of sandwiches from her.

"Come in. I see you've brought roast beef, my favorite. Tea is ready."

Othello walked to his customary place by the easy chair, circled the floor, and settled down. The Lab spent part of virtually every day in Sam's town house. When Hana was at work or on travel, canine and man enjoyed keeping each other company.

"Sam, I look forward to having tea and a snack with you once a week. But the tradition loses something when it occurs at seven o'clock at night. Why won't you let me bring you dinner?"

"When you're my age, a full meal in the evening is a mixed blessing," he said, reaching up to run his hands through snow-white hair, which he finger-combed straight back from his forehead.

Her eighty-year-old neighbor rarely alluded to his advanced years, a fact his vitality tended to make her forget.

She reminded herself not to bring up the dinner alternative again. She deliberated telling Sam about her role investigating the killing at Culmore Park, but decided to keep silent, since the retired detective had undoubtedly seen and heard his fill of gruesome murders. Reluctant to brag, she was confident he would read about her exploits in tomorrow's *Washington Post* if it hadn't been sufficiently covered in the morning paper, which she'd not yet had time to read.

Sam broke the awkward silence. "Hana, you never told me how Othello came to live with you."

"Sheer luck. Sometimes good things come out of tragedy. A little over a year ago, when I was still a uniformed officer, I saw the Lab during routine duties when I was assisting at a home invasion where his owner Maria Velasquez was murdered. Maria had lost her sight as a teenager. Her old guide dog died. Othello had been with her only a few months when he contracted an illness leading to gradual loss of his own vision. Although she finally agreed to accept a replacement, the new dog hadn't yet arrived."

Settling back in his easy chair, Sam's face reflected interest in the story.

"Gloria, the murdered woman's sibling, said her sister was reluctant to face up to Othello's declining ability to meet the exacting standards of a guide dog. Gloria claimed no one would want to adopt a retired, visually impaired seeing-eye dog. Her apartment was small, but, in memory of her sister, she was determined to keep him until a suitable owner was found."

Shrugging her shoulders, Hana said, "Despite myself, I became attached to him and kept making excuses to visit Gloria so I could spend time with him. With Gloria's encouragement, I decided to adopt Othello."

"Did you have a dog when you were a kid?"

"No."

"Considering your lack of experience with dogs, you've done an excellent job training Othello."

"As a working dog, he went through a rigorous training program. With a few pointers from the vet and a K-9 officer, Othello was my tutor."

Sam smiled at the description of the Lab as instructor.

"The hardest task was conditioning Othello to run with me in the morning on the Washington and Old Dominion trail in Vienna. I finally got the hang of easing him into the routine. The vet had emphasized the importance of carrying extra water on the belt of my fanny pack gun holster. Othello's muscled frame and endurance made him an ideal running partner."

"Impaired vision must be an obstacle," Sam said.

"Nope. Othello adapts and shadows my every movement. According to the vet, his eyesight is unlikely to deteriorate further."

She took a sip of tea, eyeing Sam thoughtfully over the top of the cup. "Let me ask you a question. You and my dad were partners when he first became a detective, right?"

"Your dad and I worked together for ten years until I retired. Mike was the best partner I ever had."

Sam leaned forward, staring at Hana.

"What's on your mind? You never talk about your parents. They were my best friends, but I get why you didn't want to talk about them. What's changed?"

Sam's intense scrutiny caused Hana to empathize with suspects who must have experienced anxiety or worse when the veteran detective had grilled them in the interrogation room.

Her chest tightened. Breathing accelerated. Her throat began to choke up.

"What's changed . . ." She paused, took a deep breath, and fought to regain her composure. "What's changed is I recently got my gold shield. Becoming a detective has forced me to face up to feelings about losing my dad."

Hana continued to breathe hard after the unaccustomed display of raw emotion.

"I've been agonizing over why my dad was targeted in Chinatown. I know he was killed by drug dealers, reportedly the largest drug gang in the metropolitan area. Did he have a history of investigating drug crimes when you were partners?"

Sam's brow creased. Hana guessed he was deciding how much to share with her.

"Not at first. But over time we began to encounter an increasing number of young kids getting hooked on heroin, a tragedy that has gotten much worse in recent years. The trigger for Mike was three teenage girls having a sleepover at one of their homes in Reston. The teens were found dead by the host parents the next morning. CSIs and the medical examiner discovered the girls had been shooting a virulent type of heroin, laced with fentanyl. Mike went ballistic. From then on, combating drug use became an obsession with him."

Gripped by tension, Hana sought to keep her body from reacting.

"After I retired and your dad began partnering with Carver Washington, the two of them ramped up anti-drug activities, which led them to make a case against the Serpiente Venenosa Banda, an offshoot of MS-13. Beats the hell out of me why anyone would want to buy drugs from a group called the "Poisonous Snake Gang." Anyway, a few members of the gang who escaped being arrested sought revenge and ambushed Mike on the evening you went out to dinner with him in Chinatown."

Hana leaned back in her chair, struggling to appear relaxed.

"I feel better knowing a bit more about the background. What was it like, partnering with my dad?"

Sam took a sip of his tea and responded after a few moments of thoughtful hesitation.

"I never met another cop like him. First rate in every way. The ace was, he believed my being gay a was a nonissue. He covered for me in a lot of ways. Some of the detectives suspected I was gay, but nobody was prepared to take on Mike. Part of my cover story was that I lived with my sister."

"She used to babysit me. I thought she was your wife."

"A lot of people jumped to that conclusion, and Ariella and I were careful never to give them reason to know our true relationship. Besides, I couldn't afford to buy my own house, even if I wanted to. After I retired, I moved into this town house with Abe."

"I remember him. You told me he was called 'Honest Abe.'"

Sam chuckled. "Yeah, the coworkers at his investment firm gave him that nickname. He joked with them he was probably the only honest employee in the outfit. If Abe were still alive, we could get married, an impossible relationship until the last few years. In his will, he left me this town house."

After a pause to respect Abe's passing and the ways he'd transformed Sam's life, she said, "The cost of home ownership was bad in the past, but now it's even worse. Houses on the street where I grew up cost twenty thousand or less when they were built. Today, they're selling for over seven hundred thousand. The buyer just tears down the old house and builds a McMansion worth more than a million dollars. There's no way cops or teachers can afford to buy a home in Vienna today. If it weren't for my mom, I'd never be able to live in this neck of the woods."

Hana puzzled over why it was only with Sam, and only in private, when she could be open about her feelings toward her mom.

CHAPTER 12

Rose Lee gazed at her reflection in the mirror while she brushed her lustrous jet-black hair the requisite one hundred strokes. Her wrist flicked automatically as the hairbrush, with its ornate handle and backing of sterling silver, worked its magic. The ceremony was part of her daily ritual. And it did the trick. Family and friends told Rose her hair was her best feature.

She thought back to her tenth birthday. Her mother had given her the hairbrush, nestled in an antique black lacquer box with a traditional mountain landscape painted in crimson on the cover. The box still occupied a place of honor on her otherwise modern, mundane dressing table.

She faced up to the inconsistency, one of many, in her relationship with her mother. Rose was scrupulous about following her mother's hair brushing guidance but went out of the way to ignore her advice on far more important matters. A fifth-generation Chinese American daughter, she sensed she was a big disappointment to her ancestors. Rose was embarrassed she had failed to develop more respect for her family's Chinese tradition. It was not for lack of effort on her mother's part.

The young woman turned to look at the bookcase in her bedroom where Stephen E. Ambrose's autographed classic, *Nothing Like It in the World*, was showcased. Ambrose chronicled heroic efforts of immigrant Chinese and other laborers to build the transcontinental railroad from 1863–1869. Her ancestors were among those immigrants a century and a half ago. Her mother had approached the author on a lecture tour at Barnes and Noble in Tysons and had the copy personally inscribed to Rosalind Lee.

Her hair-brushing ritual was interrupted by the ringing of her home phone. She strolled into the living room and peered at caller ID, then picked up the receiver.

"Hi, Ma."

She listened a moment. "Yeah. I know taxes are due this month. I've already filed, way ahead of time. Thanks for reminding me I filed late last year and had to pay a penalty. Give me a break. I was in the hospital with a broken leg caused by that asshole in the SUV who ran the light."

Rose waited, expecting the usual admonition against swearing. She heard none. The enterprising young woman refrained from gloating about the hefty refund she expected. Such news would only trigger a lengthy and contentious dialogue about how much, what was she going to buy, and why didn't she save more for her old age.

"Look Ma, I've got to go. Remember, I've got a date tonight."

She attempted to preempt her mother's predictable response. "Yeah. Yeah. I know. I go out too much. And I should spend time with Jimmy Chew . . . He drives me up the wall. All he talks about is himself, and he can't dance worth a damn."

Sensing she'd gone too far, Rose said, "Ma, I really do have to go. I love you. I'll see you Sunday."

After each conversation with her mother, Rose experienced guilt about her lack of interest in family history and tradition. The future was her thing. The past was past. Her imagination was captured by a vision of China regaining superpower status. Rose and her colleagues at the China Future Society worked to foster a revitalized China—a China that would challenge the United States for world dominance. She was a member of the faction in the Society who favored more aggressive actions on China's part to take her rightful place in the world, including, as a last resort, military conflict.

Rose, who thought of herself a hard-headed, practical woman-of-the-world, had written a poem about China's growing prominence in Asia, inspired by the recurring tension over disputed islands in the East China Sea, called Senkaku in Japan and Diaoyu in China. Her poem had been published in the Society's latest journal.

She recalled the poem, as she admired the dozen roses in a Waterford crystal vase on a table against the far wall of the living room. The mirror behind the bouquet enhanced the effect, creating the illusion of a profusion of flowers. She mentally congratulated herself on the staging of the arrangement.

The roses had been delivered from the florist shop of the Mandarin Oriental Hotel. Rose remembered the evening earlier in the month when she'd attended a magnificent dinner in the hotel's gourmet restaurant hosted by the Society's Board of Directors.

Enclosed with the flowers was an embossed card with a poem:
Petals on the mountain path, flowers blooming on the slope,
Lights the weary traveler's eye and lightens his step.

A second card in a sealed envelope extended an invitation from an "Anonymous Admirer" to meet at the Top Hat, a fashionable nightclub in Fairfax.

Rose smiled as she imagined her mother's reaction if she knew her only daughter had accepted a blind date.

She had her own misgivings about meeting an anonymous stranger in a nightclub, but nervousness was matched by the thrill of being admired and, she had to admit, the sexual overtones of a secret assignation.

Little effort was required to convince herself any man who wrote poetry and was capable of such a romantic gesture would hardly be a threat. The Top Hat was a public place. She could always leave if things didn't click.

Rose slipped into a green silk Cheongsam, well aware the slit up the side from mid-calf exposed a sexy view of shapely thigh. In accordance with instructions in the invitation, she snipped a rose from the bouquet and arranged it in her hair with the pearl-studded hairpin attached to the florist's card.

Flushed with anticipation and fantasies of a longed-for sexual encounter, Rose stepped out of the Uber car upon arrival at the Top Hat, just before ten o'clock.

CHAPTER 13

Around midnight, an attractive couple in their early twenties motored into Culmore Park in a beat-up Honda. Two casually dressed Hispanics, Juanita and Manuel, staggered out. Juanita grabbed the car door handle so she wouldn't fall. The pair were tipsy, but not too drunk.

"You sure this is the place?" Juanita asked.

"No doubt about it. See the *DO NOT CROSS* yellow police tape."

Her voice took on a wheedling tone. "I want to see where the body was found."

"This is it."

She pouted. "On the TV news, the commentator said the body was back in the woods."

Manuel sounded uneasy. "This is far enough. No way we're gonna cross the police tape, there might be cops around. Besides, I don't have a flashlight." The only light was a quarter moon shining weakly through the tree cover.

With the attitude of a child used to getting her way, she pulled his arm. "Aren't any cops. They don't hang around in the dark. Come on."

"Screw that."

She turned coquettish. "All I want is to stand where she was killed. That'd turn me on."

As she expected, the thought turned him on. Hand in hand they stumbled forward up the dimly lit path toward the dense woods.

"Dammit," she said as she tripped and fell over a branch obstructing the path.

Breaking her fall with her hands as she landed on her knees, Juanita now found herself staring at the bloody body of a stark-naked woman.

CHAPTER 14

Snatching the receiver on the third ring, Detective Al Sweeney glared at Nadine's empty chair. As he was prone to do, he jumped to the conclusion she was on her midmorning coffee break or in the john. She was not Sweeney's favorite person in the squad room.

Nadine Ciaccio's main job as administrative assistant to Lieutenant Walter Krause was to triage phone calls and visitors and steer them to the proper detective or, in rare cases, to Krause himself.

"Major Crimes, Detective Sweeney." Pen in hand, he dragged his ample girth across the desk and stretched to reach his notepad.

"Hana, telephone call for you," he yelled across the room, smothering the mouthpiece with his mammoth paw. "Some woman about the Ripper case." Hana was also high on Sweeney's list of colleagues.

Content he could continue struggling with the crossword puzzle he'd been working on, the detective hung up.

—

"Morning. Detective Brown here. How can I help you?"

"Detective Brown, I'm An-Mei Lee. I'm calling regarding the murders in Culmore Park. I believe . . ." Her calm cultivated voice faltered slightly. "No. I'm certain. My daughter, Rosalind Lee, is one of the young Asian women whose murder is all over the news."

Struggling to maintain the facade of a thoughtful interrogation, Hana began scribbling notes. "What leads you to suspect your daughter's one of the victims, Mrs. Lee?"

I don't suspect it. I'm sure. But my evidence, as you'd call it, is somewhat complicated. I can't explain over the phone. Please come to my home." The mother phrased the invitation politely, but it had the ring of someone accustomed to giving orders and expecting them to be obeyed.

Staring at the phone, Hana pondered Mrs. Lee's invitation. This was the department's eighth call of the morning with a tip about the victims found in Culmore Park. She weighed the pros and cons of a half day spent to produce a dramatic breakthrough on her case versus a wild-goose chase comforting an anxious mother who was doubtless reacting to media-induced hysteria over a daughter who may or may not be missing.

The woman didn't sound hysterical. If anything, Hana had the feeling Mrs. Lee was trying to control herself. The dignity and composure in the older woman's voice almost, but not quite, masked her obvious stress.

Her intuition convinced Hana of the rightness of Mrs. Lee's fears in the same way the mother was convinced of her daughter's fate. She felt an immediate connection to the woman on the other end of the line.

"What is your address, Mrs. Lee?"

Jotting down the Great Falls address, she realized Mrs. Lee lived in an exclusive neighborhood of multimillion-dollar homes situated on densely wooded estates near historic Great Falls National Park.

"I'll be there in half an hour."

"Thank you. Just press the intercom button at the front gate. We'll buzz you in."

By the time Hana drove through the mushrooming business sector at Tysons on the way to Great Falls, she'd rationalized meeting with Mrs. Lee was the right move.

Fifteen minutes later, she motored up the winding driveway before dead-ending in front of a formidable steel gate. The fence was twelve feet high and appeared to circle the entire property, which was much larger than the five acres occupied by many of the nearby mansions.

Hana looked over the setup and wondered about the compelling need for all the security.

Signs posted on the fence warned: *HIGH VOLTAGE ELECTRIFIED FENCE. KEEP OFF. TRESPASSERS WILL BE PROSECUTED.* She surveyed the closed-circuit cameras that bracketed the gate and continued at intervals along the fence.

She pushed the imposing red button mounted by the gate and said, "Detective Brown to see Mrs. Lee."

A husky male voice with a pronounced Chinese accent responded. "Mrs. Lee is expecting you. Drive to the front. Leave your car in the porte cochere."

"What the hell is a porte cochere?" she mumbled aloud.

Hana drove forward until she saw the roofed structure extending over the driveway.

A Chinese goliath met her as she walked up to the impressive front entrance.

He bowed her through an immense foyer toward a large, but surprisingly intimate, sitting room.

Mrs. Lee sat in a comfortable easy chair, her back ramrod straight. The seat's ornate brocade was a perfect complement to her Armani executive suit, which the uninitiated would call gray, but which Hana knew to be the color "gun," since her mom had worn a virtually identical outfit when giving a speech at an academic conference. A green jade dragon was suspended from her throat by an intricate gold chain.

Her small figure exuded power and defied easy description— Empress dowager? CEO? Cultural icon? Rich suburbanite?

The detective pegged her as a person who required careful handling.

Mrs. Lee spoke before her visitor had a chance to open her mouth. "Thank you for honoring my request."

Hana crossed the room in quick strides to shake hands with the older woman. Mrs. Lee grasped Hana's powerful hand so tightly with both of her own hands, the athletic young woman almost winced. Talons of steel.

The matriarch held on and said, "Join me for tea in the Sun Room."

Hana expected Mrs. Lee to voice her concerns about her daughter's fate at the outset of the encounter. The gracious invitation came as a surprise. She remembered her mom explaining how the Chinese, in common with the Japanese, often put off critical business or emotionally fraught moments with social niceties.

The women strolled through a wide archway into the red-tiled Sun Room, furnished with wicker furniture covered by a profusion of flowered cushions and pillows. The room evoked an atmosphere of peace and relaxation.

Floor to ceiling windows let in the scintillating morning light. Hana gazed out at the spectacular view of a Chinese garden of immense size and classic style. Flowers and plants were complemented by Oriental stone gardens, raked in intricate patterns. In the near distance, where some might place a gazebo, she glimpsed a tea room, surrounded by a moat.

"Your magnificent garden reminds me of the Chinese Garden of Dr. Sun Yat-Sen I toured in Vancouver a decade ago when I was there for an international judo meet between Canada and the US."

"You have a good eye," Mrs. Lee said, obviously pleased the garden's genesis was appreciated. "A few of the landscape architects who worked on Dr. Sun Yat-Sen's garden designed these grounds."

The goliath who met Hana when she arrived carried in a lacquer tray loaded with tea service and pastry. Her practiced gaze observed the slight bulge not even his expertly tailored suit could hide. She'd missed the concealed carry when he welcomed her to the residence.

The weapon was holstered on the servant's right hip, as was her own, hidden beneath her blue blazer.

The gracious hostess pointed to a white wicker chair offering the best view of the garden. "Please be seated,"

Treating the ritual with proper respect, the women sipped their tea, allowing ample time for silent contemplation. Hana was pleased to discover the tea, served in exquisite pottery cups, was a delicious blend of Japanese sencha, rather than the more fragrant Chinese tea she'd expected. She picked up on the signal her hostess was aware of her background and was taking pains to impress her.

"Tell me about your relationship with your mother," Mrs. Lee said.

Hana blinked at the directness of the unexpected query. She struggled to think how to sum up the complexities of the Brown family's mother-daughter relationship.

"I was a gifted athlete from an early age, and my mom attended all of my sports events. She tutored me every Saturday so I could both read and speak Japanese fluently. I was able to take a semester abroad in high school and again in college. I had the good fortune of studying at Tokyo University, where my grandfather had been a professor of English. I was a child steeped in two cultures. My mom encouraged me at every turn. We were extremely close."

Hana heaved a sigh. "My relationship with my mom went to hell in Chinatown. You probably know I was with my dad when he was killed there six years ago."

Mrs. Lee gave a nod to indicate she was aware of the tragedy.

"Neither my mom nor I have gotten over his death."

The truth of the statement struck Hana like a hammer blow. She'd never acknowledged to another person the extent to which her life, and her mom's, had been devastated by her dad's killing.

"I was hospitalized for two weeks. Forced to drop out of the Olympics, I gave up tournament judo, although I continued to train as hard as ever in all types of martial arts. My goal was to become a cop; not just any cop, but Supercop. A life of police work was my way of atoning for the sin of living on the day my dad died. The psychiatrists call it 'survivor's guilt.'"

Mrs. Lee's rapt attention encouraged her to continue.

"I became a loner and fenced my mom out of the center of my life. Since she's a professor at George Mason University, I rationalized I shouldn't burden her with my problems. In fact, it was impossible for me to admit I had any problems. Since Chinatown, I've worn a mask to shield my true feelings from the world."

Hana stopped talking, aware of the deep emotional wellspring Mrs. Lee's penetrating question tapped. She stammered, embarrassed to let her mask slip. "I'm sorry . . . I got carried away."

"You spoke with your heart. My message to you also flows from the mother-daughter bond. My daughter Rosalind—Rose as her father chose to call her, and she came to prefer—was a headstrong child, the kind who turn their mother's hair prematurely gray. She wasn't flagrantly disobedient. That's not the Chinese way. She had an uncanny instinct, even as a toddler, about how far she could go and still get away with whatever mischief she had in mind."

Rose's mother sighed at the memories.

"Rosalind was a brilliant child, but an indifferent student. She studied what pleased her, deaf to guidance from her teachers and especially me. But she read voraciously and was able to squeak into Harvard, where she graduated magna cum laude. Having demonstrated her independence of spirit, she was content to kneel at the academic altar when necessary to succeed. She declined my invitation to join the family firm I've headed in the decade since my husband died. Asian Pacific Enterprises is a multibillion-dollar international trade conglomerate."

"What'd she choose to do?" Hana asked, troubled Mrs. Lee continued to refer to her daughter in the past tense and anxious to cut to the chase and find out if she was one of the Culmore Park victims.

"Rosalind joined the staff of the China Future Society, an organization that shared her vision of a resurgent China. She became a person of influence there and was on the editorial board of their journal."

The detective sensed the mother disapproved of her daughter's activities on behalf of the Society.

Mrs. Lee shook her head. "From time to time, she came home. In fact, she promised to join us for our monthly family dinner on Sunday, a gathering of my other children and Rosalind's uncles, aunts, and cousins. My daughter and I talked every day despite our political differences. Not that our daily chats had any substantive content. Rosalind was a bit patronizing and standoffish. Still, it's important to keep in touch, don't you think?"

Without waiting for an answer to the ticklish question, Mrs. Lee pressed on. "This morning, when I called her, there was no answer. Somehow, I knew in my heart she would never again answer my calls, just as I knew that my mother had died on her trip back to China before I received the fatal call from overseas relatives."

Sensing Mrs. Lee was leading to a conclusion, Hana leaned forward.

"Rosalind had a date last night. A blind date. She thought I was oblivious to what was going on, but I could always read her every mood. The stranger murdered her. He's your killer."

Hana felt a bolt of electricity charge her body, hairs standing on end. She shivered at the denouement of Mrs. Lee's tale. Her rational mind was at war with the thrill of instinctive belief in what she'd just heard. The investigator in her struggled to regain a sense of balance.

Groping for a foothold in reality, she said, "Describe Rosalind for me, Mrs. Lee."

"She was twenty-eight, five-six, one hundred and fifteen pounds, attractive, with shoulder-length black hair, styled very much like yours." Reaching into her jacket pocket, Mrs. Lee pulled out a picture of Rose.

Hana stared at the photograph. Her heart lurched. She put a hand in her blazer pocket, retrieved a morgue photo, and handed the gruesome image to the woman who, with obvious effort, was holding herself erect.

"I'm so sorry, Mrs. Lee. Can you confirm this is your daughter?"
With a strangled sob, the mother merely inclined her head.

CHAPTER 15

Hana arrived at her favorite Tysons restaurant, looking forward to ordering the chef's signature fried shrimp. She scanned the room and spied Wilhelmina Williams seated in a booth, buttering a French roll.

"Sorry I'm late, Hook. It's been a bitch of a day."

Once Hana and Wilhelmina ordered, they got down to business.

Hana filled her in on the Great Falls encounter. "Jane Doe number two was Rosalind Lee, Rose. She worked for an organization called the China Future Society. I'd never heard of the Society, which is written up on the internet as a cross between a think tank and a quasi-lobbying group."

Wilhelmina took a bite of her roll, listening, but not yet engaged.

"Her mom astonished me when she speculated Rose had been killed by a blind date."

The ME put down the roll, visibly surprised by the revelation.

"So far, we've found nothing that either confirms or contradicts her theory, which she regards as an established fact. I talked with the young Hispanic couple who discovered Rose Lee's corpse. They were a little high when they got the idea to sneak onto the Culmore Park crime scene for thrills. In a break for us, they called 911 and confessed to going beyond the yellow tape. We got a fresh look at the slightly compromised crime scene, which resembled that of Jane Doe number one."

"The autopsy was uncanny," Wilhelmina said. "The victims were alike in appearance. The murders were virtual carbon copies. The wounds were identical—ligature strangulation, throat cut ear to ear, crosses carved on both breasts, loins gouged viciously. A parchment message was hidden in Rose Lee's vagina, in the same fashion as Jane Doe number one."

Hana raised her eyebrows, remembering the note left in her Toyota.

The ME continued. "CSI photos and measurements confirmed the body's positioning and the surrounding area were the same. Lividity, no blood spatter, the whole thing. It's like our perp read my autopsy report. There was one major difference. Rose had Rohypnol in her system; Jane Doe number one didn't."

"Rohypnol . . . the date-rape drug," Hana echoed.

"One of them, anyway. They all exhibit similar symptoms, akin to a sleepy, queasy, drunkenness. Victims have no memory of what occurred, not that Rose Lee would have lived long enough to realize what was happening to her. The drug was ingested a short time before she died, which was an hour or so before midnight."

"Let me see if I have the timeline for the second murder straight," Hana said. She took a bite of shrimp, paused a moment to chew, and started to think out loud.

"Rose talked with her mother around eight. Later that evening, she met Mr. Blind Date, who, we'll presume for now, is the perp. He gave her the drug at a nightclub or restaurant. She was 'taken ill.' He helped her outside. Took her to his favorite murder spot. Strangled her. Cut her throat. Stripped her . . . maybe the striptease came first. Vandalized her breasts and vagina. Wrapped her body in plastic or something equally convenient. Transported the corpse to Culmore Park. He arranged the body just so; that required time. He left no trace evidence and got away unobserved. All that between eight in the evening and sometime around midnight."

"Your timeline jibes with what we know," Wilhelmina said.

"Anything else significant about the second victim?" Hana asked.

"Dr. Edison made you a copy of the parchment I recovered from her vagina. It contained another message from Jack, written in red like the earlier messages." Wilhelmina slipped the note across the table.

Hana read:

What do you think about Saucy Jacky's work now, lovey? Thanks for hiding my artistry from the media until I could do this one. Now you have double-trouble. You'll have double that again before I'm done.

Jack the Ripper

Wilhelmina retrieved the note. "Edwina's colorful comment was, 'Jack's fucking with us and loving every minute.' She confirmed this message, like the first, is similar to the historical Jack the Ripper's letters and postcards, including the flippant reference to himself as 'Saucy Jacky.' Neither one of us has been able to decipher any meaning beyond the obvious. She's shipped off a copy to a team of FBI cryptologists in hopes they can come up with something, but she's not optimistic."

"One message comes through loud and clear," Hana said. "Jack's going to kill again. My guess would be soon."

CHAPTER 16

The luncheon's goal achieved, Wilhelmina stirred in her seat, anxious to get back to the morgue. Hana held up her hand and cleared her throat.

"Actually, Hook, there's something else I want to ask you—not for myself, but for a friend . . . Jesus, why is this so hard to say?" Not normally tongue-tied, she found herself floundering. She took a swig of coffee and started over.

"Let me be direct. I apologize in advance for any offense. Officer Manley has a crush on you. He looks like a tower of strength, but underneath he's very shy. He asked me to check out the possibility you'd be interested in going on a date with him. There, I've said it."

"George?" Wilhelmina asked, as though there might be some other Officer Manley involved.

"George."

"Hana, you mean you don't know?"

"Know what?"

"I'm gay."

Hana took a deep breath. "I had no idea. You tend to hear locker room gossip about gay relationships, even though the brass likes them kept quiet. An outdated replay of, 'don't ask, don't tell.'"

Wilhelmina reflected a moment. "There's a good reason why no one said anything to you. Some rumors have it you are my partner."

"You mean they think I'm a lesbian?"

"It's not so far-fetched. You've a reputation as a loner, even though most everyone likes you. You're sexy as hell, but you never date any of the guys in the department when they hit on you."

"I may be a loner, but I do date guys," Hana said. "Just no cops."

She hated to face the brutal truth her only close relationships—apart from her childhood friend Jane, currently on a six-month assignment in Paris covering financial news for the *Washington Post*, and Carver Washington, her rabbi in the department—were with Othello and Sam, a half-blind black Lab and an eighty-year-old gay neighbor.

She recalled the one time, early in her career, when she'd made an exception to her rule of not dating cops. She was riding shotgun with her senior partner Larry Ballard. Coworkers warned her about Larry's reputation as a ladies' man, but she ignored the warnings.

One night, late into their routine, when the action had quieted down, he leaned over and unexpectedly kissed her on the cheek. Startled, she nonetheless returned the kiss, full on his lips. One thing led to another and soon his hand was inside her uniform fondling her breasts. Liking the sensation and wanting the flirtation to continue and evolve, Hana reached for his groin and stroked until the hardness made his intentions unmistakable. Eventually, the lovemaking progressed to the back seat of the cruiser and established a pattern of sexual activity that filled sleepless moments during otherwise quiet shifts.

Larry fed her the line he and his wife were separated. Still emotionally fragile—suffering from her dad's death and estranged from her mom—she fell for his suave approach. The sex was memorable, but what mattered most was the chance to be close to another person, and to set aside angst about the Chinatown tragedy.

Before she could get over being smitten by her savvy partner, he'd wined, dined, and bedded her on several occasions. The affair was short-lived. Larry's wandering eye moved on. He told her he and his wife were reconciling. She learned the hard way that people are rife with contradictions. Larry could act with competence and integrity on the job and be a philanderer in his personal life. To this day, Brut aftershave brought back memories of Larry Ballard.

Her former partner and lover later made detective and would have been senior to her in Major Crimes. When she was put in charge of the Ripper case, she was thankful Larry had transferred to the Federal Drug Enforcement Administration.

Wilhelmina interrupted Hana's reminiscences. "Time to get the check. My treat. Break the news gently to George. I think he's a great guy, but I swing the other way. Ask him to be discreet."

They headed for their separate cars in the parking garage.

Once back on the road, Hana's thoughts were preoccupied by forebodings of yet more murders.

CHAPTER 17

Carver Washington entered Fire Engine Red Mahoney's munificent office, prompting the chief of police to rise from her red leather executive chair and circle her mammoth redwood desk. She gestured for him to take one of the club chairs grouped around a matching redwood coffee table. She sat down when he did.

Captain Washington, who headed Financial Crimes, remained an enigma to Mahoney.

The chief replayed her thoughts in setting up the early morning meeting. She was determined to figure Carver out, and, with his help, determine whether Hana Brown should continue as the lead detective on the Culmore Park killings.

Sizing Carver up with a critical gaze, she recalled he'd been a Golden Gloves welterweight champion who proudly bore his African ancestry. Carver was medium height with a lean toughness, square-jawed, erect and self-assured in his well-tailored uniform. A few years older than Mahoney, close-cropped black hair was sprinkled with white flecks. His muscular frame mirrored a self-disciplined practice of staying in shape.

She'd been surprised to learn his family farm had been carved out of the countryside near Leesburg by successive generations of Washingtons, former slaves who'd settled in Northern Virginia in the post-Civil War period—the holdings growing larger with each generation. Carver no longer farmed the spread. He broke with the tradition of his forebears to become a cop. She suspected his ambition was to sit in the red leather chair she occupied and wondered whether he would turn out to be friend or foe.

"Have a seat, Captain. What we discuss this morning is strictly between us. This meeting never happened."

"Understood."

"I asked you here at the crack of dawn to pick your brain about the Ripper case. This morning at eight o'clock I'm meeting with Captain McNab and Lieutenant Krause. I intend to be prepared."

"Why me? Most of what I know about the case I've picked up from the media. Some reporters suspect there's a serial killer at work because two bodies have turned up on consecutive nights at Culmore Park. Apart from the location and the fact that both victims are young Asian women, nothing is known publicly. Only a few people in the department are even aware of a Jack the Ripper connection."

"You're Detective Brown's rabbi," Mahoney said, shifting the focus of the conversation to Hana.

"True. I've watched over Hana since she joined the department. I was Mike's partner, and I'm a close friend of the family."

"You've smoothed the way for her to move up and make detective in record time."

"Nothing she hasn't earned. Hana's smart, getting top marks in all her tests. She's almost completed a master's degree in criminology at George Mason University. She works hard and has excellent evaluations from Captain Goldman, her former supervisor."

He concluded praising Hana, with a look that said this final bit of news settled the matter: "Rescuing Lizzie Jackson, the teenage kidnap victim, was a major achievement that convinced Chief Field she was ready to be promoted to detective. Lizzie's mom, chair of the Board of Supervisors, supported Hana behind-the-scenes, which was a major plus for the Fairfax police."

Mahoney nodded. "Since it happened just before I was recruited to replace Field, I didn't follow the kidnapping case. I recall two young Korean kidnappers were convicted last month. They claimed 'Mr. Big' was the mastermind behind the crime."

Carver frowned. "Mr. Big's identity is still a mystery. Based on my office's work with the FBI to follow the money, he got off scot-free with five million dollars of Hazel Jackson's ransom payoff stashed in offshore accounts. But that wasn't Hana's responsibility. She had nothing to do with investigating the kidnapping or the ransom arrangements."

"Still careful to watch over her image, aren't you."

"Always."

"Word in the department is you've done more than watch. You've deep-sixed a few people who impeded Hana's advancement." Mahoney eyed Carver for his reaction.

"An organization needs someone to level the playing field. A few people play hardball to help their friends and cronies get the plum jobs. For far too long there was a good old boy network running the department. Whenever I saw a chance to block someone from gaining an unfair advantage over Hana, I took it. My philosophy is *those who live by the sword, die by the sword*."

"The scuttlebutt is your career blossomed following that philosophy."

"Where are you going with this?"

Mahoney felt the heat of Carver's glare, thankful she was the chief of police and not a suspect being questioned about a felony.

"How'd you get the career boost that helped you shatter the glass ceiling maintained by those good old White boys?"

"You know the answer, Chief. Mike Brown and I uncovered the largest drug ring in the DC area, more Mike's work than mine. In the weeks following his execution, I caught the perps responsible for the Chinatown drive-by shooting."

Mahoney sat quietly for a moment, then gave Carver an accusing look. "You tracked down the three gang members who did the actual killing and, one by one, eliminated them. The *Washington Post* lionized you for avenging your partner. 'Justice from the barrel of a 9 mm' was the headline, I recall."

"Righteous shootings." Carver's voice tightened as anger flared.

"You were officially exonerated, but the rumor is some of the old guard tried but failed to crucify you. Even your strongest supporters speculated you executed those men, always adding 'good riddance.'"

She got up, walked back to the area across from Carver, standing over him. "Is that an example of what you mean when you say to 'die by the sword?'"

"Are you asking me if I committed murder to help my career?" Carver glowered and leaned forward in a pugnacious stance that echoed his boxing prowess. Confusion replacing anger, he eased back in his chair. "What does this have to do with Hana and the Ripper case?"

"Everything. It's essential I understand you and your take on Hana." She sighed and sat down, waving her hand aimlessly in the air.

"We've painted ourselves into a corner. No. Let's be honest. I've painted the department into a corner. Captain McNab assigned Hana to the first murder. Given her role with Asian gangs and the assumption Jane Doe number one was a routine killing of a Vietnamese gangbanger, the move was logical—even if the victim turned out to be neither Vietnamese nor a gangbanger. I did a little grandstanding with the media and announced Detective Brown would protect our Asian citizenry."

"I get it," he said. "You're stuck with a rookie detective in charge of what's going to become the highest profile murder case in Fairfax County history. If you're asking me, 'Is she up to the job?' the answer is yes."

"If only things were that simple. Once the media figures out what a ball-breaker we're up against, we're going to get roasted for not having our A-team on the field. The Fairfax County Board will cook my ass for breakfast. And the holdovers from the good old boys' club will be happy to fan the flames."

"I don't give a damn. Hana *is* the A-team," he said, voice rising as his temper, never quite in check, heated up.

"Not by herself, she isn't. Even if she were, reality will never catch up to perception. Hana will always be on the defensive, fighting the belief, shouted or unspoken, that she's not up to the task."

"You're right." Carver's shoulders slumped. "She'll be so busy protecting her flank, there'll be no time to catch Fairfax's Jack the Ripper."

Mahoney pointed her fist, finger out, like a pistol aimed at Carver. "The classic solution to this dilemma would be to partner Hana with an experienced detective. The question is who?"

His fists clenched, Carver stared straight ahead.

The trophy wall of awards and celebrity photos Mahoney had assembled to impress visitors provided no answers. Heaving a sigh, he turned to the chief.

"We can start by ruling out potential candidates. No one in Major Crimes has the unique skills this case requires. They're all senior to Hana and, for that reason alone, would resent working under her."

Shaking his head, he said, "In fact, I can't think of anyone in the department who's qualified for the job. Sorry to disappoint you, chief, but I'm not much help."

"On the contrary, captain, you've given me just what I need. You've confirmed my hunch Hana is capable of taking the lead, but she needs a partner. I agree there are no suitable candidates in the department. One possibility comes to mind."

"Who?"

"The FBI approached Fairfax with a request for an exchange of staff under the Intergovernmental Personnel Act. One of our people would work in the Hoover Building for a year. In exchange, an FBI special agent would work in our department for a year."

She stood up, walked to retrieve the briefcase beside her desk, took out a file folder, and waved it like a marching baton.

"Special Agent Brent Sasser is scheduled to start next week. He thinks he's coming to head up an intergovernmental task force on gang violence. He's in for a rude awakening. Instead, he'd going to be Hana's partner."

CHAPTER 18

A reluctant Brent Sasser entered the security screening area at the Fairfax County Court building. A deputy sheriff, sporting the name Brubaker on his uniform, eyed Brent's FBI credentials and gave him "special treatment," the main focus of which was to ensure that the agent's weapons—a 9 mm SIG SAUER in a shoulder holster and a .357 Magnum S&W with a two-and-a-half-inch barrel in a paddle holster in the small of his back—were tucked away in a lockbox.

"We'll return these when you leave," Brubaker said. "Only authorized court personnel and sheriff's staff are armed in this building."

Looking down at the shorter deputy, Brent suspected the official was enjoying his moment of lording it over a federal agent.

Not thrilled at having been detailed to Fairfax County to head up a joint FBI-Fairfax task force, Brent was even less thrilled when he learned he would be helping track down a suspected serial killer. He was forty-two. Been there. Done that.

The Ripper case was certain to become a high-profile murder investigation. Working with a rookie detective was a recipe for career disaster. His relationship with FBI higher-ups was already rocky.

His reluctance to being involved was despite his unspoken assumption he'd be the lead detective on the case. Mahoney had done nothing to clarify his role.

During his first meeting with Chief Mahoney, he'd said, "I'm not sure the Ripper case is the right placement for me. I agreed to take this IPA tour, somewhat reluctantly I might add . . ." he recalled the shouting match with his supervisor when informed he'd been selected, ". . . because I wanted to learn how a sophisticated police department like Fairfax operates."

He got nowhere playing that record with Mahoney or Captain McNab. The top brass passed the buck to Lieutenant Krause.

Krause was pleasant, but unyielding. "Officially, you'll be a detective out of Major Crimes. You're going to have to work things out with Detective Brown. She's your partner on the Ripper case. She'll be at the courthouse this afternoon. Meet her there."

Krause handed Brent a copy of Hana's personnel photo.

"Talk to her. Sort things out. Get back to me and we'll decide how to proceed. Hana's a good cop, and she's got good blood."

On his way through the squad room, Brent had overheard one of the detectives say Krause raised horses, which the FBI special agent supposed accounted for the lieutenant's faith in breeding.

Krause elaborated. "Hana's cleaning up some loose ends so she can devote full-time to the Ripper killings. We relieved her of her part-time instructional duties at the Academy where she teaches unarmed combat. But she still has to testify in the case of a Korean, Kim Shin, who beat an eighty-year-old woman nearly to death when she fought him during a robbery. He stole the woman's purse for a measly forty bucks."

Not interested in the details of Hana's caseload, Brent pretended to listen attentively.

"Shin has a reputation as a tough guy who knows some kung fu shit. He made the mistake of resisting arrest when Hana went to pick him up at his home in Annandale about two months ago. She broke both of his arms and a couple of ribs. The bastard gets off if Hana and the old woman don't testify in court."

Krause shrugged his shoulders. "I said to her, 'Hana, you can't do that. One arm you can get away with, but two begins to look like police brutality.' She looked at me like butter wouldn't melt in her mouth and tried a con job."

Mimicking a female voice, "'But Lieutenant, he's a big guy and he's trained in kung fu,' or whatever the fuck she called it. She knew and I knew, and she knew that I knew, she did it just to get back at the creep for what he did attacking an old lady. The son of a bitch deserved what he got and more, so I gave her a pass."

Brent grinned to reveal his basic agreement with the attitude among police officers everywhere: criminals deserve all the retribution society could dish out.

Waving off the lapse of discipline, Krause said, "I warned her, 'Suppose the case comes up before Judge Jessie Parker?' We call her Hanging Judge Parker around here because of the tough sentences she imposes on criminals. But she's just as tough on lawyers or law enforcement personnel if she feels they've crossed the line."

Krause barked a laugh.

"The damnedest thing. The case is on Judge Parker's docket for today. Hana is scheduled to testify at three o'clock. Hurry and you can catch up with her at the Fairfax Courthouse, assuming the Hanging Judge hasn't already thrown her ass in a cell just for the hell of it."

Judge Jessie Parker moved toward her dais. All rose in respect. Hana realized Her Honor's stern visage made her look every inch the Hanging Judge described in local folklore. Glancing around, she observed her partner-to-be coming into the courtroom, recognizing him from the photo in his personnel file she'd received from Krause. Her eyes locked briefly with Brent's.

She placed her textbook on the bench next to her. Court personnel frowned on the general public bringing in reading materials. But Hana rationalized her transgression. She was using every spare moment to keep from falling behind in her evening graduate studies. She hoped *Serial Killers*, the weighty text by her criminology professor Cheryl Livingstone, would prove helpful in the Ripper case.

Without warning, a side door of the courtroom flew open. Kim Shin rushed out, brandishing a large revolver. Deputy Karwalski, standing near Judge Parker, reached for his holster. He never had a chance. Two shots rang out. The deputy grabbed his chest, leaking scarlet, and collapsed. A deputy on the far side of the courtroom stood paralyzed.

Shin pointed his weapon at Judge Parker.

"You bitch. You won't get another chance to cage me."

Before he could fire, Hana leaped over the barrier separating the public from officials in the courtroom, hurling her copy of *Serial Killers*. The weighty tome struck the shooter on the arm, deflecting his aim. The bullet impacted the wall scant inches above the judge's head.

Wild-eyed, Shin snarled at the detective, "I'll send you to hell."

He drew dead aim between heaving breasts, prepared to shoot. Moving at Mach speed, Brent smashed into Shin's back. The revolver swung upward. The wild shot shattered overhead lighting.

The brute contorted his body to point the revolver's barrel at Brent's head.

Charging the attacker, Hana grabbed Shin's right wrist with both of her hands and twisted. The crack of breaking bone echoed in the room. The second arm snapped like dry kindling. About to kick Shin in the ribs, she spied the judge in her peripheral vision and remembered Krause's advice about when enough is enough.

Panicked spectators in the courtroom fled for the exits.

Better late than never, the second deputy hurried to the aid of Deputy Karwalski, yelling, "Someone call 911!"

A visibly shaken Judge Parker approached the trio of bodies grouped in the center of the courtroom. Her black robes fluttered. She looked like the scales of justice personified.

"Detective Brown, I'm sure you're aware of the laws protecting defendants in custody from police brutality."

"Yes, Your Honor."

She conjured up a mental image of Lieutenant Krause saying, "I told you so."

The judge stood before Hana. "I'll be happy to testify any time, before any tribunal, that you understand these laws and scrupulously abide by them. Please accept the thanks of the court for your courageous action."

CHAPTER 19

Brent and Hana endured the interviews and ubiquitous red tape at the courthouse following the shooting incident. Once the routine was over, he said, "Let's grab a cup of coffee in the cafeteria and compare notes."

"Let's not," she said. "We need to get past the law enforcement zone for a private talk. Any place within a mile of this building—half the patrons are lawyers, and the other half are law enforcement. I'm craving a beer. I know a quiet bar not far from here."

"Good idea."

She drove to Maplewood Bar, which was outside the area patronized by cops and lawyers, and ushered Brent to a quiet booth at the rear of the establishment.

Waiting for the busy waitress to circle around to their booth, Hana looked agitated.

"Normally, I limit myself to one beer a week when in training. And I try to keep in training. Today, to hell with training. I'm going to have two beers, maybe three."

It wasn't every day someone took a shot at her. Echoes of the Chinatown shootout overwhelmed her emotions.

Blinking in surprise at the outburst, Brent turned to the waitress who'd just arrived, order pad in hand. "Coffee, black. She'll have Asahi beer."

Hana wondered how he'd known to order her favorite beer, or if he somehow knew it was the most popular brew in Japan. Hell, why would he even be aware she was Nisei (second generation Japanese American)?

Hana and Brent shared the bowl of roasted salted peanuts on the table in their booth, absentmindedly shucking the peanuts and adding the shells to the piles that littered the floor around booths throughout the bar.

Regaining her composure once the drinks were delivered, Hana gave her new partner the once-over. A black-haired curly-headed Irishman wearing a midnight blue suit, strictly page one of the FBI fashion book. Only the faint red stripes in the pale blue shirt and the red silk tie decorated with miniature images of Picasso's *Interior with Easel* gave a hint of rebellion.

Tall and rangy, Brent outweighed Hana by a good forty pounds and was at least three inches taller. He looked hard all over. It was obvious his nose had been broken in the distant past and badly set.

Except for those physical attributes, he didn't look the sort who killed men in a firefight. But she'd read his file and knew about the bank robbery in Boston where he'd faced down two robbers who were fleeing after one of the men shot a guard inside. The robbers opened fire at police and FBI on the sidewalk. Brent returned fire, killing one man, and disabling the other.

He struck her as a bit long in the tooth, but still sexy and extremely fit. She couldn't believe how fast he'd moved in tackling Shin. She imagined an evening staring into his green and somewhat sad eyes.

With a jolt, she remembered they were together as partners in the Ripper case. This was not a date. She chided herself for forgetting even for a moment that her role was to track down a serial killer. For that, she needed Brent's help. She decided to start with the attack on Judge Parker as a transition to getting down to business.

"While you were being interviewed about the incident in the courtroom, one of the deputies filled me in on Shin's background. Like many athletes, Shin's a quick healer, but he feigned chronic problems with one of the arms I broke when he resisted arrest for robbing an elderly woman. The doc let him continue to wear a sling. The two armed deputies escorting him through the corridors from the holding cell to the courtroom assumed they were more than a match for someone who was partially disabled. Shin was a big man, but the deputies were bigger, which made them overconfident. They didn't cuff him because Judge Parker didn't permit defendants to wear handcuffs in her courtroom."

She shook her head. "The poor guys had no idea how dangerous someone with Shin's training could be. I saw him one time competing in taekwon-do. Taekwon-do is—"

Before she could describe the Korean martial art, Brent cut her off. "I know what taekwon-do is."

She ignored his brusque comment. "From time to time, I train with the sensei of various schools of martial arts. The master at Shin's school invited me to conduct a demonstration for the students. Shin was in one of the prelim demos. He humiliated his opponent."

Brent settled back in a listening posture.

"With Shin's expertise in martial arts, it would have been an easy matter for him to overpower the deputies. When they were escorting him to the courtroom, he brutally beat them and took their weapons. He emptied one revolver into the two men, killing one, and wounding the other. He took the second revolver with him to the courtroom. Revenge was more important to him than the chance to escape. Several years back, Shin received a severe sentence from Judge Parker for another armed robbery."

Brent interrupted. "I couldn't believe my eyes when Shin charged into the courtroom waving a revolver and you hurled your book at him to disrupt his aim. If you hadn't reacted when you did, Judge Parker would be history. By the way, how'd you break his arms with so little apparent effort? I've never seen moves like that before."

"Aikido." Hana hesitated, looking at Brent. She could tell from his expression, he may know about taekwon-do, but he was clueless about the Japanese martial art of aikido.

"Aikido has much in common with other forms of self-defense. But many of the throws focus on use of the wrists to apply leverage.

Extraordinary power is concentrated. An aikido master can break an arm quicker than you can snap your fingers."

"Are you a master?" he asked.

"I haven't competed formally for many years, so I have no idea what level I might be."

Deciding that was enough transition chitchat, she got to the point. "Let's talk about the Ripper case. I'm the lead detective and we have to decide how we're going to work together."

"Work together? With *you* the lead detective? I haven't agreed to that."

"What?" the flabbergasted detective said. "Captain McNab informed me my partner would be this hotshot FBI special agent . . . meaning you. He made your arrival sound like Christmas was coming twice this year. Having second thoughts now you've noticed I'm a woman?"

Brent rose halfway out of his seat in protest.

"You being female is beside the point. The fact is you're a rookie detective. Riding shotgun on this case strikes me as a shortcut to career suicide."

"Hell, Brent, why don't you say what's really on your mind? Thinking of me as the lead detective kills you. I'm young, you're old. I'm an Asian female, you're an Anglo male. I heard you Fibbies were big on discrimination. Congratulations. You just won the trifecta—gender, age, and race."

"Wait a goddamn minute. This is not about you. I've got a right to protect my future. I didn't want to come to this chicken-shit police department. And I sure as hell don't plan to play Sancho Panza to your Don Quixote."

They glared at each other across the table. Eyes locked in a silent war to see who would blink.

Hana was first to break the silence.

"Hold on. Truce. This is getting us nowhere. My bosses made it clear I have to have a partner. I'm told you're the man. You're stuck here on an IPA tour. I don't know much about how the FBI works, but I would guess it's 'whether you like it or not.'"

He nodded.

"Let's take stock of the pros and cons of making the best of the situation." She paused to see if he'd object.

Brent gave a grudging shrug of acknowledgment.

"I'm a lifelong resident of Fairfax County. I know the Asian community better than anyone in the department. Being a cop who's the daughter of a Fairfax cop, I can decipher the politics of law enforcement. The Ripper case is going to be mired in politics." She knew she'd have the backing of Carver Washington as a pipeline to developments throughout FCPD and in the broader Fairfax power structure.

She took a moment to confirm he was taking in what she was saying. "And I bring the fresh perspective of youth."

Hana detected the hint of a smile.

She was relieved to discover Brent had a sense of humor.

"We've both proven we can react quickly and keep our heads in a crisis."

She waited to see whether Brent would disagree with the comment. He kept silent.

"A lot of pros. Not many cons, except you were taken by surprise that I'm the lead and we don't seem to have hit it off."

More silence.

"What say we have a one-month trial partnership? If we can't agree on continuing to work together, I'll back you in trying to change your assignment."

She decided to interpret a grudging silence as agreement.

CHAPTER 20

Eriko Brown was trying to plow through the *New York Times* and the *Washington Post*. When the phone rang, she picked up on the second ring.

"Mom—"

"Hana, what's wrong?" Eriko said, cutting off her daughter.

Eriko had named her offspring Hana Murasaki Brown after her favorite character, Hanako, in a Japanese historical novel. Murasaki, coupled with her paternal family name, Shikibu, called to mind Murasaki Shikibu, the nickname of the woman credited in the eleventh century with authoring *The Tale of Genji*, the first Japanese novel.

"Nothing," Hana said, a refrain certain to trouble a caring parent. "I just wanted to talk."

Eriko resonated to the altered rhythm of the unexpected call. Since Mike's death, their mother-daughter conversations had become choreographed, like a Kabuki play where the actors' stylized movements mask their real intent and deeper feelings.

"Is now a good time for me to come over?"

The mother sprang to the window and peered outside. Hana's gray Camry was parked in the driveway behind her white Lexus IS 300.

"Now is the best time of all."

Giving her mother a warm embrace, Hana moved to her accustomed seat on the couch near her mother's easy chair.

Eriko shoved aside her newspapers and settled back. Hana knew she had her dad to thank for her size. Vibrant and petite, the professor wore a maroon jogging outfit that suited her slight frame. Raven hair sprinkled with strands of gray was pulled straight back in a chic knot on top of her head, creating the illusion of increasing her height. Her eyes followed her daughter's every movement.

Hana's hands fluttered like butterflies trying to decide where to alight. "I don't know how to begin. So much is happening. You know about the murders?"

Eriko kept silent, waiting for her daughter to come to the point.

"Since I was named lead detective on the Ripper case, I've been assigned a partner. We don't get along. He's much older, but that's not the reason. Things are really complicated. Office politics and all that." She waved her hand and struggled to get control of her mindless rambling.

"The thing is: I went to interview An-Mei Lee, the mother of the second victim, at her home in Great Falls. Mrs. Lee spoke about her ties to her daughter, Rose. She also encouraged me to speak about my relationship with you. For the first time, I talked about how our lives changed when Dad was killed. She understood. In telling her, I saw how selfish and destructive my behavior has been."

In response to her daughter's distress and pent-up emotion, Eriko held up a hand to halt the tide of self-recrimination.

Hana shook her head.

"Please, Mom. I have to get this off my chest. When Dad died, all I could feel was my own pain. How I missed him. How my life changed. Why I *had* to become a cop. To avenge him and as penance for the sin of living. Everything was me, me, me."

She took a deep breath and continued. "At one level, I knew you were suffering. How much you loved and missed Dad. The changes in your life. The many ways you tried to reach out to comfort me, forgiving my lack of response. But you always seemed so together. Supermom. Successful professor, writer, consultant to the five major film studios. You had money. You had your friends. I rationalized you didn't need me."

Hana paused and reached out her hand.

"I refused to admit I needed you . . . I was wrong. I do need you."

Eriko leaped to her feet and rushed to the couch. The two women embraced, weeping.

Mother and daughter talked for hours, reliving anecdotes from their past, laughing and crying with the rhythm of their moods. They shared stories about Mike, reminiscing about him as husband, father, and companion on a million outings. Incidents from family trips, particularly Mike's tendency to get lost every time the car ventured more than fifty miles outside Fairfax County, seemed hilarious in retrospect.

Hana spoke of her grandparents' simple residence in Bunkyo-ku, with its tatami mat floors and translucent shoji walls. "Tokyo was my second home, especially during the summer. I used to love walking with Granddad to his office at Tokyo University. He always made me feel so important. The students going by would pause to bow respectfully to him and to acknowledge me."

"He was a great man," Eriko said.

"Granddad took me to the park to play catch as soon as I was able to hold a glove. Even better were our visits to Korakuen Garden and Korakuen Stadium, where they played professional baseball games. Kodokan Judo Hall was my absolute favorite. I was mesmerized by the *judoka* in their white coats, white trousers, and black belts. Grandad taught me judo was not mainly a test of strength, but most of all a contest of brains and will. How to leverage your opponent's force to win. Kodokan Judo Hall was where I first imagined a girl could beat any man if she had the brains and the will. Later, I realized technique and training were needed."

"Your granddad was so proud of you. He saw you following in his footsteps as a scholar-athlete. His greatest satisfaction was living long enough to see you earn a black belt and go on to gain second dan and third dan rankings. He would be even more gratified had he seen how far you've come."

Mother and daughter went into the kitchen. Eriko made coffee and thawed out some blueberry bagels.

Hana smiled, pleased her mom always kept her favorite bagels on hand.

As she bit into the second half of her bagel, she told her mom everything about the Ripper case. She talked in the way she remembered hearing her dad and Carver rehash their cases, in the belief new insights would be sparked in the telling.

"I expect to go to Philadelphia to look into a case that seems to be related to the killings in Fairfax. Sam will keep Othello company. They love hanging out together. It's a load off my mind knowing Othello is being looked after. Buying the town house so I could move in next door to Sam is the best of the many good things you've done for me."

"What's the relevance of Philly to your work here in Fairfax?" Eriko asked.

"Wilhelmina told me about a killing in Philly with a similar MO. She thought it might shed light on the Fairfax murders. That is if I can persuade Krause to authorize the trip," she said, with a bitter edge to the comment.

"Don't be so hard on your boss, Hana. Let me tell you a story about Lieutenant Krause from when he was a new cop. Just as green as Officer Yardley, with whom, I was pleased to hear, you were gentle. 'Cut him a little slack' was the phrase I believe you used when Yardley made the mistake of identifying Jane Doe number one as a Vietnamese gangbanger."

Hana laughed at the recollection. She'd forgotten she'd told her mom so much about the first visit to her crime scene.

"Your father and Carver went to a redneck bar on Route 29 to pick up a suspect. Things got out of hand. Relatives and friends of their target, Rufus Slater, were primed for a fight. They managed to disarm Carver. Rufus, who outweighed Carver by a hundred pounds, had him in a choke hold and was threatening to cut him with a broken beer bottle. Your father drew down on Rufus and told him he would shoot to kill. The mob was pretty drunk, and they were ready to attack."

Hearing the anecdote, Hana realized it must have occurred the first summer she studied in Japan.

"One of Rufus's cousins, Ezekial Slater . . . I'll never forget that name . . . worked his way behind your father, creeping toward him from the other side of the bar. Ezekial was about to crown your father with the bung starter mallet the bartender kept handy in case of a fracas. Walter was in the neighborhood on routine patrol when one of the patrons, who'd sneaked out of the bar to avoid trouble, waved him down to alert him about the brawl. He came to the rescue in the nick of time."

Eriko paused, overcome by emotion at thoughts of what might have been.

"Walter shot Ezekial in the leg. Rufus was caught off guard. He loosened his grip on Carver. Carver hit Rufus so hard he broke his jaw and knocked out two of his front teeth. He went on to fracture three ribs. You remember all the boxing trophies on the mantel over the fireplace at the Washington's farm?"

Hana winced at Rufus's imagined pain, remembering the boxing statues.

"Walter and your father held off the other rednecks at gunpoint. By then, all the starch had gone out of them. Carver and your father owed their lives to your boss's quick thinking and decisive action. We all became good friends. Walter visited the house several times, the semester you were in Japan during high school."

Eriko shook her head. "Soon after, Walter began dating a woman from Middleburg. He married old money. He discovered politics was another way to get ahead in the Fairfax County Police Department. His wife's family pulled strings, eventually helping Krause make lieutenant. Your dad and Carver argued with Walter about the family's improper influence, and the three men had a falling out. Even today, Carver and Walter barely speak."

"I never knew," Hana said.

"All things considered, I think you should cut Walter a little slack."

CHAPTER 21

Parking the wad of gum adroitly in the hollow of her cheek so she could talk clearly, Nadine Ciaccio answered her phone on the first ring. She thought of herself as tough and smart, adept at seeing through bullshit. And there was never a shortage of BS in the Major Crimes squad room.

The administrative assistant put the caller on hold and yelled across the room, "Brent, this guy asked for Detective Brown, but she's not here. He's from some embassy. You wanna talk to him?"

"Detective Sasser. How can I help you?" Brent went along with Hana's suggestion he go by the designation "detective," during the period he was working the Ripper case, to avoid the confusion if he were to identify himself as an FBI special agent.

"Good morning, Detective Sasser. I'm Counselor Pei of the Embassy of the People's Republic of China in Washington, DC. I was trying to reach Detective Brown. I understand she's in charge of the Ripper case."

Brent did a double take. Nobody outside the department was supposed to know these killings were called the Ripper case or that the department suspected a serial killer was behind them.

"Detective Brown is out at the moment. I'm her partner. Perhaps I can assist you. What was the case you mentioned?"

"Detective Sasser, please don't play games. You know exactly what I'm talking about."

"Of course, Counselor Pei. Please accept my apologies. I'm certain Detective Brown will be anxious to see you. I expect her back later this morning. Would it be convenient for you to meet with us at the Embassy in the early afternoon?"

"The time is okay. But not at the Embassy. I prefer neutral ground where we won't attract attention. Would you and Detective Brown be agreeable to meet at Great Falls National Park?"

"Yes."

"Meet me at the scenic overlook closest to the Park Ranger pavilion at two o'clock. You'll recognize me by my khaki Tilley hat and blue shirt. You'll call me Pei. I'll call you Sasser and Brown. No official titles. We'll walk the trails until we find a secluded spot where we can talk privately."

"Sounds like a plan. Give me a number where I can reach you."

"If there's a need, I'll contact you. Goodbye, Detective Sasser, until two."

Hana pulled up at the kiosk guarding the entrance to Great Falls National Park. She flashed her creds, and the ranger waved them through. She maneuvered around the winding road and parked in the lot nearest the overlook. The Potomac, swollen with spring rains, crashed through the narrow gorge and over the falls. Despite the dangers, or perhaps because of them, a half dozen intrepid kayakers were testing their skills against the onrushing current, reminding her of salmon swimming upstream.

She wondered how many drowning victims the river would claim this year near the spot where she was standing.

The detectives met with Pei at the appointed rendezvous. The trio set out on the trail in the direction of the remains of the canal, a major transportation artery around the time of the birth of the

American Republic.

Pei steered the group toward a remote section of cliff overlooking the Potomac River. He paused to light a cigarette and said, "You're wondering why I called you."

"We're here at your request," Hana said.

"Deborah Chu, an employee of our Embassy, is missing. I suspect she's Jane Doe number one. The main purpose of our meeting is to confirm whether or not she was the first victim of the serial killer who calls himself, somewhat melodramatically, *Jack the Ripper.*"

Hana stirred, about to say something.

Pei held up a hand to forestall her.

"Don't be distracted by my detailed knowledge of what you think of as 'inside information.' Consider for a moment the dim prospect of keeping secret details of these notorious killings in the Fairfax County Police Department which employs nearly two thousand people. They're certain to become front-page news within a few days. I'd wager some reporter is writing the story of a serial killer as we speak."

Hana didn't press Counselor Pei about the source of the leak because she knew diplomatic immunity would protect him from telling any more than would serve his goals.

Pei continued. "The second purpose of the meeting is to brainstorm an alternative interpretation of the nature of the crime."

Reaching into his pocket, he produced a photo. "This is a picture of Deborah Chu. She was not actually an Embassy employee and lacks diplomatic status. Dr. Chu was a contract worker, a university professor conducting economic analyses of US-China trade."

Hana reached into her blazer pocket for the morgue photo of Jane Doe number one. The two photos were placed side by side in the dappled sunlight filtering through the trees. Birds chirped a melancholy dirge in the background.

"No question," Brent said. "Dr. Chu is our first victim."

"How'd you learn she was missing?" Hana asked.

"She disappeared after her evening seminar at Georgetown

University where she taught international trade. Security guards found her unlocked car in the faculty garage. The Embassy was notified soon thereafter."

Crushing out his cigarette in the dirt, Pei continued. "Dr. Chu owned a condo at the Rotonda near Tysons. I'll arrange for someone who lives in her building to confirm her identity at the morgue. Her parents live in Seattle and are traveling in China; there may be a considerable delay before they return to the US."

Hana nodded.

"If you could avoid mentioning her connection to the Embassy, my government would be appreciative. She can rightly be described as an economist who specialized in US trade with countries in the Pacific Rim. In return, I'll ensure you have access to all the information you need in your investigation of her death."

Given the limits to which foreign embassies go in hiding sensitive information under the cloak of diplomatic immunity, Hana was confident however little she could glean through this quid pro quo was more than she could learn without Pei's cooperation.

"You mentioned an alternative theory," she said.

"The official record indicates similarities between Deborah and Rose consistent with a serial killer theory. Both Chinese American young women, attractive, alike in build and appearance, well-to-do, and residing in Fairfax County. Both with connections to the China Future Society. The MO, to quote your eminent medical examiner, Dr. Wilhelmina Williams, is 'virtually identical.'"

Pei waved a hand to dismiss the detectives looks of amazement at the extent of the diplomat's knowledge of inner workings of the FCPD.

"I would like to point out the not so obvious," Pei said. "Dr. Chu and Ms. Lee both played important, behind-the-scenes, roles related to China. Both played important roles in the China Future Society. Dr. Chu was a major contributor to the Society's journal. Ms. Lee was the staff liaison who requested and edited her articles."

Brent sat down on a large rock. Hana and Pei sat on nearby rocks.

"Ms. Lee's mother is the CEO of an influential trade conglomerate," Pei said.

"Yes. We've met," Hana said.

"What you don't know is Dr. Chu's family owns an international shipping company, based in Seattle, specializing in transportation of goods to and from China."

Hana hid her astonishment behind a bland look. She had little faith in coincidence as an explanation when criminal behavior was involved.

"Could these killings be part of some bizarre business scheme?" she asked.

"I believe it's a scheme of a different sort. Your Jack the Ripper is simply an actor in a conspiracy against China. There are elements in the United States who fear the People's Republic of China. Our country has regained its stature as the dominant power in Asia. Our population is four times that of the US. Our rate of economic growth is two to three times yours."

Pei ignored Hana's expression of annoyance at the diplomat's tirade.

"America is the sick partner in a chronic imbalance of trade. Your economists scream 'China must bail out your country by manipulating our exchange rate,' or 'instability of US currency will trigger a worldwide depression.' Your Pentagon generals see a threat in China's military budget, which has become second in the world only to their own—financial wherewithal for a Chinese army of unlimited size, equipped with the most advanced technology—"

Determined to stem Pei's fusillade of words, Hana interrupted. "What you suggest is too far-fetched to be believed. There's no hard evidence to support such a conspiracy. I'll concede there may be a business motive. But that doesn't explain the nature of the crimes. If the purpose is to put pressure on companies controlled by the Chu and Lee families, why go to the extreme of making the killer the reincarnation of Jack the Ripper?"

"I don't have all the answers. My purpose is simply to alert you to the deep roots of these murders. You'll get nowhere just scratching around the surface. Dig deeper. You're the detectives."

CHAPTER 22

Following the meeting with Counselor Pei, Hana and Brent headed to the cafeteria, which served as the second office of Major Crimes. They didn't expect to be interrupted in the late afternoon, a time their fellow detectives rarely visited the cafeteria. If any colleagues showed up, the grim countenances of the partners would discourage sociability. They sat across from each other, saying nothing, staring at two untouched cups of coffee.

Brent broke the silence. "We need to figure out a strategy for investigating this case."

"Umm."

"Could you flesh out the *umm* a little, Hana? I missed some of the finer points."

"Shut up a minute. I'm thinking."

They remained mute, sipped their coffee, and stared at the laminate tabletop.

She grunted. "China."

"China? Our serial killer's from China? Pei's right, the killings are a plot to harm China? What?"

Hana shook her head. "None of the above. But this case hinges on China in some crucial way we've yet to figure out. Makes more sense than focusing on a sex-crazed serial killer."

"Say I buy your hunch China is the key." Noting Hana's raised eyebrows, he amended, "All right, it's not a hunch, it's a theory. What does that mean for our investigation?"

"We focus on ethnicity of the victims: Chinese American. We

focus on the families: wealthy entrepreneurs engaged in trade with China. We focus on the common denominator of both victims: the China Future Society. What we don't focus on is the phony drama of the bizarre crime scenes, sexual mutilation of the bodies, and notes from Jack the Ripper—all red herrings."

"I'll be damned, Hana. I'm starting to be intrigued by your theory. Where do we begin?"

"We begin at the beginning, with the China Future Society."

The elevator hissed open to an opulent foyer. The detectives stepped out of the elevator on the top floor of a midrise building in the heart of Tysons. Hana looked wide-eyed at the magnificent Chinese art and antiques.

An immense gold plaque on the wall read *China Future Society*.

A stunning, thirtysomething Chinese woman, wearing a fashionable Yves St. Laurent suit with a hint of Asian styling, came from behind her imposing desk in the foyer to meet them. A string of matched gray pearls the size of children's marbles graced her slender throat. Coordinating earrings nested in a fetching hairdo that set off her long raven hair to optimum advantage.

"You must be Detectives Brown and Sasser." She extended her hand and greeted each of them with a firm grip.

In a silky voice marked by a distinctive British accent, she said "I am Pearl Chen, special assistant to Executive Director Wang. Dr. Wang will be with you directly."

Hana took in two diplomas in elaborate frames on the wall. One honored Pearl Chen for graduate work at the London School of Economics. A second was evidence of a doctorate in Asian Studies from the University of California.

Dr. Wang strode through massive mahogany double doors, which opened at the far end of the foyer. A handsome man of medium height, his dynamic personality dominated the room. "Welcome to the China Future Society. I see you've met Dr. Chen. Let's talk in the board room," he said in a mellifluous voice, steering them toward the entrance on the right.

An oval table with gold decorations etched in red granite dominated the board room. High-back black leather chairs were spaced at equal intervals around the meeting table.

Tea service with four porcelain cups was set out on a nearby credenza. Hana recognized this as a signal Dr. Chen would be joining them.

She gazed out the window, pretending to admire the late afternoon view so she could reflect on the atmospherics of the meeting. The Washington Monument and US Capitol caught her eye as she mulled over Wang's motivation for meeting them in the board room rather than in his office. She reasoned the setting was a subtle reminder of the power of the organization and resolved to look into who else was on the board.

Exercising her prerogative as lead detective, Hana got right to business, addressing her remarks to the executive director. She had coached Brent regarding the Asian practice of virtually ignoring subordinates during a meeting.

"Dr. Wang, I'm Detective Brown, this is Detective Sasser. We're here to investigate the tragic murder of your colleague Rose Lee. We're sorry for your loss."

Hana and Brent had agreed to focus on Rose's role and to defer any mention of Deborah Chu's involvement they had learned from Counselor Pei.

"Rose was a valuable member of the China Future Society. A gifted writer and poet, she contributed to our journal. More than a colleague, she was a close friend."

Hana noticed Brent gazing intently at Pearl Chen during Wang's remarks. "When did you last see Rose?"

"On the day she was murdered."

"Did she do or say anything unusual? Mention having an engagement for the evening?"

"No. Everything was normal. Rose never talked about her personal life when she was at work. She was focused, professional, dedicated to the mission of the Society."

"What is the mission?"

"Ah. The mission is complex and difficult to explain, even to an Asian American such as yourself."

"Try me," Hanna said dryly. The remark, which would have been interpreted as rude in a strictly Asian context, was a reminder to the executive director of who was in charge of the investigation.

Wang inclined his head in acquiescence. "The Society's mission is to promote the future of China. We seek to dispel misunderstandings concerning China that are widely shared in the United States. Consider trade. Americans love to buy things made in China. Your countrymen appreciate a good deal, high quality goods at a fair price. But your Congress questions the advantages of commerce. Politicians blame over a billion Chinese for not buying more 'Made in America' products. The Society's publications present the facts of US trade with China and shed light on other controversial issues, such as the strategic balance between the two nations."

He took a sip of tea. He appeared to be satisfied with the detectives' attentiveness, even though they remained poker-faced.

"Chinese business is criticized over investments in American companies—oil, computers, banks, autos, and other essentials of a modern industrial society. Your president trumpets the virtues of free trade with Mexico and Canada. But all China hears is threats of sanctions if she doesn't restrain trade and manipulate the exchange rate to support the American dollar."

"Is the Society affiliated with the Chinese government?" Hana asked, careful not to show any reaction to Wang's polemic.

"Certainly not. We're a private concern. A nonprofit corporation under the laws of the Commonwealth of Virginia. Our board members are prominent US citizens. We're as American as apple pie."

"We'd appreciate a list of board members."

"No problem. All of our activities are a matter of public record."

Wang gestured to his special assistant, who left the room, returning with two folders. Pearl Chen gave one to each detective.

"The folder has the information you requested," she said. "We've included background on the Society and a copy of our journal. Please give me a call if you require anything else."

Dr. Wang bowed, easing the detectives out of the board room.

Once back on the road, Hana said, "Either of them could be the assassin."

"I agree. Did you see the look on Pearl's face when Wang described Rose as a 'close friend?'"

"Hard to miss. In the 'if looks could kill' category."

CHAPTER 23

The alarm rang at five o'clock. Hana woke, thankful she'd been spared the Chinatown nightmare. Feeling rested for the first time in a week, she looked forward to a run on the Washington and Old Dominion trail. She jumped out of bed and bent down to stroke Othello's head.

"Are you ready for a run, boy?"

The Lab nuzzled her leg, signifying he too was eager to hit the trail for their early morning outing. His tail thumped the floor.

She checked her fanny pack gun holster to ensure she'd put in extra water for Othello, her cell phone, a tactical flashlight, and her dad's snub-nose revolver. Good to go.

Before heading out the door, she adjusted the dog's leash for optimum flexibility.

Mindful sunrise was an hour away, she navigated Vienna's streets with care, knowing the greatest threat to running while it was still dark was a careless (or drunk) driver. Othello's collar and her jogging suit were marked with reflective tape, but she believed vigilance was the best safeguard.

Othello ran at her side, now and then distracted by other dogs on the trail. A quick tug on the leash was sufficient reminder to stay on his best behavior.

During the run, she thought about Brent and their somewhat rocky relationship. She wondered what he'd done to get on the bad side of higher-ups in the Bureau, triggering the bizarre assignment to Fairfax.

Five miles marked her typical route. Running a six-minute

mile enabled Othello to keep pace so she could complete her daily workout in a half hour.

Recognizing her halfway landmarks in the distance, she prepared to reverse direction. It had been some time since she'd encountered bikers or other runners on the trail. At that moment, she spied a dark shape sprawled in the center of the path.

Flicking on her tactical light, she moved cautiously forward, identifying the shape as the body of a large man.

"Are you okay?"

She pulled out her cell phone, ready to dial 911 if the person were injured or seriously ill.

Othello commenced barking and gave a warning growl. The Lab jerked the leash out of his mistress's hand and charged at an attacker wielding a club who sprang toward them from the side of the path. Seventy-five pounds of snarling dog hit the aggressor and knocked him to the ground.

Hana reacted in time to block a second attacker's club on its downswing. Dropping her light, she struck her assailant in the throat with her left hand, grabbed the man's wrist with her right, and pivoted to force him to the ground. The club fell to the path. The man gave a choked scream of pain.

The prone man yelled, "Get this dog off me."

A quick glance at Othello confirmed her expectation that the Lab had subdued her attacker's partner by sinking his teeth into the man's lower arm. Her relief at having turned the tables on their two attackers was short-lived.

The supposed victim she'd started out to rescue plowed into her from behind, giving her the sensation she'd been on the receiving end of a pro football tackle. Knocked away from her first attacker, Hana found herself crushed under the weight of the tackler. Leverage on her neck forced her to realize she was in a chokehold capable of producing unconsciousness followed by death in less than a minute if she couldn't break free of the pressure on her carotid arteries.

She gasped, "Othello, *help!*"

The Lab responded immediately, releasing the man he was biting and lunging for Hana's tackler. Othello's jaws seized the large man's leg. The dog spun viciously, jerking the assailant away from Hana, and throwing him to the path.

Once freed of the chokehold, she drew her revolver and backed up a couple of steps where she could cover all three men.

"Don't move. I'm a police officer. All of you are under arrest. Lie on your stomach and spread your arms wide."

She stared at each of her attackers. Reassured that none of them looked about to resist arrest, she said, "Reach for a weapon or try to flee and I'll shoot to kill."

The tackler screamed, "This dog's murdering me. Make it stop."

"Othello, heel."

The Lab hesitated to open his jaws, looking in disbelief at the mistress he'd just saved at her request.

She repeated the command in a stern voice. "Othello, HEEL!"

With what Hana interpreted as disappointment at her failure to understand the situation, the Lab came to heel, parking his bum on the path by her left leg.

She rewarded his behavior, bending down and stroking his head and back.

"You're a brave dog, Othello. You protected me when I needed you."

She picked up her cell, which she'd dropped on the path and dialed 911.

"Officer needs assistance."

In a few minutes, she saw the flashing lights of a police cruiser stop on a nearby street. Two police officers, following the signal of her blinking tactical light, cut through the brush to join her on the path.

Hana recognized Officer Eva Sanchez and explained how she'd been ambushed, detailing the steps she and Othello had taken to defend themselves.

"Take them into custody. I've got to get together with my partner for breakfast. We're preparing for a meeting with Chief Mahoney later this morning. When that's over, I'll come by your district to give a formal statement." She squeezed Sanchez's hand to acknowledge their close friendship.

On the return run, twilight tinted Virginia's eastern skyline a rosy hue when she passed the freshly painted red caboose that housed the W&OD railroad museum exhibit, the sole reminder of the old railroad track that had been turned into a jogging and bike trail. She turned left on Church Street, heading toward her town house, ending the run with a quick sprint up her steps. Othello panted along beside her, stride for stride.

After a few minutes roughhousing with Othello, Hana took a refreshing shower, dressed, and went into the kitchen to make coffee. Humming, she thought ahead to the working breakfast with Brent at his hotel. She bustled about the kitchen, half-listening to the TV tuned to ABC on Channel 7. Hearing mention of the killings, she focused on the news report.

"ABC News has just learned notes signed by Jack the Ripper were discovered by Fairfax police on the bodies of the two Asian victims left in Culmore Park. The Washington area is being terrorized by a serial killer," the announcer proclaimed.

Hana's eyes riveted on the screen.

"The shit's really hit the fan," she said aloud.

Othello came over in response to Hana's tone of distress, not sure if his mistress's remarks were directed at him.

"Everything's okay, fellow. My own little world just went to hell. You're the best thing in my life right now. You're my hero." She scratched the Lab behind his ears, continuing to listen to the rest of the newscast.

"Fairfax County Police Chief Erin Mahoney declined comment when contacted by a reporter who tried to question her when she went outside her home to pick up her *Washington Post*. She promised the department would hold a press conference at noon." The screen featured a stoic-faced Mahoney, barely recognizable in the dawn light, grabbing the morning paper like an accused felon and scurrying up the driveway to escape any further contact with the media.

Reaching for her copy of the *Post*, Hana skimmed the story. She confirmed the media had access to the main facts in the official file.

Pei was right. The department was leaking.

She reached for the phone and dialed the Ritz-Carlton Hotel at Tysons. "Please connect me to Brent Sasser's room."

Without preamble, she asked, "Have you seen the news?"

"Yes. Can we meet earlier than planned? I'll order room service and we can eat breakfast in my suite."

"I'll be there in fifteen minutes."

She gave him her order—pancakes and coffee. Just as she hung up, her phone rang.

Lieutenant Krause was on the line. "You know?"

"I know."

"Mahoney wants to move up our briefing to seven thirty. Be there with Brent. Do we need Officers Manley and Yardley?"

"No."

Hana had been surprised when Krause agreed to her request to detail the two patrolmen to the Ripper case. The cops were assigned preliminary legwork, including interviewing neighbors near condos owned by the victims, interrogating rank-and-file employees of the China Future Society, following up with the florist at the Mandarin Oriental Hotel, and tracking down the Uber driver Rose Lee had called.

She wrote a quick text message for Sam to let him know her schedule change, gave Othello a final pat, and left to meet Brent. She thought about how far removed the Ripper case had come from the homicide she and everyone else in the department thought would be routine.

—¶

Hana rang the buzzer of Room 1207 at the Ritz-Carlton Hotel. Brent opened the door almost immediately.

She entered the luxurious suite. "Wow. Not too shabby."

The spacious sitting room featured a couch, a comfortable chair, and a desk with a laptop open to a news screen. The TV was tuned to CNN, with the sound muted. A cozy kitchenette adjoined the sitting area. Through a half-opened door, she spied the unmade bed.

"A hotel's convenient when working odd hours," Brent said. "Besides, I don't know how long I'll be around, so permanent arrangements are out of the question."

She sidestepped the oblique reference to their agreement the partnership was a one-month trial period. "Are you keeping your place in Boston?" She knew Brent had been the Special Agent in Charge of the Boston Field Office, but she knew nothing of his personal life.

"I'm not doing any long-range planning, including whether I'll stay in the Bureau." Brent flinched. "Please forget I just said that. I haven't told anyone I've been thinking about leaving."

"My lips are sealed." She mimed a zip-the-lip gesture, still baffled about what was bothering him. To change the subject and kill time until room service arrived, she asked, "Do you have family in Boston?"

"No."

An awkward silence followed. Waving an apology for his brusque manner, he said, "I was married. Abigail Louise was my wife. She was from Savannah. We met when we were students at Boston University. We were married soon after graduation and had two children, a boy and a girl. Cute kids, Steve and Annette. They were my life."

His voice began to quaver, but he fought for control. "When I was still pretty new to the Bureau, I was working a case, tracking down a serial bomber. He thought I was getting too close. He blew up our home one night when I'd been called out of town unexpectedly. My wife and children were killed. We caught the bastard. He's on death row, but his lawyer keeps getting stays of execution. "Should have shot him when I had the chance," he said, in a barely audible mumble.

"I'm so sorry. I had no business prying into your personal life."

"I don't know what happens around you Hana Brown, but everything that goes through my mind comes out my mouth. Don't be sorry. The shrinks tell me most of my problems come from keeping my feelings bottled up. I haven't talked about my family's tragedy for years."

The mood was broken by the buzzer sounding the arrival of room service.

Chowing down breakfast, they tackled preparations for the morning briefing. Hana knew from experience to expect the unexpected from Fire Engine Red Mahoney.

CHAPTER 24

E rin Mahoney cursed under her breath. "Why does the goddamn media always show up at the crack of dawn?"

She picked up her red phone's receiver, hit speed dial for Carver Washington's direct line, and, with unaccustomed weariness, leaned back in her executive chair.

Hearing a response on the line, she forced herself to focus.

"Carver, I need your help." She thought of the feisty captain in Financial Crimes as a friend and trusted confidant, an unusual feeling for her, and one she had trouble explaining to herself.

"Sure Chief. You name it."

"I need information about the two Chinese American firms controlled by the families of the victims. Rose Lee's mother is the CEO of Asian Pacific Enterprises. Deborah Chu's family owns a shipping firm based in Seattle. I have no reason to suspect fraud is involved, but it would be helpful if you could do a routine economic profile on them."

"Done. Hana already requested that information."

Mahoney congratulated herself on the acumen of her team.

"Eastern Waters Shipping is the name of the Seattle outfit. I can email you a report on both firms in the next few minutes. The companies appear to be on the up-and-up, at least by the somewhat relaxed standards of international traders. They play in the big leagues, handling transactions in the millions with the frequency we shop at Starbucks for coffee. Both organizations retain top-drawer law firms in the District and on the West Coast. They're represented by K Street lobbyists, with heavy-hitter connections on Capitol Hill and in the White House."

"Thanks Carver. I'll share your email at the meeting."

Captain McNab and Lieutenant Krause were first to arrive, followed by Hana and Brent. After helping themselves to drinks and pastry, they sat around the table.

Handing out Carver's email, Chief Mahoney said, "Look over this report I requested with background on the firms linked to the two victims. While you're doing that, let's begin by discussing a possible motive for the murders raised by Counselor Pei."

She nodded at Hana to take the lead.

"Pei speculated the women were killed as an indirect way of attacking China. We have no reason to buy into his theory. He added little to what's been on the news. There's no love lost between powerful interests in the US and Communist China. Linking those global issues to the murder victims just because they're both associated with the China Future Society sounds far-fetched to me."

"I agree," Mahoney said. "Anyone believe Pei's motive has legs?"

There were no takers.

"We'll table those considerations for now. If new info turns up, we can always review the bidding. Maybe arrange another meeting with Pei and see if he has hard evidence he didn't share.

"What about the business connection, Hana?"

"Seems more plausible." The detective flipped through the email. "Captain Washington's analysis confirms our thoughts on the subject. The Lee and Chu firms are major brokers of trade with the Pacific Rim. Megabucks are at stake. Checking out a business motive for the killings should be given priority."

"I disagree," Brent said.

Hana shot Brent a look, annoyed she and her partner were on opposite sides of an important issue. Planning for the briefing at the hotel focused on how to present the forensic evidence and findings of the two beat cops investigating. She and Brent had not explored other theories of the crimes.

She fumed. *Highlighting the China connection in the cafeteria should have had more impact. He doesn't get it.*

Brent continued. "In my experience, serial killings are exactly what they seem. We shouldn't waste scarce resources on exotic motives when there's no foundation. We're law enforcement. We should stick to what we do best. There's a sick killer out there. All the evidence at the scene suggests his sickness is the immediate cause of the crimes. We have to track him down with good old-fashioned police work."

Hana kept silent, waiting to hear the chief's reaction,

Mahoney nodded. "The Ripper Task Force will focus on the murders as 'straightforward' serial killings, assuming there is such a thing. If and when hard evidence comes to light, we'll address other angles."

Agreement around the table was acknowledged by a gesture from the chief indicating the motive issue was closed for now.

Angered as Hana was by Brent breaking ranks, she felt a jolt of pleasure at Mahoney's remarks. She was surprised and delighted to learn she was now heading a "task force"—a good headline for today's press briefing.

CHAPTER 25

Captain McNab and Lieutenant Krause filed out of Mahoney's office. Hana and Brent remained seated.

"If you have a few minutes, Chief, Brent and I have some questions about another issue."

"Okay."

"Dr. Williams told me about a murder in Philadelphia with a similar MO. She suggested a visit there to check out the case face-to-face with the medical examiner and the detective in charge. Brent and I have gone over the evidence emailed to us by Detective Bertucci and concluded a trip would be worth the time. The loo approved," Hana said.

Mahoney listened, waiting for the punch line.

"You came here from Philadelphia a few months ago, just after the murder occurred. Can you suggest anyone we should meet with in addition to the ME and Bertucci?"

"Back then, I was in short-timer mode, awaiting final approval of the Fairfax Board of Supervisors. The case was not on my radar screen. The murder was described as gruesome. Ethnicity was not Asian; Hispanic I believe—a departure from the Blacks who make up most of the two- to three-hundred killings in Philadelphia each year. No hint of a serial killer. No note from Jack. Nothing I can add."

"What about Rambo?" Hana asked. "He also transferred here from Philadelphia about the same time."

"Officer Gustav Sorenson," Mahoney said, chuckling. "What a piece of work. I heard about your little run-in with Rambo at the gym."

"Just a routine demonstration of unarmed combat for the class," Hana said.

"Sure," the chief replied sotto voce.

Hana fought to present a poker face. She shouldn't have been surprised. Mahoney didn't miss a thing and would have learned about what happened in the gym, even though she'd tried to keep the incident quiet. Rambo didn't complain. She felt a twinge of guilt at being rougher on him than she'd normally be in an unarmed combat class. But he'd asked for it. And the cadets had to learn that violence has consequences.

"Don't concern yourself, Hana," Mahoney said. "Whatever you did, Rambo did far worse to plenty of people. His file was full of complaints about police brutality, just nothing anyone could make stick, which explains the reason we took nearly a year to get rid of him. 'Anywhere but Philly,' was our motto. What a shock when he showed up in Fairfax, even as a recruit on probation."

"But would he know anything about the Philly killing?" Hana asked.

Mahoney deliberated a moment.

"The killing was in his section of town. To follow proper procedure, interview him."

CHAPTER 26

Allowing herself a few extra moments, Hana luxuriated in the shower. The past two weeks' tensions flowed down the drain. The combination of a satisfying early run with Othello and refreshing spray sparked her with renewed enthusiasm.

Today's schedule centered on the trip to Philadelphia to check out Wilhelmina's hunch the murder there might be related to the Ripper case. She was determined to set her partner straight about the need to stay on the same page when discussing sensitive issues with the top brass. Despite that irritant, she concluded, Brent was proving to be a valuable asset.

Othello barked a warning.

Emerging from the shower dripping wet, she realized the Lab was reacting to the ringing doorbell.

"Othello, quiet."

Slipping on a terry cloth robe, she hurried through her bedroom, leaving a trail of damp footprints. She removed her SIG SAUER from its holster, double-checking that a round was in the chamber. The cautious cop looked through the curtains in the bay window, where she had an unobtrusive view of the front steps.

The man standing on her doorstep looked vaguely familiar, but she couldn't place either him or the black Range Rover parked in front of her condo.

Holding the pistol behind her right hip, she opened the door several inches.

"Good morning, Hana."

"I'm sorry. Have we met?"

In a flash, she remembered. A few months ago, her neighbor and childhood friend, Jane Fabrizi, had introduced her to the boyfriend of the moment, a fellow reporter at the *Washington Post*, whose name she struggled to recall.

"I'm Lincoln Bartlett, a friend of Jane's."

"Ahhh, Jane introduced us last fall." She adroitly shifted the pistol to her left hand. She shook the reporter's powerful hand and felt hard calluses. Her memory was starting to return. She recalled Jane mentioning Lincoln was a rock climber, which explained why shaking hands with him felt like getting a massage with sandpaper.

An awkward pause ensued.

"Around six is early for a house call."

Standing nude under the robe and holding a gun hidden behind her hip left Hana feeling increasingly ill at ease. She eyed her unexpected caller, liking what she saw despite her discomfort.

Lincoln was lean, tall, and broad-shouldered. She visualized hard, well-used muscle under the blue herringbone tweed jacket. Brown hair, which had not seen a barber in far too long, was flecked with premature silver. The cool gray eyes seemed to be laughing at her, but there was no smile on his lips.

"I need to talk with you. May I come in?"

"It's not a good time. I'm getting ready for work."

"I apologize for the unannounced visit. But I remember Jane telling me you finish your run about this time every morning. I wanted to catch you before you take off."

She appraised him. "You still haven't said why you want to talk with me."

"I think you know—the Ripper case."

"I can't comment on any case. Contact public affairs. They have all the information the department is prepared to give the media."

"You and I both know public affairs tells only a fraction of the story being leaked."

"Not my problem."

She was growing uncomfortable under his level gaze. Somehow she knew he was aware of her bare skin beneath the robe. Her mind conjured an image of rough hands caressing her body. Embarrassment caused her face to flush.

She began to shut the door, but he put out a hand to stop it. Hana was bowled over by the rapidity and strength of his movement.

"Please let go. I don't want to have to force you."

"I have no doubt you could. But hear me out for a second. I only want to talk off-the-record. And I have vital information to share. If Jane were here, she'd be contacting you instead of me."

Recalling her friend's letters relating explicit and hilarious tales of her sexual adventures in Europe, Hana fought to keep from grinning.

The reporter released his hold on the door. Her hesitation signaled he'd piqued her curiosity.

"What information do you have?"

"Mind if I come in? This chilly air is getting to me."

She waved him into the kitchen area. Othello, who was standing guard, followed them into the room, sensing Lincoln had passed some sort of test.

The reluctant hostess pulled out a chair by the kitchen table. "Would you like a cup of coffee?"

"I'd love one."

He took a seat and reached down to pat the Lab. In response, Othello curled up at the visitor's feet to enjoy the attention.

Holding her robe together with one hand, she tipped her head to the coffeemaker. "Help yourself to milk and sugar. I'll take mine black."

Hana headed down the hall toward the bedroom, calling back, "Bagels are in the bread box. I like mine toasted."

On her return, she saw Lincoln busying himself with the fixings for a breakfast snack.

"Wow! So that's what a well-dressed Fairfax detective wears."

The outfit had the desired effect. She'd saved a chic black leather blazer for a special occasion. She wore the jacket over wide-legged charcoal gray pants. Her white Armani Jacquard tank top was a gift from her mom.

Pretending to ignore the compliment, she said, "Drink up. We need to talk fast. I have to hit the road in a few minutes."

She grabbed a toasted bagel, slathered on butter, and began chewing. She peered expectantly at the reporter.

"You know about the leaks?" he asked.

"Old news. What can you add?"

"Information is coming to the *Post* from an unidentified source in the department. What's not coming through, and what we can't print at this time, is the political angle."

"Do you mean the controversy over US-China trade? Some see economics and global politics as underlying issues accounting for the murders."

"I'm not talking about global issues," he said. "The crucial point is domestic politics. Rumors of blackmail and bribery going all the way to Vice President Costello. The next election for president could be at stake."

"Off-the-record?" She looked him hard in the eye.

"Yes."

"The department doesn't believe there's any political rationale for the murders. We're treating them as straightforward—in quotes—serial killings."

"You may want to keep an open mind. My bet is the murders in Fairfax are connected to Congress, and beyond that to Vice President Costello."

"An intriguing theory. I need facts. How about you pull together background information you think might help my investigation?"

"Glad to. Just remember. I'm a reporter. My editor will expect some payoff if I spend time on this."

"Fair enough. I'll talk to Chief Mahoney and see if we can arrange priority coverage for the *Post* if your information helps us solve the Ripper case."

After scribbling his cell phone number on the back, Lincoln handed Hana his card. "Let's keep in touch."

Watching Lincoln walk to his SUV, the fantasy of sleeping with the desirable reporter echoed in her mind. This time she smiled and didn't repress it.

CHAPTER 27

Hana and Brent Sasser were scheduled for the Acela 9:00 a.m. express train from DC to Philadelphia, with return tickets for that evening. The Acela was perfect for their purposes. After a quick trip to the snack area, they settled in. The comfortable seating made working and conferring convenient.

Hana decided the time had come to confront Brent for contradicting her in the meeting with Chief Mahoney.

"You cut me off at the knees with the top brass when I proposed we give priority to a business motive in the Ripper case. I'm the lead detective. Your job is to back me. If you don't agree, that's fine. But tell me privately, so we can talk the issue through."

"Hold on. How was I to know you were going to throw out that cockamamie idea in Mahoney's office?"

"Where were you when I was meeting with Pei at Great Falls? We talked about political and business motives for the crimes. He pushed political. I said that was far-fetched, but there might be some basis for considering a business conspiracy."

"I was there. You asked Pei if he was suggesting 'some bizarre business scheme.' Those were your words. You went on to concede there may be a 'business motive.' I thought you were stringing him along. Never occurred to me you were taking that crazy notion seriously."

"Crazy notion? With the big bucks at play in the Chu and Lee families, a business conspiracy has to be considered."

"If you thought a business motive played such a major role in the crime, why didn't you bring that up when we rehearsed for the meeting in my suite at the Ritz-Carlton?"

She considered the question, wrinkling her brow. "Because we were focused on the nitty-gritty of our investigation. Besides, have you forgotten our conversation in the cafeteria about how central China is to our investigation?"

"I can see now why you've earned the reputation of being so damn stubborn."

"You're confusing the issue. The point is how we work together as partners. I've got your back. I have to know you've got mine."

"It doesn't mean I have to lie and say 'I think you're right' when I know you're wrong. One of the things I've always hated about the Bureau is how higher-ups get bent out of shape if anyone tells the truth, even when it's unpopular."

Hana glared at Brent.

Assessing her reaction, Brent said, "How's this for a compromise? I'll make every effort to keep us from getting in a situation where we're on opposite sides of an issue. If one of us slips up and stakes out a position the other can't support, appear to go along. Later, we'll compare notes. We'll go back and lay out a revised version that conforms to what we both believe."

"Works for me," she said.

The detectives got off the Acela at the 30th Street Train Station and took a taxi to the Philadelphia Police Department, where Detective Bertucci had arranged for them to be escorted to his office.

Hana mused how the pandemonium in Philly contrasted with the relative order in the Fairfax squad room.

"Let's get out of here and go someplace where we can get a mug of java and talk," Bertucci said.

They walked to the nearest cop hangout, appropriately named

the Blue Bar and Grill.

Coffee was served, black all around.

Hana opened her briefcase and began spreading documents and pictures on the table. She was a bit self-conscious about her burgundy Hermès briefcase, but she enjoyed showing off her mom's generosity, a closeness she'd been reluctant to acknowledge until the encounter with Mrs. Lee.

Bertucci raised his eyebrows at the classy luggage but said nothing. He focused his attention on the assembled evidence, which was more extensive than anything already forwarded by email.

He whistled softly.

"This is one sick bastard."

"We need to know if the MO is the same," Brent said.

"Not the same, but similar," Bertucci said of the method of operation, skimming the file.

"The cuts on the breasts were done in the same fashion, a sharply defined cross. The gouges on the vagina were different, not as many, and the feeling was less violent, less out of control. The ligature markings and cut on the throat were identical. The positioning of the corpse was unusual, like Jack was posing a model for a painting."

"I had the same impression when I saw Deborah Chu's corpse," Hana said. She recounted how the Fairfax crime scenes called to mind paintings by Henri Matisse.

Bertucci's reaction signaled he'd never heard of the classic French painter and couldn't care less.

"The significance of our victim being Hispanic, not Chinese, is unclear," Bertucci said. "She's a Jane Doe. We never did identify her. In overall size and appearance, she resembled the Fairfax victims. They were upper-crust; she wasn't. Her hands were rough from manual labor. She hadn't been to a beauty salon to have her hair done professionally. We thought, and I still believe, that she was an illegal immigrant."

"If you had to guess, would you say it's the same doer?" she asked.

"Oh yeah. I'd put money on it. If you want a wild guess, I'd say Philly was Jack's dress rehearsal for what went down in Fairfax."

Brent and Hana exchanged glances.

Bertucci drove them out to view the scene of the crime, and on to the appointment with Dr. Chou, the medical examiner. They went through the same routine, albeit from the ME's perspective.

When they returned to the station, Bertucci provided them with a full set of evidence in the case, augmenting what had been emailed. The documentation provided more detail, without changing the overall picture.

Just as they were thanking the Philly detective for a productive day, the station's public address system announced the 30th Street Train Station had been closed due to reports of terrorist threats.

The loudspeaker continued to blare: "Amtrak halted operations on the New York to Washington run. No trains will be stopping in Philadelphia. Rail traffic is at a standstill along the Eastern Seaboard. All personnel are directed to meet with their supervisors to receive orders regarding this emergency."

Bertucci excused himself and hurried off to an evening meeting with the top brass.

Hana threw up her hands. "I've used up the travel budget and now we have no way to get back. Rental cars will disappear like snowflakes in a heat wave. A hotel is our only option. It'll break the bank, and I'll catch hell from the loo. We can only pray rail service is restored tomorrow."

"I have an idea," Brent said.

"We need one."

"My book publisher, who's based in Philadelphia, arranged for me to have access to a suite at the Four Seasons Hotel. I can stay there free, whenever I'm in town, if they have a vacancy. Would you be willing to share? You can have the bed; I'll take the couch."

Hana was too distracted to pursue the opening about his book. "Right now, I'm so tired, I'd share a park bench."

The Four Seasons reservation desk confirmed availability, and they grabbed a taxi to the hotel.

They requested complimentary toiletry kits from the front desk. Once in their room, they divided the evidence files and settled down, Hana in the bedroom and Brent on the couch in the living room. Sometime later, files were swapped, and they continued to burn the midnight oil.

CHAPTER 28

Officer Gustav Sorenson threw away his half-smoked cigar, thrust open the swinging doors, and swaggered into the Horseshoe Bar. A pudgy bartender in his midforties stood behind the broad horseshoe-shaped cherrywood counter and gave the welcoming nod reserved for familiar patrons.

Rambo had heard the bar was once a favorite hangout of the Redskins, now called the Washington Commanders. Pictures of the players wearing their football jerseys were hung around the room. Two of the star quarterbacks from the Redskins' heyday—Sonny Jergensen, number 9, and Joe Theisman, number 7—were displayed in full-size posters.

A football fan occasionally wandered in, someone who hadn't gotten the word the current watering hole for the Washington team was no longer in Bailey's Crossroads. These days the main crowd was made up of Asians, among whom country and western music was the latest fad.

Asians were the attraction for Rambo. Asian women of a particular type: young, slim, and sexy. This was his haunt, where he trolled for quarry.

Having learned from experience that the popular Chinese imported Tsingtao beer provided a conversation icebreaker for Asian women on the make, Rambo bellied up to the bar and ordered a Tsingtao brew. He favored the brand's distinctive taste. Stronger than US beers.

His come-on was working. A woman slipped onto the bar stool

next to him and put a hand on his arm. She was tall, perhaps five-nine. Her breasts were fuller than he preferred, but exquisitely shaped. Her figure caught stares from several men and not a few women.

"I see you like Tsingtao beer. The Tsingtao brewery is close to where my ancestors lived in China. Have you been to China?"

"No. Are you from China? You speak really good English."

"I should speak good English. I was born in San Francisco. I'm a student at George Mason University. English is my major. My name's April. My dream is to become an author and write books like Amy Tan."

Rambo puzzled over who the hell Amy Tan was. He realized he didn't give a fuck.

"April, they call me Rambo. What's a nice girl like you doing in a place like this?"

Through trial and error, he'd discovered the hackneyed line quickly sorted willing partners from those who sought the cheap thrills of harmless flirtation.

"What makes you think I'm a nice girl?" She reached over and kneaded his thigh.

Bingo.

The successful gambit triggered a surge of sexual arousal. He leaned into her hand. Her fingers brushed his groin.

A few moments later, they left the bar together.

CHAPTER 29

Putting aside the well-read files, Brent grew conscious of the bedroom TV tuned to CNN. Too tired to watch television and too wound up to sleep, he lay on the couch and stared out the window at the lights of nearby buildings.

He noticed when Hana turned off her TV and, a short time later, turned on the shower. When the drum of the shower stopped, the suite grew silent.

⌐

After her shower, Hana was on the verge of falling asleep when her cell phone rang.

It was well after midnight. Annoyed, she punched the green accept button without bothering to check caller ID.

"Brown here. What do you want?"

"This is Krause. There's been a third murder in Fairfax. What I want is you and Brent here ASAP."

She modulated her voice. "It's not feasible, Lieutenant." She started to explain the lack of transportation and the budgetary issue.

He cut her off.

"I know all about problems caused by the terror threat. The chief and McNab are on my ass to make something happen. Screw the budget. Take a cab to Fairfax. Be here in three hours."

CHAPTER 30

The Philly taxi came to a screeching stop. A broad grin cracked the tired driver's face as he received the fare, plus the generous tip he was promised if he made good time. Hana's watch showed four o'clock sharp. They didn't meet the lieutenant's three-hour target, but hadn't missed the deadline by much. They left their parked vehicles at Union Station in the District so they could come directly to the meeting.

The detectives sprinted into the new facility at the heart of the Fairfax County Police Department. Officer Rickey Watson was waiting outside the chief's office and hurried them into the conference room.

Despite the early hour, the entire task force was assembled. Chief Mahoney sat at the head of the table, looking fresh. Everyone else looked wilted. Captain McNab and Lieutenant Krause flanked their boss. Drs. Wilhelmina Williams and Edwina Edison sat together on one side of the room. Officers George Manley and Pete Yardley, both bleary-eyed, stared at the ME and CSI tech from across the table.

The new arrivals took their seats next to Wilhelmina and Edwina. Hana psyched herself for the briefing and gained a spurt of energy.

Despite the early hour, the ME had the group's attention.

Wilhelmina shifted into surgeon persona. Traces of fatigue disappeared when she switched on the afterburners physicians magically activate when coping with an emergency.

"A third victim was discovered around midnight, this time in Lake Braddock Park. The crime scene is a little over a mile from Culmore Park, where the first two victims were showcased."

"Jane Doe number three was also Asian. She resembled Deborah Chu and Rose Lee, and, like them, she was beautiful. But she was younger, several inches taller, with fulsome breasts. She was killed earlier in the evening, somewhere between nine and eleven. We haven't completed a full autopsy, but I gave her a cursory examination, looking for similarities and differences among the three murders."

Hana started to raise her hand to ask a question, then gestured to Wilhelmina to continue.

"Jane Doe number three was killed elsewhere and transported to the park. The MO was similar to the other two victims. The ligature marks and slash on the throat were the same. So were crosses carved on the breasts and wounds in the vagina. There was no obvious indication of Rohypnol."

Wilhelmina paused to dramatize the next point.

"There was one major difference—Jane Doe number three had intercourse before she was killed. Sperm in her vagina and anus. Intercourse was consensual, although it was rough sex. There were several bruises on her body, but nothing of the severity we see in forcible rape. My guess is she didn't make a habit of participating in kinky sex. This may have been a first for her."

"So we have DNA," Hana said.

"We do. Once we have a suspect, we can tell if he's a match."

When Wilhelmina concluded her remarks, she asked Edwina to pass out copies of the latest parchment message from Jack.

Jack has a bonus for you. Don't count on any more like this.
Jack the Ripper

"What does it mean?" Hana asked.

"You're not gonna like my answer."

"For God's sake, Edwina," Wilhelmina said, glaring at the CSI tech, "it's too damn early to be coy. Give us your best guess."

Edwina nodded her head. "The words *bonus* and *don't count* suggest this murder is not part of the *double-trouble* mentioned in Rose Lee's note."

"If that's correct, we still have two murders to go," Chief Mahoney said.

"Precisely. Another meaning of *Don't count on any more like this* could refer to the abundance of clues left this time."

"You mean the presence of semen? Or something else?" Hana asked, struggling to follow the bouncing ball.

"We got an anonymous 911 call shortly before midnight telling us the location of the victim," George Manley said. "Officer Yardley and I responded. We called in other officers and cordoned off the crime scene. CSI found a coaster that came from the Horseshoe Bar in Bailey's Crossroads."

George stood to emphasize his points.

"The coaster was a major break. Officer Yardley and I interrogated the bartender. He ID'd a photo of Jane Doe number three. In his words, she was a 'babe' he'd never seen before, and he kept his eye on her. He recalled she paired up with a big dude who comes in occasionally to pick up young Asian women. The barkeep described a guy wearing blue jeans with a blue and white Western shirt. The kind with pearl snaps rather than buttons. Big. Six-three or more, over two hundred thirty pounds. Extremely muscular. Blond, close-cropped hair. Clean shaven. Sort of a 'wise-ass attitude.'"

Hana glanced closely at Mahoney. The chief nodded confirmation.

"You just described Rambo," Hanna said of her unarmed combat opponent. "Print out a personnel photo of Officer Gustav Sorenson. Show it to the bartender with the usual set of pictures. If he confirms the ID, we'll pick up Rambo. Brent and I will go with you to make the arrest. Rambo is nobody to fool with. Whether he has a weapon or not, he's armed and dangerous."

"Get moving," McNab said. "In a couple of hours, we're going to have a community in turmoil, even more terrified of Jack the Ripper. The panic will throw a monkey wrench in our investigation. The sooner we make an arrest, the sooner things will calm down."

The patrolmen hurried out.

"Let's not jump to conclusions," Hana said.

"Whaddya mean?" McNab half rose, face flushed with nascent anger. Muscles bulged in arms that were bigger than some men's thighs. The street cop he'd been for a decade was never far below the surface.

"We have enough evidence to arrest Rambo if he's identified by the bartender, but that doesn't mean he's Jack," Hana clarified.

"Why the hell not?"

"Everything feels too easy. Like we're being spoon fed. There's this anonymous tip. Next, the Horseshoe Bar coaster is found. We get a perfect description of Rambo, who picked up the victim at a bar where he's known to hang out. Rambo may not be the sharpest knife in the drawer, but he's still a cop. No way he's that dumb."

"Right," Brent said. "We've gone from a careful, controlled killer who leaves two crime scenes with no usable clues to a nearly identical killing with a bucket of clues dropped in our lap."

"A common denominator of all three killings is Jack's fucking with us," Edwina said. "I agree with Hana and Brent. Things are not what they seem."

"Let the DNA evidence do the talking," Wilhelmina said. "If Rambo is a match, we'll confirm it's his semen."

The chief stood to signal the meeting was winding down. "We'll check out Rambo, from ID to DNA. But we're not going to put all our bets on the same hand. Our search for a serial killer will continue. We're covered whether or not Rambo turns out to be Jack."

CHAPTER 31

When Rambo answered the knock on his apartment door, his eyes locked on Hana.

"Whatcha doin' here, bitch?" He took a step forward as though about to attack but did a double take when he took in the four bodies in aggressive stances bracing him. George and Pete's hands hovered near still-holstered weapons.

"Gustav Sorenson, you're under arrest for murder." Hana read him his rights and confirmed the handcuffs were clamped tight.

Rambo looked disgusted but made no attempt to resist. "I don't know what the fuck you're talking about. I want a lawyer. A public defender is okay. The next time I open my mouth will be to him."

Hana wondered, *Why isn't he asking questions? Is it because he's guilty of murder or is it the instinctive reaction of a cynical cop who hates my guts?*

Once the holding cell door in the Fairfax jail slammed shut behind Rambo, Hana said to her team, "Go home. Get some sleep. We'll meet in the squad room in six hours."

She followed her own advice. Went home, went through the motions of playing with Othello, napped restlessly, and returned early to the Major Crimes squad room only slightly revived. The others trickled in.

"Let's review the evidence and make sure we've covered all the bases. Things have been moving so fast, there's not been enough time to pool our ideas. We need to keep the top brass informed, but the squad room is where cases get solved."

She turned to the two patrolmen. "Before we get started, I want to commend you both. You've worked hard and smart. Your reports are outstanding—well written, concise, following the proper format, and no typos."

Pete blushed. "Well, truth is we've had some help from Nadine. She goes over our rough drafts on the computer and cleans them up."

Hana stared in amazement at the administrative assistant. Who'd have thought she had a motherly instinct? She eyed the two cops. *Or is some other instinct at work here?*

Lieutenant Krause strode up to the group and spoke to George and Pete. "You officers are doing a great job. Your reports are the best of any I've read in years. When this case is over, I'm gonna have you tutor the detectives."

Krause left. The four collapsed in laughter. Nadine peered over, doubtless wondering, what could be so funny.

Hana waited until the laughter subsided and continued. "Finish briefing me about your interviews with Deborah Chu and Rose Lee's neighbors. You reported that witnesses in each building mentioned seeing two Asian men who visited late at night. Is that a coincidence? Or could the same two men have been visiting both women?"

George recapped the vague and inconsistent descriptions of the nocturnal visitors.

Hana reflected a moment and shared a look with Brent. "One of them could be Executive Director Wang of the China Future Society. We wondered whether he had a thing going with Rose Lee."

She opened the China Future Society folder given them by Pearl Chen, hustled to the copier, and ran off some duplicates. "Look over these pictures of key staff and board members. Show them to the witnesses. See if they recognize anyone."

She remembered Brent telling her about the look on Pearl Chen's face when Dr. Wang talked about Rose Lee. "And check if any of the women in the pictures visited the victims."

Hana thought of Rambo and said, "Also ask if they saw a White male visiting or hanging around the premises of the victims."

She turned to Brent. "What've you heard from the FBI? Have the gurus at the Behavioral Analysis Unit come up with any answers?"

"So far, BAU has struck out. We may have to rely on the classic profile of serial killers: White male, single, aged twenty to forty, anti-social, victim of childhood abuse and/or substance abuse, yada, yada, yada."

"If BAU can't shed any light on the case, perhaps we should consult with Dr. Livingstone, my criminology professor at George Mason. My mom has been urging me to involve her. I've been toying with the idea of going for a PhD and asking her to be my thesis adviser. Not only is Livingstone an authority on serial killers, but she's very knowledgeable about China, having spent time there in her youth."

Brent lit up with enthusiasm. "She's probably the foremost expert on serial killers. I attended one of her lectures at the Academy when she was on a consult with BAU. Thinks light years out of the box."

CHAPTER 32

Cheryl Livingstone welcomed Hana. Taking in Brent, she said, "You must be Detective Sasser." Penetrating blue eyes lingered on Brent.

The professor was stately, almost regal in bearing, standing eye-to-eye with her visitors. She looked fetching and professional in a smartly tailored mocha pantsuit. Blond tresses crowned her image, her striking eyes bracketing a patrician nose.

"Thank you for meeting with us on such short notice, Dr. Livingstone," Hana said.

"Cheryl. No more Professor or Doctor. You're here as a colleague, not a student. May I call you Brent, Detective, so we're all on a first name basis, or can an FBI special agent stand that much informality?"

"My pleasure, Cheryl. One of the advantages of working with Hana is that I can dispense with the Bureau's protocol."

Hana gaped at Brent, stupefied to hear him acknowledge there were any pluses in their partnership. She noticed how taken he was with the professor. The attraction seemed to be mutual.

She blinked, suddenly aware of how gorgeous Cheryl was. No wonder Brent was captivated by her.

Brent looked around the room. "This looks more like a museum than an office. Is that Thompson submachine gun operational?"

"It is a museum, privately funded, but sanctioned by the university. Unfortunately, to comply with federal firearms regulations, the weapon has been rendered inoperative. The Thompson belonged to a member of the Chicago Capone gang. Everything displayed here is to help students understand the diverse worlds of serial killers."

Raising his eyebrows, Brent said, "I'm astounded to hear you classify old style gangsters as serial killers."

"*Now* I remember where I saw you," Cheryl said. "One of my lectures at the FBI Academy. You sat in the front row. Your comments on that occasion were similarly thoughtful."

Tuned in by now to the dynamic interplay between Cheryl and Brent, Hana stared open-mouthed. Brent was actually preening in response to the professor's stroking, like he'd been voted Teacher's Pet for the day. Hana wondered whether every male student reacted that way to Cheryl's magnetism. She resolved to pay more attention to all that goes on in the classroom.

Cheryl shifted into lecture mode. "Let's not echo the stereotypes about serial killers. They're not all young male loners who had traumatic childhoods. The dynamics of their behavior are complex and vary with the individual. A common denominator of serial killers is he or she murders a number of people—at least two, sometimes dozens, in separate events."

Hana recognized the information as coming straight out of Cheryl's tome, *Serial Killers*.

"The act of killing grows out of their psychological compulsions. The killing provides release. They 'get off' on the mechanics of murder, often experiencing orgasm during the event. Male serial killers may ejaculate on the victim even when no intercourse has taken place. The irresistible impulse that compels them to commit each crime is satisfied by the killing itself. Sometimes they prolong the satisfaction by reliving the event over and over in their minds. To do this, they may take pictures or other souvenirs. Regrettably, the psychic release is only temporary. The compulsions return in a never-ending cycle, which accelerates in tempo and intensity with each slaughter."

Cheryl gazed at her visitors to underscore her next comments. "This is as true of professional killers, like the gangsters of the 1920s and 1930s, as it is of Ted Bundy, the Son of Sam, or Jack the Ripper. The difference is the gangster has no motive to conceal his true character. On the contrary, the more horrible and inhumane his acts, the more his services are valued."

Brent nodded. "If you agree to help us, I'd like to hear you relate your theories about serial killers to our case."

He pointed to the next display. "This looks like a miniature replica of Unabomber David Kaczynski's cabin."

"Correct. The bomber is a special type of serial killer. He has no personal contact with his victims. Often, the person killed is a matter of chance. The bomber may, and Kaczynski certainly did, have a broader 'cause' that provides a partial rationale for the slaughter. Quoting Freud, human behavior is 'multiply determined.' We struggle to identify simple explanations for the actions of serial killers. 'He was sexually abused as a child,' or whatever. The truth is more complex. Analyzing a serial killer like the Unabomber forces us to tease out the multiple strands of what made him kill."

Hana eyed Brent. She sensed he was shaken by memories of how another serial bomber had destroyed his family. She identified with his struggle to focus on the present.

Brent stopped before a trophy case of sports memorabilia. "By the looks of this, you were a champion fencer. How does this display jibe with your comment that everything here is designed to help the students understand serial killers?"

"Students must come to know not only the subject matter, but also the perspective of the teacher. Otherwise they will never comprehend the topic. This exhibit illuminates a formative period of my life that shaped my character and aspirations."

Pointing to the display case, Cheryl said, "I was a champion fencer, coming out number one in US and several international meets. I expected to be a member of the US Olympic Team. My situation was similar to Hana's. A tragic event disabled me and prevented me from competing. Unlike Hana, however, the tragedy was of my own making. Out of pride, arrogance, and stupidity, I went skiing before the Olympic competition. Not satisfied with taking a foolish risk, I had to ski the most difficult course, and to race at top speed. I was out of control and had an accident, a compound fracture of the leg. Hana and I both lost the chance to win a gold medal in a sport we loved."

Hana, who had noticed the trophy case on previous visits but never heard the story, asked, "Did you compete after the accident?"

"No. I could never regain championship form. The problem was I fenced right-handed and my right leg was the injured limb. With fencers, the dominant leg, the right in my case, becomes hyperdeveloped from constant strenuous use. My leg never recovered its former power. My movements were slowed a fraction of a second and lost a bit of fluidity. That doesn't sound like much, but, as you know, Hana, in world-class competition, it's the margin separating winners from losers. I tried to shift to fencing with my left hand, but never quite got the knack. I accepted the inevitable and retired from competitive fencing."

Hana concluded the Cook's tour had gone on far too long, and the information was a replay of Cheryl's book. The byplay between her partner and the professor, which she interpreted as borderline flirting, was becoming more and more irritating.

"Cheryl, we've taken up too much of your time. We should focus on the Ripper case."

The criminologist waved them toward her office where they settled into comfortable leather chairs around an Asian black lacquer table.

Opening her briefcase, Hana pulled out a large manila envelope containing the principal files on the Ripper case. "We'd like you to be a consultant to the department. However, there's no funding for this purpose. If you help us, the work will have to be pro bono."

"Don't give the fee issue another thought. Any criminologist would give her eye teeth for a chance to be involved in a case of this magnitude."

Hana breathed a sigh of relief. She was uneasy about asking her professor to volunteer. Such services often elicited handsome consulting fees from jurisdictions far less well-endowed than Fairfax County.

Cheryl examined the contents of the envelope, focusing on a file folder marked Philadelphia. "What does the City of Brotherly Love have to do with killings in Fairfax?"

"Our theory is the killing in Philly was a dress rehearsal for Jack's killings here." Hana went on to spell out Rambo's arrest pursuant to his involvement with Jane Doe number three and how he was still in Philadelphia when the Hispanic victim was assassinated.

"The puzzling thing about the Philly connection is nothing has appeared in our media," Cheryl said. "Someone in the department is leaking to the *Washington Post*. The other reporters pick up the thread from the Post and add a little embroidery and local color of their own, but they don't seem privy to any critical facts. One way to track down the leaker would be to determine what sensitive information, like the Philadelphia story, is not being leaked, and to identify the people in the know. The *Post*'s source will be someone outside that inner circle."

"We'll pass on that tip to Chief Mahoney. Our job is to catch Jack, not the leaker."

Cheryl hurried to her desk and rummaged through some drawers. She came back carrying a powerful magnifying glass. She examined photos from the crime scenes, starting with the first, Deborah Chu, and jumping back and forth from the second, Rose Lee. Review of the visual evidence was interspersed with skimming portions of the medical examiner's autopsy reports.

"Some things stand out. We get hints about the nature of the killer. Most serial killers are either organized or disorganized, but Jack seems to display a complex mix of both traits. During the crime, Jack gets caught up in the event, starting off planful and in control, next losing it, regaining control at the end. When Jack is in control, he has the impressive ability to subdue and to assassinate the victim and transport her to Culmore Park, leaving no traces. The cuts on the breasts are amazingly precise; a surgeon would be hard put to do as well under similar conditions. Posing the victims and escaping without a trace are also features of an organized killer."

Hana noted Brent was transfixed listening to Cheryl's cogent explanation.

"In contrast, consider the stabbing of the vagina, perhaps twenty gouges in all. Such a frenzy almost always occurs with the disorganized killer, and often one with a personal relationship with the victim. I'm not sure how to interpret the manner of leaving the note, but serial killers often leave messages to provoke the police. One way of flaunting their superiority. Of course, for some, leaving a note is a manifestation of a secret urge to get caught. My guess would be that's not the case with Jack."

"Our CSI tech, Dr. Edwina Edison, keeps emphasizing, that Jack's fucking with us," Hana said.

"The language in the notes is an example of taunting behavior. Possibly sleight of hand to throw us off."

"What else stands out?" Brent asked.

"The parchment. I've never heard of another case in modern times where parchment was used by a serial killer. Parchment is hard to make, relatively rare, and there are a limited number of places where it can be acquired. Consider the possibility the parchment used may date from Victorian England, a century and a half ago."

Turning her attention to the remaining documents on the table, Cheryl began to peruse the file on Jane Doe number three.

"Christ," she exclaimed in horror, "I know the victim."

Stunned, the detectives looked at her with anticipation.

"She was a student at George Mason. Her name is April Kwan. Last semester she took my class on Criminology 101. April was a gifted writer. She saw herself as the future author of the Great American Novel, and she might have pulled it off. Her term paper was the best written of any I've read in years. I gave her an A- because she was a little weak on subject matter. She could never quite grasp the subtleties of the criminal mind."

"Do you know anything about her family?" Hana asked, anxious to determine whether April fit the profile of rich parents engaged in trade between the US and China.

"I never met them. They're Chinese Americans of modest circumstances from San Francisco. April was on scholarship. She tended to live beyond her means. Next to literature, her favorite activity was shopping at Tysons stores like Saks and Neiman Marcus. She was full-figured, but beautiful enough to be a model. The downside of having a fabulous wardrobe was she had to pinch pennies for everything else. The title of her paper was 'The Lives and Motivations of High-Class Call Girls."

"April's interest in call girls is a clue to vulnerability," Hana said.

Cheryl nodded. "Rambo is your suspect. Tell me more about him."

Hana filled her in.

Cheryl shook her head. "Even with the Philadelphia connection, I find it hard to picture Rambo as Jack. But you have DNA evidence, which should narrow things a bit."

She looked at Hana, a perplexed frown creasing her forehead. "Why are you consulting me when you already have a suspect in custody with the prospect of being able to confirm a link to the victim?"

"Like you, we have misgivings about Rambo being our serial killer. The department wants to pursue all lines of inquiry."

"I'm pleased to be involved. We've gone about as far as we can today."

As Brent was preparing to leave her office, Cheryl said, "Here's my card. Give me a call when you have a spare moment, and we'll swap stories about the Academy."

CHAPTER 33

Pearl Chen was obsessed with trying to guess Jack the Ripper's identity. Her greatest fear was whether she was destined to be Jack's next victim. Two of the women killed were affiliated with the China Future Society, and she was the most prominent woman on the Society's staff. Not for the first time, she resolved not to let anyone know her fears and the litany of her reasons for being afraid.

She'd seized on the notion one of the board members might be the assassin. Raymond Malik, the sole Caucasian on the China Future Society's board, was her prime suspect.

Pearl's eyes darted around from the closed mahogany entrance into the board room to Chairman Zhao and back again. She was standing by her high-back black leather chair, waiting for Malik, the only member of the board yet to arrive.

As usual, Zhao had come long before the scheduled start time and greeted other members as they entered the board room.

Watching Zhao fidgeting at the head of the massive red granite oval table, Pearl realized he looked less formidable than his ruthless accomplishments testified. Executive Director Wang sat at his right hand. Pearl, Wang's special assistant, would take her place to the chairman's left once things got under way. The eight board members who'd already arrived were grouped around the table looking bored and annoyed.

At the edge of Pearl's peripheral vision, she recognized Zhao's telltale signs of nervousness prior to the start of a meeting. The stakes for the current meeting were higher than any previous one in her memory. Having quickly exhausted his feeble supply of small talk, the chairman was growing increasingly restless. Body language left no doubt of his impatience for Malik to appear.

Pearl knew Raymond Malik was prone to believe he could make his own rules, and he was probably right. Strict about starting meetings precisely on time, the chairman usually allowed Malik more latitude than his peers.

She'd devoted countless hours of research to uncover Malik's background. The billionaire had won his place on the board by virtue of the contributions of his firm, based in Shanghai, to China's economic growth. Malik played the voice of reason in the Society, balancing the hotheads who advocated a militant course for China's reemergence as a major power with an argument for continued economic growth as the path to greatness. Pearl was suspicious when someone as ruthless as Malik in his business dealings acted as a peacemaker on policy issues. She had no doubt Zhao treated Malik with kid gloves because the entrepreneur could swing a majority of the board his way on almost any issue.

"When Mr. Malik arrives, we'll begin our meeting." Zhao looked around the room as though seeking approval for his pronouncement.

William Qian spoke up. "Our business is too important to delay. The Society is threatened. Through us, China is in jeopardy. Malik was informed of the meeting schedule along with the rest of us. A quorum is present. Let's begin."

His pinched countenance and blue pin-striped suit made Qian look every inch the lawyer he had been for over thirty years. Pearl often heard members speak of him as a royal pain in the ass. Qian was a lightweight on the board. Everyone knew the conflict between Qian and Malik grew out of a decade-old battle the attorney had lost. Pearl couldn't picture Qian as a killer—certainly not if he had to get blood on his hands.

Zhao ignored the lawyer's argument for starting the meeting.

The door to the boardroom flew open. Malik strode in, as if it were his private domain. Pearl noted the chairman relaxed when the missing member arrived.

Apart from a curt nod to the chairman, the latecomer gave no acknowledgment that his tardy arrival had delayed the meeting. He plunked down in his chair, which emitted a palpable groan from the three hundred plus pounds concealed beneath the exquisite tailoring of his custom-made cashmere suit. His broad shoulders and massive arms were clues to the champion athlete he had been before gluttony became his favorite sport.

Clearing his throat, Zhao said, "Dr. Wang suggested we hold this special meeting to discuss the extraordinary developments related to the Ripper murders. Today we must settle on a course of action to protect the Society's reputation and influence."

Mireille Sun tapped the table with a gold pen. "We speak of threats to the Society. Let us remember it is women who have been killed. Deborah Chu and Rose Lee were affiliated with the Society. Let us consider the possibility others, perhaps members of the board, may be at risk."

"Thank you, Madam Sun." Zhao nodded in assent. "We're concerned for the people at risk in equal measure to any threat to the Society's ability to achieve its goal of furthering China's interests."

Of all the board members, Mireille Sun was the one Pearl most admired and sought to emulate. She was the elder of the two women on the board. In her sixties, echoes of her youthful beauty were evident. Her model-thin silhouette was imposing in an Oscar de la Renta cobalt floral taffeta gown with matching slim pants. The aroma of custom-designed perfume—an exotic blend of jasmine and Oriental flowers—announced her presence. She had grown super-rich as CEO of one of the largest cosmetic companies in the world, the principal supplier of beauty products to Asians everywhere.

Other than Malik, Sun was the most influential voice in the Society's leadership. When provoked, she could be fierce—a true dragon. Although reluctant to cast Mireille Sun in the role of assassin, Pearl admitted to herself the dragon lady matched Malik in sheer ruthlessness.

Pearl watched Kathy Wu's hands flutter nervously, waiting for her turn to comment. Wu was the other female board member. A colorful TV commentator, both in dress and forthright manner, she'd been getting a lot of airtime on Sunday talk shows, especially since controversy over US-China relations began to heat up. The Ripper case gave media producers added incentive to showcase her.

A fashionable long silver dress coat fell to mid-calf and set off a black silk gown that hit just above Kathy's knees. Knee-high silver boots with spiked heels completed the ensemble. Her once-black hair was now a dramatic vermilion and hung midway down her back, accenting her exotic appeal.

Given her close friendship with Kathy, Pearl wondered if she could be objective about the possibility the TV commentator was an assassin. Once more, upon reflection, Pearl assured herself there was no way Kathy could have murdered the three victims.

Pearl was aware the chairman almost always called on more powerful members first. Kathy was near the bottom of the pecking order, so she had good reason to fidget.

To Pearl's surprise, Zhao said, "Ms. Wu, you have your delicate finger on the pulse of the press. Please summarize how the spin given recent events is likely to impact the Society."

CHAPTER 34

Television persona took command. Kathy Wu stood and paced the room, eyeing each of her listeners in turn. "This is a time of destiny for China. Her military power is surpassed only by that of the United States. The Pentagon is terrified of confronting a China that possesses both unlimited troops and sophisticated weaponry."

Crossing the room to face the chairman, she posed dramatically and continued. "China's economy is the second largest in the world. China is the only Communist country to succeed economically. Everyone marvels at the synthesis of our political system and the unique forms of dynamic capitalism that have evolved. Americans are awed and frightened by the leverage of the 1.4 billion Chinese people on the balance of trade and the strength or weakness of the US economy."

Pearl marveled as she watched Kathy's tricks in capturing the attention of her audience.

"We are at the dawn of another era when the world will once again be dominated by two Great Powers, China and the US. Opinion makers speculate whether this contest will be played out on the chessboard of economic rivalry or explode in military chaos."

Rudely interrupting Kathy's discourse, Raymond Malik said, "Many of us in the Society believe our influence in promoting trade between the United States and China promotes peaceful coexistence and avoids the threat of a Cold War-type conflict."

Ignoring Malik, Kathy addressed Zhao's initial question. "The spin is twofold. One school fears the worst. Many in Congress are in this camp, which appeals to isolationism, protectionism, and White nationalism. These sentiments have been on the rise since the onset of radical Muslim terrorism. A second school points to benefits from access to China as a virtually unlimited market for American goods, including autos and computers, and a source of inexpensive imports. Were the flow of these Chinese goods to Walmart, Amazon, and other outlets to cease, the domestic economy would be crippled, triggering an international depression. The Society must find ways to support the second school, which is in the best interest of China's economy and global influence."

Malik's body language presaged another interruption, but Kathy's cold stare kept him silent.

"Against this backdrop, how have the murders of three Chinese women . . ."

Pearl noticed Kathy's calculated failure to describe the victims as Chinese Americans.

". . . affected US-China relations? You might expect sympathy for the murdered women to tip the balance more favorably toward China. You would be wrong. The crimes and associated media coverage are a reminder of China's prominence and presumed threat. Such sentiments have been exploited by the isolationists, egged on by Senator Jimenez from California."

"Well said," Robert Li stood, pounding the table in a form of applause. Others nodded in affirmation.

Malik's tight grimace signaled she'd won the day.

Kathy made a slight bow of acknowledgment.

Li elaborated. "You have summed up the situation. But how do these murders fit in? Only two seem related to the Society; perhaps that is just a coincidence. The third was a student of no consequence. These killings may have nothing to do with our interests."

"Li, you are the perennial Pollyanna," Qian scoffed. "To you nothing is ever a problem, so you never need to trouble your mind with finding a solution. Face facts. The Society is being assaulted. We must retaliate by unmasking the attacker and discovering his motive."

Pearl noticed the chairman hesitate, perhaps deliberating whether he should intervene in the incessant squabbling. In classic form, Zhao did nothing.

Madam Sun rose to her feet and strode to the bar at the back of the room. With everyone's attention riveted on her movements, she chose a bottle of Evian and returned to her seat.

The cosmetic baroness threw her hands theatrically in the air. "We are making a mystery of an issue that is crystal clear. These murders were committed by someone who calls himself 'Jack the Ripper.' He chose this nom de plume for a reason. Ask yourself, for what is Jack the Ripper famous? The answer is . . . killing prostitutes. The triviality that we are in Fairfax and he was in London is irrelevant. So is the race of the victims—Chinese in place of Caucasians."

The room grew quiet with her listeners awaiting her next words.

"The essential element is the social role of the women murdered. They were all whores. In some way, our modern Jack saw Deborah, Rose, and April as whores. I would conjecture he believes the Society is a pimp for harlots. I can't explain how April fits the scenario, since she may have actually *been* a harlot, but she had no association with the Society."

"My dear Madam Sun," Qian began, "why do you suppose Jack selected Deborah Chu and Rose Lee? They were affiliated with the Society, but hardly first rank. I would have thought he would have picked you if the motive were to make the point you theorize."

Madam Sun scoffed. "Is it a tribute to the effectiveness of my makeup or a result of fading eyesight that it has escaped your notice I've been too long on the vine? The choicest grapes turn to raisins in time. Were Jack to aim high, targeting a board member, Kathy Wu would be the logical choice."

Kathy looked startled, glancing behind her. Pearl wondered if she was expecting an assassin to leap from a dark corner of the room.

"Why women at all?" Mah Ho said, never making a secret of his homosexual predilections. "Jack is discriminating against males. In the modern era, there's no longer a distinction between the sexes."

Barely audible, Madam Sun said, "Vive la différence."

Daniel Ming, one of the richest members of the board, said, "We should take seriously the potential threat to Kathy Wu. For that matter, Pearl Chen may also be at risk. Her article in the latest issue of our journal was a brilliant analysis of the inexorable forces that will project China to world leadership in the near future. Dr. Chen is not a board member, but she is the most influential staff in the Society, apart from Dr. Wang, of course."

On Pearl's list of potential assassins, Ming ranked just behind Malik and Madam Sun. She discounted his seeming concern for her well-being.

She had ample evidence Ming was a pirate in his business dealings. He wouldn't hesitate to kill if it were to his advantage.

Executive Director Wang responded to Ming's mention of his name, doubtless to underscore his relevance. "With the board's permission, and assuming the ladies agree, I will take immediate steps to arrange for bodyguards. We should take every precaution until we ascertain what's behind all this."

The group's body language signaled assent. "It shall be done. Madam Sun, perhaps . . ."

With a look that would have heated liquid nitrogen, the dragon lady killed the thought before it was uttered.

Jin Yang, who had remained as silent as a Buddha during the deliberations, lifted his hand and prepared to speak. Pearl knew Yang played two roles, depending on the issues under discussion. He headed a worldwide construction company and was a wealthy businessman. He was also the conduit for the thinking of Counselor Pei, serving, at times, in the role of an unofficial, but de facto, representative of the Chinese government.

"We are allowing ourselves to be distracted by the colorful sideshow of these serial killings. I have no objection to providing protection for the lovely ladies but let us not lose sight of the main goal. The Society is being threatened because of what we represent. The vital interests of China are in jeopardy. Safeguarding China is where we should focus our efforts. Jack the Ripper is nothing but a puppet for the enemies of China."

"Yang is right, of course," Ming said. "Powerful forces are instigating these killings to arouse public fears against China."

Near the conclusion of the meeting, Pearl made a final decision on her roster of suspects.

CHAPTER 35

Raymond Malik was Pearl Chen's first choice as the assassin, closely followed by Daniel Ming. To be honest with herself, she'd have to include Mireille Sun, reluctantly admitting Sun may even rank ahead of Ming. None of the others on the China Future Society's board could make their bones.

Pearl recognized her speculation about who might be the assassin would have little impact in the real world. She resolved to keep her own counsel. Although she knew her role in these meetings was to remain quiet and provide support, on this occasion, she believed it necessary to speak out.

"The Fairfax police task force assigned to the Ripper case is only modestly competent. Hana Brown, a Nisei rookie detective, is the lead. She's able, but inexperienced. Her partner, Brent Sasser, is an FBI special agent, reputedly out of favor with the Bureau leadership because of a book he wrote critical of the FBI's response to international and domestic terrorism. He's been exiled to a one-year, dead-end assignment in Fairfax where he's second-in-command to Brown. The detectives have sought help from Cheryl Livingstone, Brown's professor at George Mason University. She's a leading authority on serial killers, but thus far has come up with nothing tangible."

She slammed her hand on the table.

"The police are getting nowhere. They've arrested a cop nicknamed Rambo, but neither Brown nor Sasser think he's Jack. I recommend we hire our own investigators and track down Jack. The Wellerton Agency has the resources to provide bodyguard protection and private investigators."

"I agree with Dr. Chen's proposal," Malik said. "We should commission the Wellerton Agency to investigate Jack the Ripper."

"I disagree," Qian said. "Catching Jack is the job of the Fairfax police."

Prolonged and meandering discussion followed. When the chairman put Pearl Chen's proposal to a vote, there was only one dissent.

CHAPTER 36

Cheryl Livingstone spun the Black Sapphire BMW Z4 roadster into the parking lot under the Ritz-Carlton Hotel. She ascended to the twelfth floor and pushed the buzzer for room 1207.

Brent gaped open-mouthed when he opened the door. The professor was decked out in a blue silk dress with spring flowers embroidered in delicate colors. The gown's cut accented her statuesque body. Pale blue Manolos with stiletto heels left her looking down on him.

"Well, are you going to invite me in or just stand there and stare?"

He stammered like a schoolboy, backing up to wave her into the suite. Eyeing her, he said, "I thought you wanted to meet me here to discuss—"

She put a hand on his arm. "We're going out to dinner. Afterward, I'll show you my home, which is near the university. Whenever we decide the evening is over, I'll drive you back here."

Cheryl steered the BMW through winding rural roads, zooming over hills so steep it was impossible to see oncoming cars until the last moment.

"We're headed to L'Auberge Chez Francois in Great Falls. The restaurant is famous for gourmet French country cuisine. The owner died a few years ago in his nineties after an amazing career. He was imprisoned by the Nazis during World War II and forced to work as a chef at the Four Seasons Hotel in Munich. One can imagine worse sentences for a POW. The restaurant is about twenty minutes from Tysons."

She squealed the BMW into the restaurant parking lot. She parked in the only remaining space in front of a quaint white structure with red trim. Once inside, Brent and Cheryl were transported to a charming Alsatian country inn.

"Bonsoir professeur le docteur Livingstone."

Pleasantries were exchanged and the couple was escorted to a table with a window view of the moonlit garden. Sipping wine, Brent said, "I've heard getting a reservation here takes a month. How'd you get us in on such short notice?"

"They treat me like family. Better than some families treat their own. I did them a small professional service as a business consultant once and refused to bill them since they are my friends. Anytime I want to come, they make a choice table available. I rarely dine here on the spur of the moment because I don't want special treatment. Tonight . . . well, let's just say tonight is an extra-special occasion."

Brent and Cheryl lingered over a gourmet six-course dinner, during which they shared their personal backgrounds and chatted about their various experiences with the FBI. Once the dinner was over, Cheryl drove toward Fairfax City. Less than a mile past George Mason University, she turned off a secluded street onto a long driveway and parked outside a two-car garage. She exited the roadster, circled to the passenger side, and grasped Brent's hand. Hand in hand she led him up the slate sidewalk into the house.

She escorted him through the foyer into the living room. One wall was dominated by a display of fencing equipment: shields, swords, and other edged weapons.

"This room is my private sanctum. Few people have been here. Students are never invited."

She gestured at the wall. "This is an extension of the fencing display you remarked on in my office, a reflection of my character and aspirations."

"I recognize the fencing gear. The pirate's cutlass. A rapier like the Three Musketeers used. A broadsword from the days of King

Arthur. And a cavalry officer's saber from the Civil War."

"Confederate Army, since we're in Virginia," she said, smiling at his enthusiastic interest.

Brent pointed to a long single-edge blade with an ornate handle big enough to be held by two hands. "That's a Japanese Samurai sword. Tom Cruise fought with one of those in *The Last Samurai*. The Samurai sword reputedly has the sharpest blade of any sword."

Cheryl smiled. "And a well-deserved reputation. The Japanese call it a katana. Samurai also carried a short sword, a wakizashi, which you see hanging under the longer one."

"What's this?" he asked. "Looks like a bamboo fishing pole."

"A sword used in kendo, Japanese-style fencing. The mask, body armor, padding, and gloves displayed with the kendo bamboo sword are all part of the fencer's equipment—somewhat parallel, if you use your imagination, to Western fencing gear. If you recall, Tom Cruise practiced kendo in the movie and took a lot of hard knocks before he mastered it."

"And these over here," he said, pointing to the display at the far end of the wall, "medieval weapons—axe and mace—used in the movie *Timeline* based on Michael Crichton's book."

"Brent, you've a pretty fair knowledge of edged weapons. But you seem a bit unclear about the boundaries of where history leaves off and fantasy begins. Except for the Civil War and the cutlass, all the examples you gave—King Arthur, The Three Musketeers, *The Last Samurai*, and *Timeline*—are fictional. Let me assure you, these weapons are lethal and were used by real people." She waved her hand. "Enough talk of weaponry. Let me show you the rest of the house."

They walked down the stairs to the recreation room, which was divided into two main areas: a small theater and a billiard room.

She pointed to the theater. "Here's where I prepare the audiovisuals for my lectures."

He cast a look at the lectern stored in a corner.

Noting his interest she said, "I use the lectern for a full dress rehearsal when I'm getting ready for a formal speech, such as at the FBI Academy."

"But do you watch TV or movies here?"

"Sometimes to relax I watch old movies or classic thrillers. My favorite is Hitchcock. Perhaps you could join me some evening."

"It would be my pleasure . . . I see you have a professional pool table." Examining the pool cues in the wall rack, he added, "Excellent equipment, too."

"How is it you know so much about billiards?"

"My dad owned a pool hall." Brent grinned. "My misspent youth was dedicated to playing pool. By age fifteen, I could beat anyone in our small town except my dad. He was a pool shark who played in a lot of exhibitions."

"Do you still play?"

"Not really. I haven't touched a pool cue in over a dozen years."

"Would you like to try? Say a friendly game of eight ball?"

"I know I'm being hustled when anyone starts talking about a 'friendly game.' Sure. Let's give it a go."

While Brent racked for eight ball, Cheryl walked to a small refrigerator, pulled out a bottle of Merlot, opened it, and filled two glasses.

He realized the bottle was the same as the wine they had imbibed copiously at the restaurant.

It dawned on him; Cheryl left nothing to chance. Life to her was an elaborate chess match.

They played a few games. She won every time. The wine did nothing to improve his performance, but it helped to ease the chagrin at his long-lost virtuosity.

Checking his watch, he said, "Time to throw in the towel, wave the white flag, or whatever I must do to surrender. The last time I looked at the eight ball, I imagined there were two of them."

She opened a fresh bottle of wine. "Now, on to the rest of the house."

They walked up the staircase to the second floor, which led to an immense bedroom. An inset floodlight in the ceiling provided the only illumination, shining on a king bed covered by a golden down quilt.

The seductive woman reached behind her neck, seized the fastener, and undid the zipper with one fluid motion. The blue silk fluttered to the floor. Her bare breasts reflected alabaster white. Stripping, layer by layer, she unveiled the image of a Greek goddess.

Brent's blood raced with the stimulation from the wine he'd consumed, catalyzed by the sensual attractiveness of his companion for the evening. Sexual excitement prompted him to overcome his last inhibitions. He began removing his clothes, hurrying as she moved toward him, her hips swaying.

As Cheryl walked past the end of the bed, she reached over and yanked the quilt, tossing it toward a corner of the room. She sprawled on the bed, spreading her legs wide in an unmistakable invitation.

Sexually intoxicated, Brent embraced her, showering kisses on her body.

CHAPTER 37

Hana glanced at her watch and noted the time was 6:25 a.m. She buzzed her partner's hotel suite and was startled to see a haggard Brent appear.

"Holy shit. Carver Washington has the words for your condition: 'you look like you've been rode hard and put away wet.'"

"I didn't get much rest last night," he mumbled, showing the combined effects of sleep deprivation and a brain-frying hangover.

She guessed what must have transpired overnight, asking, "Were you putting in a little overtime with our consultant?"

"Don't start with me Hana. I'm not in the mood."

Hana raised her eyebrows.

In an uncomfortable silence, they headed toward the car. She'd scheduled a seven thirty meeting at Carver Washington's Leesburg area farm. The flustered young woman was determined to make it on time.

This was her first trip to the Leesburg farm since her dad had been killed six years earlier. Prior to the Chinatown tragedy, she'd accompanied her parents several times a year to visit Carver, his wife Fatima, and their children. After Carver and her dad became partners, the visits grew more frequent. But since Chinatown, she couldn't bring herself to face the memories a trip to the rural retreat would rekindle. Today's trip was essential. Only a sense of duty would prompt her to overcome six years of ambivalence and travel to the farm.

A lingering concern about calling undue police attention to their presence in Loudoun County led her to mute the siren, content with winking blue lights to help them squeeze through the grudging openings in traffic. On the dot of seven thirty, she pulled into the road leading to the farm.

Still giving her partner the silent treatment, she walked up on the porch, knocked once, and entered in the time-honored manner of friends accustomed to country hospitality. She had barely crossed the threshold when her misgivings about the visit evaporated.

She felt like she'd come home.

Carver had already reached the foyer and gave her a warm hug. He offered Brent a welcoming handshake.

"So you're Hana's heralded partner. Come in. Before Fatima left for work, she baked cinnamon rolls." He led them to the kitchen and pointed to pastry and coffee on the farm table.

"Is Clennie on the way?" Hana asked.

Taking pity on Brent for being left out of this family-oriented dialogue, she explained: "Clennie is Carver's oldest. He's a legislative assistant to John Blair, the first Black senator from Virginia. Clennie has some 'off-the-record' information to share with us. McNab and Krause would blow a gasket if they knew we were taking Carver, and not them, into our confidence."

She turned back to their host. "Have you heard from Edwina? She should've been here by now."

"Dr. Edison's coming with Clennie."

Hana gave Carver a questioning look.

"Been dating a few months. Fatima says they're living together."

Pondering the unexpected news, she heard the approaching sound of Clennie's Chevy Silverado pickup.

A few moments later, Edwina entered the kitchen, looking harried.

"I'm so sorry to be late Hana. There was car trouble."

"Not my truck," Clennie said. "A couple was stalled on the side of the road. The driver waved for help. We stopped. He said he was rushing his pregnant wife to the hospital. In the excitement, he forgot his cell phone. We called 911. A deputy sheriff arrived within a couple of minutes to give them a lift."

"Our arrival was a godsend," Edwina said, picking up the refrain. "The wife was more than ready. She promised to name the baby Clennie, if it's a boy, and Edwina, if it's a girl."

"Where were you when you stopped to help them?" Hana asked.

"Don't worry," Edwina said. "We crossed the Fairfax line and were in Loudoun County. No way anyone from the sheriff's office here would recognize me."

The newcomers were already washing down cinnamon rolls with the Washington's unique blend of Blue Mountain and Columbian coffee.

Hana marveled, even though Clennie and Edwina appeared to be an odd couple, they were at ease with each other. She fantasized about having a similar relationship with Lincoln Bartlett. Forcing herself back to reality, she repressed any further thought of her unsatisfactory love life.

"Here's the situation . . ." Hana said. "Officers George Manley and Pete Yardley went to Jane Doe number one, Deborah Chu's, condo in the Rotonda and interviewed neighbors who ID'd three visitors from photos given us by the China Future Society: Executive Director Wang, Wang's special assistant Pearl Chen, and board member Daniel Ming. All were regular visitors."

Beginning to show signs of life, Brent nodded as though that was what he had expected.

"Much to the officers' surprise, the neighbors at Jane Doe number two, Rose Lee's, condo near Government Center also reported frequent visits by the same three visitors: Wang, Chen, and Ming. Neighbors at both places described a Caucasian who was a frequent visitor to the two victims. We had a description but no photo. This could have presented a problem, but we got a lucky break. Edwina . . ."

Edwina beamed. "George and Pete confiscated laptop computers that belonged to each of the victims. The computers contained encrypted files. I cracked the code and discovered Rose Lee and Deborah Chu were conspiring in a blackmail plot. They had a third partner in the intrigue identified only as X."

"Who were they blackmailing?" Brent asked, fully alert at the prospect of making tangible progress on the Ripper case.

"Albert Johnston, who's a legislative assistant to Senator Raphael Jimenez from California. The senator may be the real target because it's his voting power that Johnston leverages."

"Here's another break," Hana said, "George discovered Johnston's Jag was given a parking ticket around the block from Rose Lee's condo early in the evening the night she was murdered. When the officers went back to the witnesses with a photo lineup, several of them ID'd Johnston."

"Sounds like we have probable cause. Why don't we pick him up?" Brent said.

"Not so fast," Hana said. "There are major political complications."

Clennie explained. "Hana alerted my dad, who touched base with me to ask what was going on in Congress. Senator Blair—he's my boss—and Jimenez are both on the Senate Committee on Foreign Relations. Both men have played leadership roles on opposite sides of the controversy over US relations with China."

Brent nodded to further confirmation of Hana's theory that the Ripper killings were linked to China.

"The basis for the blackmail appears to be Jimenez's swing vote on key issues. He's made no secret of his anti-China position, but he has the power to tip the scales either way on vital legislation. Johnston, Jimenez's main man on China, was taking bribes from organizations that stood to gain or lose billions depending on Congress's action. The two women threatened to expose Johnston and Jimenez if they didn't rig the system to support the Society's point of view."

Hana reasoned Clennie's interpretation of events was as much a reflection of "pillow talk" with Edwina as his insider's take on developments in the Senate.

"The politics get worse," Clennie said. "Senator Jimenez is a close ally of Vice President Bernard Costello. The vice president has been a wheeler-dealer on negotiations concerning China, putting his thumb on the scale to support the protectionists. There's no conclusive evidence implicating Costello in anything illegal at this point, but, if the bribery is exposed, it would result in a major political scandal. The next election for president could be determined by the way the China card is played."

Echoes of Lincoln Bartlett's comments in her kitchen about a domestic political connection to the killings reverberated in Hana's memory. She mused whether Lincoln and Clennie could be right, aware Jack the Ripper's killings could determine the outcome of the upcoming presidential election.

She turned to Brent and said, "Someone in the department is leaking information about the Ripper case. That's why it was necessary to meet at the farm. I was hesitant to alert Captain McNab or Lieutenant Krause because the leaks could be coming from their offices. I propose we hold off arresting Johnston but keep him under surveillance."

"I agree with Hana," Carver said. "Once we pick up Johnston, the lid gets blown. The media will have a field day. I'll update Chief Mahoney. This new evidence underscores our doubts about whether Rambo is the perp. We should put a twenty-four-seven tail on Johnston to be sure he stays out of trouble until the chief gives us instructions how to proceed."

CHAPTER 38

Kathy Wu picked up the study phone in her McLean home, hit speed dial, and was connected to Pearl Chen.

"Pearl, I'm glad I caught you. Are those Wellerton bodyguards still following you?"

Complaints from Dr. Wang's special assistant echoed her own experiences.

"I just got back from interviews at CNN in Atlanta and NBC in New York. The guards flew on the plane with me, even insisted on remaining in the other room of my hotel suite. When I was at the TV studios, they hung around, making a nuisance of themselves. They freaked me out."

Continuing her litany of discontent, Kathy said, "These Wellerton goons don't even know how to behave around a woman. Half of them act like they want to get me in the sack. Tonight's pair of guards take the cake."

She paused for emphasis.

"Bulldog, the short one—he's probably five-and-a-half-feet tall and weighs over two hundred pounds—is in the living room securing the front of the house. The tall one—called Tiny, even though he's six-six and three hundred pounds—is in the kitchen, eating everything in the refrigerator. If I'm attacked, all Tiny would have to do is lie down on the Ripper and it's all over."

She laughed at her own joke.

"This whole bodyguard shtick is just a way for the board to act like they're doing something. I'll give it a week. If nothing happens, and I doubt anything will, I'm telling Wang to wrap it up."

After listening to Pearl respond in a similar vein, Kathy said, "The word on the media grapevine is the cops are getting nowhere. Thanks for suggesting the Society commission Wellerton to investigate Jack. Wellerton's bodyguards may leave something to be desired, but the company's investigators are supposed to be top drawer. I'm going to sign off now and see if I can sneak into my kitchen and steal a cup of tea without getting raped by Tiny. Sometimes, I feel like I need protection from my bodyguards."

Kathy hung up. She reflected on how much she enjoyed talking and hanging out with Pearl and resolved to call her tomorrow to propose they take a weekend trip to Annapolis and spend the day on the water.

Bulldog eyed the grandfather clock as it tolled twice, mouthing, "Christ. Two in the morning."

He blanched at the thought of enduring two more hours before the next bodyguard shift was due to arrive. He was ambivalent about his attraction to "the Chinese broad" as he and Tiny called Kathy Wu.

Around midnight, Bulldog had complained to his partner, "The Chinese broad is a stuck-up TV mannequin. She wears those 'fuck me' clothes but when I look interested acts like I'm dog shit waiting for a pooper scooper."

Now he started walking toward the kitchen to touch base with Tiny who had gone to get his second "midnight snack," wondering why the hell his partner was taking so damn long.

Tiny checked out the refrigerator, debating the relative merits of another ham and Swiss on rye versus third helpings of roast beef. Unable to decide, his massive hand picked up a jar of kosher dills.

He heard a noise and started to turn around.

The blade entered the left side of his neck and slashed, ripping through his Adam's apple. Tiny lunged backward, groping for his attacker with hands flailing empty space. The pickle jar sailed through the air, smashed on the tile floor, and spewed kosher dills across the room.

Bulldog heard the commotion, drew his Glock, and hurried to the kitchen. He burst into the room, weapon pointed forward. He felt a knife slash his gun hand. His pistol flew from nerveless fingers. He screamed.

Reacting instinctively from years of training and combat experience, the veteran bodyguard pulled the Baby Glock from the holster over his spine and tried to aim it at a blur of motion that seemed to be everywhere.

He staggered from the impact of a knife thrust in his left shoulder and watched his backup pistol spin across the room.

With two useless arms, Bulldog knew legs were his only weapons. A powerful karate kick struck empty air. He felt his leg seized in a viselike grip. He howled as a blade sliced through his right Achilles tendon. He staggered, fell back against the refrigerator, and slid to the floor. Added pain barely registered as his left Achilles was severed.

Helpless, he lay on the tile resigned to the coup de grâce, which was not long in coming. The knife slipped between ribs and entered his heart. Racked with pain, he watched as blood pumped out and mingled with pickle juice. Bulldog's last image was his assassin's back heading for the stairs leading to the level with the four bedrooms.

Awakened by the crash of the pickle jar hitting the tile floor, followed by Bulldog's scream, Kathy sat up in bed. She'd faced danger when she was a cub reporter on the crime beat and took pride in knowing how to react in a crisis. Without hesitation, the plucky TV commentator dialed 911 on the bedside phone and reported an armed home intruder.

With her left hand, she grabbed the tactical light on the table by the phone and pointed its powerful beam toward the closed bedroom door. Her right hand drew a loaded Colt .357 magnum from the drawer in the table.

Kathy aimed the revolver toward the center of the zone of light targeting the door. She held her breath and waited. Either there would be an "all clear" from the bodyguards, or Jack would open the door and enter the room.

Kathy's nervous system felt the cumulative chemical effects of adrenaline. During a brief but far-too-scary tour in Afghanistan as a war correspondent, she'd been coached how soldiers reacted to fear and tension: peripheral vision narrowed, muscles clenched, and hands trembled. She didn't have the benefit of the months of training and experience necessary for soldiers and first responders to learn to control their reflexes under extreme stress. She remembered being lectured that an hour a month at the range, firing at a static target, didn't cut it.

Unconsciously, she held her breath.

Running out of air, she gasped. Upon hearing footsteps and seeing the bedroom door fly open, she fired three shots in quick succession. Her wrist, unused to one-handed fire with the powerful revolver, pained from the recoil. To Kathy's credit, the first bullet went where she'd aimed. The other two ripped gaping holes in the door frame and the adjacent wall. The target, still unseen, was missed. The doorway remained empty.

A shadow swooped through the doorway, crossed the flashlight's beam, and leaped to the far side of the room. Two more shots. Both misses.

Kathy was very good at counting her shots. One bullet remained.

Near panic, she debated whether to wait until she was attacked and fire at close range, or risk her only remaining shot.

Kathy waved the flashlight beam around the room, trying to spot her assailant. "The beam is bright enough to blind your attacker," the ads asserted. No one told her how difficult it was to pinpoint the eyes of a shadow flitting across your bedroom in the dark.

The shadow lunged toward the bed. The Colt exploded. A wild shot drilled the ceiling.

Strong hands seized her. She struggled to break free of the iron grip. Thrown on her back atop the bedclothes, she could smell the blood from the killer's knife. The pictures of the Fairfax victims she'd seen replayed in the privacy of the studio flashed through her mind.

"Please," she begged, "Not like that."

The knife stabbing into her pubic area was the worst pain she could imagine. She whimpered, pleading with her assailant to stop the unending torment.

Staring at her attacker's face, even in the dim light of the bedroom, dawn of recognition caused Kathy to gasp.

"I know you . . ."

Her strong, trained voice grew weaker in response to the thrusts in the vagina becoming increasingly frenzied. Suddenly, her body was flipped. The killer grasped her hair, pulled back on vermilion tresses, and exposed the throat. One quick slash and Kathy was gone.

CHAPTER 39

Chief Mahoney agreed with decisions made by Hana Brown and Carver Washington during the clandestine meeting at the farm.

The chain of reasoning was simple and straightforward: Why pick up Johnston if arresting him was certain to trigger a political shit storm? The smart option was to keep him under twenty-four-seven surveillance. Why involve Hana's superiors? Briefing them increased the odds of a leak to the media. Apart from Carver and herself, the brass had no "need to know."

That was yesterday. This was today. Kathy Wu's death changed the equation. Keeping Captain McNab and Lieutenant Krause in the dark turned out to have been the wrong choice. Any murder by Jack would have been bad news, but the dramatic killing of the high-visibility TV commentator in her own home, with the Fairfax police arriving too late to prevent the crime or catch the killer, was a ring-tailed disaster. The murders of the two Wellerton bodyguards only added to the fiasco.

The chief was aware she was vulnerable to criticism for the way she'd handled the situation. To let a known suspect run free, despite a proven connection to the China Future Society, at a time when one of the Society's board members—a national celebrity, no less—was assassinated, was borderline malfeasance on her part. The strong evidence of Johnston's involvement in bribery, and suspicion of murder, didn't help matters.

Mahoney was awaiting the imminent arrival of Captain McNab and Lieutenant Krause. Meeting with them was as welcome as a trip to the dentist for a root canal.

Hearing the doorknob turn, she rose to face the music. She greeted McNab and Krause, wasted no time on preliminaries, and told them the whole story from the top. Why Rambo was no longer a suspect since he was incarcerated at the time Kathy Wu was murdered. Why Johnston was now a suspect. And why they'd been kept out of the loop.

Krause looked ready to explode. "I'm Hana's supervisor. What right does she have to keep me—"

McNab cut off the lieutenant's tirade. "Either I run Major Crimes or Carver Washington does. What the hell's going on?"

Mahoney listened to her key subordinates vent, and, as her counterarguments were summarily rejected, ate humble pie. After several minutes of fruitless back and forth, she led the captain and the lieutenant into the conference room where the task force members were waiting. The attending cops failed to mask the pretense of having ignored the shouting that had emanated from behind the chief's wall.

McNab and Krause were still visibly seething, but pained expressions communicated they were trying their level best to keep a lid on it. They glared daggers at Hana and Brent, but aimed their worst looks at Carver. When Mahoney had informed them Carver Washington would be at the meeting, their initial reaction was to refuse to attend. Only her smoothest diplomacy persuaded them Carver's help was vital at this juncture.

"Now we're all briefed," Mahoney said, trying to put a positive face on the situation.

"Yeah," McNab said. "We're all together, one big happy family, behind the eight ball."

"To some extent, that's true," she said. "Let the record show it was my decision that put us there. I accept full responsibility. If anyone has to take the fall for this, it'll be me."

Expressions around the table softened at her stand-up style of shouldering the blame. "The Buck Stops Here" was an award she'd just earned—a distinction with fewer honorees in the Washington area each year.

"Let's get down to business," she said. "We'll cut Rambo loose. Most of us were skeptical he was Jack despite the evidence he'd screwed April. We'll arrest Johnston for murder. The case is far from airtight, but we can't let him run loose any longer. He was under surveillance in his McLean home, but he could have slipped out unobserved. Any criticism we get at this juncture will be for not moving sooner. Hana, your task force will continue to pursue all leads. We're not certain Johnston is Jack. This could be another red herring."

Hana nodded.

"The media's going to have a field day. I'll brief county and state politicos, so they can be ready with the proper spin."

Hana jumped in. "One more thing, Chief. What are we doing to stop the leaks? People outside the department are learning as much about the case as I am."

Adjusting her glasses, Edwina looked like she had something to say.

"Edwina?" Mahoney prompted.

"My guess is whoever's doing the leaking is tapping the department's computer system. All the information's there. I suggest we go low tech."

"What does that mean?" Krause asked.

George and Pete looked equally blank.

"Hard copy. Paper. Numbered copies. Restricted distribution. Burn bags. Do it the old-fashioned way."

"Some of us have to access the computer," Wilhelmina said. "Our autopsy system is dependent on the machines."

"Not a problem," Edwina said. "I can set up a dedicated, password protected network for exclusive use of Dr. Williams at the morgue and myself at CSI. Except for routine reporting to the statewide medical examiner system, the Ripper case data will be like the Roach Motel. The data go in, but nothing comes out. We can print out hard copy for Detectives Brown and Sasser or anyone else with a 'need to know.'"

Krause, who had a reputation for hating computers and all modern technology, beamed vigorous agreement. The others joined in with varying degrees of enthusiasm.

"Wilhelmina, give us a heads up on the McLean autopsies findings." Brent said.

The ME reacted to her cue. "Kathy Wu's murder followed a different scenario from the first three victims. The 911 call shows she knew the attack was coming. She emptied her .357 at her assailant—six misses in the direction of the bedroom door and randomly around the room. Gunshot residue on her right hand confirms she fired the revolver. A tactical flashlight was found lit on her bedroom floor when the police arrived."

Brent raised his eyebrows at the extent to which Kathy's killing established a new pattern.

"No Rohypnol. No indication of intercourse or presence of semen. The vagina was stabbed first. Next her throat was slashed. Bleeding out from carotid arteries was the proximate cause of death. Postmortem, her breasts were carved with crosses in the pattern we've seen. The speedy arrival of the police left no time for posing the corpse."

"What about the bodyguards?" Brent asked.

Edwina spoke up. "The killer entered via the back patio. The lock was sprung with a knife blade. Tiny, a three-hundred-and-five-pound muscular giant, was attacked from behind in the kitchen. His throat was cut with one rip of the knife. I doubt he knew what killed him. Tiny's partner, Bulldog, came into the kitchen armed. Two pistols were found halfway across the room. A slash to his right hand and stab wound in his left shoulder were probably how he was disarmed. He was disabled by cutting both Achilles tendons. Defenseless, his heart was penetrated by a six-inch blade. He bled out in a few seconds. Blood spatter makes it clear the two were killed before the perp went upstairs."

"What about a note?" Hana asked.

"Jack waxed eloquent," Edwina said. "Here's a copy."

Qui custodiet ipsos custodes? I've plucked three flowers, assuming you've learned to count by now. One more to go. You think you'll catch Jack. Best you wonder when Jack will catch you.

Jack the Ripper

"What the hell does that mean?" McNab asked.

"Permit me to translate," Edwina said. "The Latin quote roughly says, 'Who guards the guards?' The usual meaning is 'Watch out for the guards, for they may be the thieves' or, in a political context, 'Who keeps an eye on those who are supposed to be looking out for us?' Jack's given the classic quote a bit of a twist to mean 'Who protects the bodyguards?' A direct challenge to Brent and Hana, taunting them for being unable to safeguard Kathy Wu's guardians. The comment 'Jack will catch you' is an explicit threat to kill Brent and Hana, maybe some of the rest of us."

"Holy shit," McNab said sotto voce.

Edwina ignored the diversion. "The one about having 'plucked three flowers' refers to Deborah Chu, Rose Lee, and Kathy Wu. April Kwan, you will remember, was the reference in the 'don't count' comment. If you 'don't count' April, there were three women—the 'three flowers'—who were 'plucked.' This is consistent with our hunch April was a red herring, presumably killed to direct attention to Rambo. Her murder may serve some deeper purpose, but my guess is it's just another instance of Jack fucking with us."

"Who's the 'one more to go?'" Hana asked.

Edwina shrugged her shoulders. "I wish I knew."

"Someone connected to the Society, an influential someone would be my guess," Brent said. "Pearl Chen and Mireille Sun get my vote."

"Pearl Chen is the target," Hana said. "Jack likes them young and sexy. Madam Sun was a beautiful woman in her prime. She's still striking, but even her cosmetics can't preserve those exquisite looks forever."

Wilhelmina spoke up, staring at the two detectives. "This is one deadly bastard. My job is to analyze, not give advice. I'm making an exception. If you get a chance to kill this perp, don't hesitate. Kill him. Don't wait to yell 'Police' or some other bullshit. Shoot first and sort it out later."

"Shoot first, and shoot to kill," Mahoney ordered.

CHAPTER 40

Albert Johnston pulled his Jaguar X-TYPE R into the driveway of his McLean residence and beeped the garage opener.

The legislative assistant hurried into his study, grabbed the Haig and Haig Pinch Bottle, and poured three fingers of blended scotch whiskey. He collapsed into the chair behind his desk, sipped the scotch, and took a deep breath. Trying to ameliorate the effects of a stressful day, his mind kept replaying the chess game with interests competing for Senator Jimenez's support for legislation that would have a decisive impact on US-China commerce.

Cursing the Chinese under his breath, he sought to conjure up moves to consolidate today's hard-won political victories.

The distinctive ringtone of the doorbell caused him to wonder who the hell would be calling at nine o'clock. Nobody he wanted to see, that's for sure. Opening the door, Johnston was faced with four threatening bodies staring back at him—two plainclothes detectives, backed by two uniformed cops. Hana had advised the patrolmen to wear official dress to prevent any ambiguity about the group's status. She and Brent had weapons drawn and hidden at their sides. George Manley and Pete Yardley's hands were on their pistols, ready to draw.

"What's going on?"

"Albert Johnston, you're under arrest for murder," Hana said.

"Do you know who I am?" he asked, a reflex attempt to assert his status, oblivious he'd been addressed by name in his own residence.

Hana ignored his protests, spun him around, and applied the handcuffs, tighter than absolutely necessary.

Johnston was booked and escorted to the interrogation room, accompanied by Hana and Brent. Hana observed he was frustrated, furious, and, despite his bluster, frightened to have been arrested.

"You've heard about good cop, bad cop," she said.

The suspect writhed in his chair and remained silent. He glared at the detectives.

"Now you're going to experience bad cop, bad cop. You killed Deborah Chu, Rose Lee, and several other women. How did you know Rose Lee?"

Johnston said, "Never heard of her. I've got a right to a phone call."

"In a minute, we'll take a break, and you can make that call." She wondered what kind of a dumbass legislative assistant he was not to have demanded a lawyer as soon as they'd arrested him.

Hana stood and leaned over Johnston. The suspect recoiled in his chair.

"You've never heard of Rose Lee? We've got witnesses who placed you at her condo on more than one occasion. Your Jaguar got a ticket near her home early on the night she was killed. I'd advise you to think before you answer." She gave Brent a look signifying he had the ball in the interrogation.

"How'd you know Deborah Chu?" he asked.

"I never heard of her either." Johnston began to sweat.

"We've got witnesses who said you were a frequent visitor."

The suspect tried to rise in protest.

Brent said, "Sit down and shut up. Rose and Deborah's computers had information implicating you in several crimes. They were blackmailing you, attempting to coerce you to slant trade legislation in China's favor. Also, their bank records confirm you were doling out substantial payoffs. Rose's safe deposit box contained documents that prove you accepted bribes from more than a dozen organizations in an attempt to influence legislation related to China. We've got you dead to rights for several crimes, including murder."

Johnston turned white. "I'm not a killer."

"You're not a killer, but . . ."

"But nothing. I didn't kill anyone. And I didn't do any of those other things."

"You admit you visited the two women at their homes," Hana said.

"No . . . yes. Suppose I did visit them? They were attractive young women. I'm a guy. What's wrong with that?"

"So you knew them," she said.

"All right. I knew them."

"And you knew they were connected to the China Future Society."

"Sure. I do a lot of legislative work related to China. They were both experts in the field," Johnston said, leaning back and relaxing. He was visibly regaining confidence, believing the interrogation was moving onto familiar ground.

"So were you seeing them personally, like on a date, or did this have to do with staff work for Senator Jimenez?" she asked.

Johnston's face broadcast he saw the trap. He was at a fork in the road where he had to define the nature of his relationship with the two women—business or pleasure. He thought of the sage advice of Yogi Berra, "When you come to a fork in the road, take it."

"Sort of both. I met with the women at their condos to discuss legislative issues related to China. They weren't exactly dates, but they cooked me dinner, and we talked about going out," his posture broadcast growing confidence the detectives wouldn't be able to disprove his claims.

"When you have a meeting with experts to discuss legislative issues, do you write up a report for the file or to share with the senator?" Brent asked.

"Sure. Routine procedure."

"Did you prepare a report on your meetings with Deborah or Rose?"

"No. Those were exploratory discussions. They didn't go far enough to need a formal report."

Brent looked skeptical. "Do you have any evidence to prove what you've told us about your connection to the two women?"

Johnston was sweating profusely. He shook his head. "No."

Hana shifted the rhythm, trying to keep the suspect off-balance. "Let's talk about your relationship with April Kwan."

"I don't know any April Kwan. Maybe she's one of those Chinese women murdered by Jack the Ripper I read about in the paper. A George Mason student. What does she have to do with me?" He looked genuinely mystified.

For the first time since Johnston opened his mouth, Hana felt his statement had the ring of truth. She looked at her partner, who appeared to share her thinking.

Switching questions and questioner in a routine intended to keep the accused constantly off-balance, Brent asked, "What about Kathy Wu?"

"Never heard of her." Johnston's knee-jerk response sounded hollow.

The detective didn't dignify the obvious lie with a reaction. He simply stared at the suspect.

The absurdity of denying any knowledge of a prominent TV commentator who was an expert on China, a board member of the Society, and lived close enough in McLean to be almost a neighbor, finally sunk in.

"I knew her. But I didn't kill her. I was home alone last night, driving back about ten o'clock from a working dinner. I watched TV, went to bed about midnight. I was sleeping at the time the media reported Kathy Wu and her bodyguards had been assassinated."

Hana decided to wrap it up for the evening.

"It's time for you to make your phone call."

CHAPTER 41

Hana and Brent entered the China Future Society's headquarters. Hana noticed everything looked the same as on their first visit, except for a pair of bodyguards from the Wellerton Agency.

The moment the detectives came into the foyer, the larger bodyguard put his hand on his pistol, ostentatiously pulling his suit coat aside so the weapon was visible.

His smaller companion saw the gesture and followed his lead.

Hana walked up to the big guy and got in his space. "I assume Dr. Chen informed you that two detectives from the Fairfax County Police Department were expected."

The Wellerton bodyguard clenched his teeth and gripped the pistol even tighter.

Brent kept a watchful eye on the smaller guy to gauge his reaction to the confrontation.

Without warning, Hana grasped the big guy by his gun hand, forcing him to remove his hand from the weapon. The bruiser found himself on his knees doing his utmost to avoid screaming from the excruciating pain in his wrist.

Brent had anticipated the aikido move and was ready. When the big guy's partner started to respond, half drawing his weapon, he found a pistol pressed against his neck. "Easy," Brent whispered in his ear and took the weapon from him.

Hana looked down at the kneeling bodyguard and asked, "What's your name?"

"Huh?" was the mumbled response through gritted teeth.

She eased the pressure on the wrist. "Your name. I'm sure you remember it."

"Bruno. Bruno Lichtenstein."

"Bruno, there are a couple of things I want you to remember. First, Virginia has a law against brandishing. That means—in case you've forgotten Concealed Carry 101—you can't flash your weapon around to intimidate people. Are we together on the first thing, Bruno?"

She increased the pressure on his joints, eliciting a repressed groan.

"Second, Brent and I, together with some fellow cops, are going to take a personal interest in Dr. Chen's survival. We will need you to work with us. Partners. Maybe even buddies. I believed we needed to have this friendly chat so we can get off on the right foot. Are you willing to work with us?"

This time, she reduced the pressure.

"Yes," the response was grudging, but with a tone of respect.

Hana helped Bruno to his feet, bent over and picked up his weapon, and handed it to him. She turned her back on Bruno, an action that caused Brent to flinch.

"And what's your name, Bruno's partner?"

"Mikey Schwartz."

"I'm Hana Brown. This is Brent Sasser. Brent, give Mikey back his firearm."

Brent complied, albeit hesitantly.

"Bruno, Brent and I are going to chat with Dr. Chen in the board room. She'll be safe with us. You guys take a break. Get some ice for that wrist. Come back in a half hour."

Bruno looked at Pearl Chen, who'd come out of the board room to observe the tail end of the confrontation. She gave a thumbs up.

Once the bodyguards left, Pearl said, "Detective Brown, you're amazing! Those two knuckle draggers frighten everyone who comes in the office. They even scare me sometimes, and I'm the one they're here to protect. After Kathy Wu was killed, I read their résumés, which prove Bruno and Mikey are as tough as they look. But you handled them with ease, and they seemed to accept the situation. How'd you pull it off?"

Hana recognized an opening to gain the special assistant's confidence.

"Part technique, part knowing what to do, and part training to be able to perform. But the more important part is psychology."

"Psychology?" Pearl echoed.

"How they think. What motivates them. What they respect."

"And how'd you figure that out?"

"Most of these guys are ex-military. Some are former cops, FBI, or Secret Service. Bruno and Mikey were Special Forces."

"Right. But how could you know?" Pearl reacted like she was watching a magician perform tricks.

"My summer job in college was training Special Forces in self-defense. You hang around those guys each season over a couple of years and you pick up their mannerisms: a little swagger in the way they walk, the air of intimidation in how they carry their bodies, and the way they look at you. They're always trying for an edge, physical and mental. Keep in mind, there are no second chances in combat. That world is strictly pass-fail, live or die. Special Forces training is dead serious. Their religion is 'no pain, no gain.' The person they respect—often the only person they respect—is someone who can compete with them and win."

"So that little scene was just another training exercise," Pearl said.

"Exactly. And, since I handled it matter-of-factly, they responded in kind. No hard feelings. We may get to be buddies. I'm glad Bruno gave me the opening. Otherwise, they'd resent our presence and feel they're better than we are. A dangerous, and possibly fatal, combination. Now, we can expect tolerance at worst, and cooperation at best."

Pearl stared at Hana with an expression approaching awe.

"Brent and I . . . okay if we use first names all around? Good. Pearl, we're here to talk about how we can protect you. We also need your help in catching the killer."

Looking puzzled, Pearl said, "I thought the police arrested a suspect, Albert Johnston, who works on Capitol Hill for Senator Jimenez. He's a longtime foe of the Society. I can't say I'm sorry to see him take the fall."

Pearl hesitated.

"Wait a minute . . . You arrested a cop earlier and let him go."

"Chief Mahoney informed the press new evidence had cleared Officer Sorenson," Hana said.

"Was Johnston also a mistake? Have you let him go?" Pearl asked, a note of alarm in her voice.

"No. We believe Johnston's for real," Hana said.

Brent chimed in. "We aren't taking anything for granted. We're checking out the evidence on Johnston, but we're also investigating other possible suspects. For a time, we even considered you on that list."

"Me? Why would I have been a suspect?"

"When we were here last time and Hana was interrogating Dr. Wang about Rose Lee, the look on your face was very much like jealousy. We wondered if Dr. Wang was having an affair with both of you. You were angry with Rose, and . . ." He let his voice trail off.

"And I killed her in a jealous rage? . . . I suppose I killed the others for the same reason?"

"Did you?" he asked.

"No. But, it's true Dr. Wang and I had a brief romantic interlude when I first started working at the Society. For me it was romance. I now know it was only sex for him. I broke off our liaison because I realized there was no way to balance personal and professional relationships on the job. I'm an ambitious woman. One day, I shall be executive director. I had to make a choice. The professional took priority."

Hana glanced out the window at the Washington Monument in the distance. She wondered if Pearl regretted her decision. Then she noticed a tear in the corner of Pearl's eye.

"I never got over my feelings for Dr. Wang. I was jealous of Rose and also of Deborah Chu. Wang had affairs with both of them. Kathy Wu told me he had hit on her, but she turned him down."

"Did anyone on the board have a relationship with either Deborah or Rose?" Hana asked.

"Not as far as I know."

"What about Ming?"

"Funny you should mention him, Hana. He did ask me some personal questions about Rose, but, at the time, they didn't ring any alarm bells. He was the one who expressed concern about Kathy's safety and mine at our last board meeting, which prompted Wang to get the board's approval for bodyguards."

"We have witnesses who claim he visited both Rose and Deborah."

"I don't know why I should be surprised, but I am. Both were attractive women. Just not 'sex on a stick,' like Kathy. She was sweet in private, and quite shy once you got past the public persona. I was fond of her. We talked a lot by phone."

Still teary-eyed, Pearl tried to compose herself. "She'd call me from the damnedest places. Once, in the middle of the night here, she rang me up just to let me know she was walking on the Great Wall of China . . . Forgive me. I didn't mean to get maudlin."

"I understand. A lot of celebrities have a private side seen only by close friends," Hana said. "Can you think of any reason—other than sex—why Ming might have visited the two women?"

"Not really. We share a common interest in the goals of the Society. But Ming wasn't involved in writing articles for the journal or any other activities that would put him in touch with them."

Brent nodded. "We researched Ming. He's a businessman who's multiplied the family fortune in recent years through commerce with China. The families of Rose and Deborah are big players in East-West trade. Could they have been competitors?"

Pearl laughed. "I'm sure they were . . . for some deals. In that world, today's enemy is tomorrow's friend. But anyone who's engaged in international trade over a long period of time comes to recognize the importance of keeping trade as free as possible."

"You're saying, on basic issues, they're all on the same side," Brent probed.

"Yes. The Chu and Lee families agree with Ming, but they would never speak out publicly about the Society, even though privately they support us. They fear the backlash of the senator Jimenez crowd, quarterbacked by Albert Johnston. Vice President Costello is a behind-the-scenes backer of Jimenez. But he never takes a clear public position, because he needs the support of big business for the next presidential campaign."

Hana shifted the discussion to Pearl's personal safety. "Your inside protection will come from Wellerton. The Fairfax police team will guard the perimeter. The police we've assembled will help keep you safe."

She looked at her watch. "Please tell Dr. Wang there's been a slight change of plans. We'll see him tomorrow. Our next stop is Daniel Ming."

CHAPTER 42

Hana, accompanied by Brent, drove west on the Dulles toll road and exited at Reston Parkway. She called Nadine back in the squad room to check that the administrative assistant had everything on track for the late afternoon meeting of the team responsible for guarding the perimeters at Pearl Chen's home and office. Nadine assured her that the team would be ready and they would arrive at Pearl's house on schedule that evening.

After wrapping up with Nadine, Hana turned to Brent. They needed to brainstorm theories of the crime.

"You think this case begins and ends with the serial killings of Chinese American women. But we can't ignore that there's more going on. I've come to believe political motivation about US relations with China is a major factor." She found herself thinking about Lincoln Bartlett more and more and wondered if that was influencing her thinking about the motive behind the Ripper killings.

Hana continued. "Rose Lee and Deborah Chu's computers had evidence of a plot to blackmail Albert Johnston. Rose and Deborah had a coconspirator, the mysterious X. One thing we want to find out at today's meeting is whether Daniel Ming is X or if he knows the identity of X."

"Okay," Brent said.

Hana sensed he remained anxious about the investigation moving away from a focus on the serial killings. "The case begins with the killings, but it doesn't end there. We keep hearing hints of the involvement of Vice President Bernard Costello in the conspiracy to rig votes on China for money. I never told you, but a *Washington Post* reporter, Lincoln Bartlett, met with me before our trip to Philly. He agreed to provide me with information about the VP and related domestic political developments in turn for giving the *Post* the inside scoop if his info proves helpful. Chief Mahoney agreed to the arrangement."

"I don't give a damn about the vice president or whether or how he might be involved in the Ripper case," Brent said. "What burns my ass is you met with a *Post* reporter and promised him a scoop without telling me! What the hell was all that talk about how you've 'got my back' and I'm supposed to have yours?"

"If you recall, you scoffed at my suggestion there was any angle other than serial killings to the Ripper case. Hardly seemed the time to brief you on my meeting with Bartlett. Besides, I didn't take his ideas seriously at the time. I was just curious whether the *Post* could come up with information to move our case forward." Hana resolved not to show any hint of her sexual interest in Lincoln.

"You've got to make up your mind, Hana. Either we're partners and we share all aspects of the case or we're not. If not, I'm out of here."

"Hold on." Her hands tightened on the wheel. She knew her behavior was indefensible. "I'm sorry. There's no excuse for not filling you in on my conversation with Bartlett."

Brent mumbled something inaudible and pointed to the monument-size *MING* at the top of the midrise building on their right. "Pull in here."

A stately middle-aged woman met the detectives at the reception area and escorted them into a small conference room. She introduced herself as Mrs. Kai.

"Make yourselves comfortable. Mr. Ming will be out directly."

Hana wandered around the room, taking in the high-tech audiovisual equipment, the glossy mahogany table, and the pervasive smell of big business.

Dressed in a bespoke navy blue business suit, Ming entered

the room. Although he was a man of average size and ordinary appearance, the impact of his charismatic presence impressed Hana.

"I'm Daniel Ming. I'm here to assist your investigation in any way I can." He shook hands with both detectives.

"Let me come right to the point," Hana said. She believed Pearl would have given Ming a heads up on what to expect from the detectives. "Witnesses reported you visited the condos of Deborah Chu and Rose Lee. Were those visits of a business or personal nature?"

"I met with each of the women to brainstorm an article for the Society's journal. They served as sounding boards and sources of help for the article."

"A Google search failed to uncover anything you've published in the past."

"Correct. Since receiving an MBA from Harvard Business School I haven't written anything longer than one page. I had no intention of authoring the article in question. My plan was for one of them to be my ghostwriter, but neither of them seemed interested."

Shifting gears, Hana said, "Chu and Lee found out Albert Johnston was accepting bribes for rigging the outcome of legislation affecting China. Based on that knowledge, they were blackmailing him."

Ming made a wry face. "Johnston is the scum of the earth. His boss, Senator Jimenez, is no better. Nothing they did would surprise me. But, what you say about Chu and Lee does. Both women came from wealthy families. They had no need of blackmail money."

"What was your relationship with Kathy Wu? She told colleagues you hit on her." Brent said.

"Pearl Chen is surely the source of the story. She's been telling tales out of school." He grinned broadly. "I admit to hitting on Ms. Wu. You look like a man of the world, Detective Sasser. I'm sure you've seen Kathy Wu on TV. She was twice as appetizing in person. If she climbed into bed with you in the middle of the night, would you throw her out?"

Brent flushed as the memory of his interlude with Cheryl

intruded in his thoughts. Professionalism kicked in. "This is not about me, Mr. Ming."

"My apologies. If my wife heard the story, she would be the first to tell you that more than a rejected sexual overture would be necessary to incite me to murder. Besides, if you're serious about unrequited love or overactive hormones as a motive, you'd be wise to investigate most of the males on the board, including our esteemed executive director."

Ming paused and eyed his visitors. "Now, I have questions for you. Be at ease, these are not of a personal nature. Did you know I was the one at the board meeting who highlighted the matter of Kathy Wu's safety? Why would I insist on her protection if I intended to kill her?"

Hana smiled. "Seems like a clever gambit for a killer to draw suspicion from himself. Jack is self-assured, arrogant. Someone who would welcome a challenge. Does the description fit, Mr. Ming?"

"Touché. I confess I fit the profile of an arrogant bastard, much like Jack. However, I have an alibi. Around the time of Ms. Wu's murder, I was in New York, speaking before hundreds of distinguished citizens. I stayed at the Waldorf Astoria. Flew back on my private jet the next day after the murder had taken place. Ms. Kai can provide you with documentation."

Hana tried, but failed, to maintain a poker face at the news Ming claimed to have an ironclad alibi.

"Another point," he said smirking. "Were you aware of the board's decision to engage the Wellerton Agency? The board took primary responsibility for tracking down your Jack. With all due respect, the consensus was the Fairfax police were 'getting nowhere.' This was at Pearl Chen's suggestion, a point I see by your faces she failed to mention when she was regaling you with my repressed sexual peccadilloes. Dr. Wang is the liaison with the investigators. You should ask him about progress in tracking down Jack."

Ming's last comment convinced Hana to wrap up the interview.

The detectives excused themselves and left. She was certain the papers provided by Ms. Kai would support Ming's alibi, but she remained skeptical about how much to trust the alleged timing of travel on a private jet.

Exiting Ming's building, she said, "He may not be X and he may not be Jack, but he's hiding something. His alibi of being in New York and flying back on his private jet sounds a bit too convenient."

"Even private jets have to clear their flight plan," Brent said. "Easy enough to check. I'll follow up."

Hana nodded. "Right now, we don't have enough to prove he's guilty of anything except lying while talking. The clock is ticking before there's another murder."

CHAPTER 43

Discouraged at the unsatisfactory outcome of their interview with Daniel Ming, Hana dropped Brent off at the Ritz-Carlton and drove into Vienna to reboot her brain by spending time with Othello.

She chatted a few minutes with Sam, reassuring her close friend and neighbor that nothing was wrong.

"I just need to decompress for a little while."

The ex-detective smiled sympathetically. "I understand how you feel, handling the pressure of a front-page case."

Hana's laugh was lacking in humor.

Energized by the afternoon surprise of his mistress's visit, Othello violated training protocol and jumped on Hana, placing heavy paws on her shoulders.

Her laugh this time reflected a heartfelt mixture of pleasure and relief. "I'm glad to see you too."

She gently reminded the Lab how to behave. "Down boy."

Gesturing to Sam, she said, "I've got to head out."

Without bothering to stop by her town house to collect jogging gear, including extra water for the Lab, she headed toward Church Street.

Othello's excitement grew with the recognition they were following the customary route for their morning jog.

When they approached the red caboose that marked the entrance to the W&OD Trail, Hana sat down on a bench in the park-like area.

Despite the unusual behavior of his mistress, Othello parked his bum on the ground in front of her, awaiting instructions. Receiving none as Hana stared into space, the Lab sprawled to rest.

After a few moments, she began stroking the dog's ears and worked her way down the back over his thick coat.

In a soft voice unintelligible to passersby, Hana said, "I haven't told you about Lincoln. You remember, the guy who showed up the other morning after my shower and stayed for bagels."

Othello assumed the attentive stance which was his unfailing response when his mistress launched into one of her soliloquies.

"Well, I've been spending a lot of time thinking about him. The brutal truth is I haven't had a real date in months. The Ripper case has gripped my attention, but today I feel burned out. Brent and I don't agree about the focus of the investigation. Is it China or a classic search for a serial killer?" She stared at the Lab as though expecting a profound answer.

Othello gave her a quizzical look, his head cocked to the side.

She chuckled.

"I know. You couldn't care less about such matters, but they tend to trouble people. Today, they're driving me crazy."

Hana jumped to her feet and headed toward home, deciding actions spoke louder than words, even when directed to a willing canine audience.

Moving rapidly, Othello kept pace.

Once back at the town house, she dropped Othello off with Sam, ignoring her neighbor's questions about what was going on. As soon as she entered her living room, she fished Lincoln Bartlett's card out of her pocket, picked up the telephone on her desk, and dialed the reporter. The ensuing conversation led to an agreement to meet for dinner at Randy's, a high-end steak and seafood restaurant in the Tysons area.

CHAPTER 44

After arranging to meet Hana for dinner, Lincoln Bartlett set about revising his schedule for the evening. He called his editor, Chad Mclanahan, to cancel their meeting to discuss a series of articles about US-China relations. He was amazed his lame excuse—something came up—was accepted at face value by his boss.

Lincoln arrived at Randy's twenty minutes ahead of time for the dinner date, only to find Hana already seated at a table in the rear of the posh restaurant sipping a cup of coffee. Her stunning off-the-shoulder black dress marked a dramatic contrast to his first memory of her in a white terry cloth that had barely covered what he was convinced was a nude and still-wet cop who was hiding a pistol behind her robe.

Laughing, Hana rose to her full height, standing eye-to-eye with Lincoln.

"I see we're both early," she said, leaning forward to kiss him on the cheek.

When the waitress scurried up to take their order, he followed Hana's lead and asked for coffee (black). He sipped the brew slowly while checking out the menu.

After a brief back and forth about the appetizing choices of meat and seafood, they both decided to try the crab and lobster cakes, which neither had experienced.

"How's the Ripper case coming along?" Lincoln asked.

Hana shook her head.

"No shop talk. I called you because I was desperate to get away from the daily grind of chasing a murderer. Tonight, I'm not a cop. I'm a woman who chose you as the one to be with to celebrate being a woman alone with a man. Can you accept that?"

In response to Hana's expression of raw need, Lincoln reached across the table and squeezed her hand.

He remembered little of the trivia they talked about, cognizant only that the crab and lobster cakes were unexpectedly delicious.

Foregoing dessert, they pushed away from the table and stood while the waitress—sensing their impatience—hurried to settle their bill. Once that formality was accomplished, Lincoln said, "I have a condo in Alexandria overlooking the Potomac. Would you like to see it?"

During the drive to Alexandria, they traded stories about youthful adventures. Hana regaled Lincoln about her travels to visit her grandparents in Japan. He talked about trips climbing the Rockies with his dad while growing up in Denver.

Active conversation came to a halt as Lincoln opened the door and they entered his condo.

Hana paused and looked around. Far from the bachelor pad she had expected, the living room look attractive and relaxing. One wall was arrayed with bookcases, showcasing books of all kinds, but heavy on history and politics. Other walls were hung with reproductions of paintings, mostly by long-dead European artists. Scanning the room more carefully, she recognized Chinese scrolls and Korean pottery. She was astonished to see a famous woodblock print by a Japanese printmaker.

"I see you have *The Snow Village at Lakeside*. My granddad took me to see an exhibition of Hide Kawanishi's artwork when I spent a semester abroad at Tokyo University."

He nodded. "For a while, I dated a Japanese journalist from the

Asahi Shimbun who was on assignment in DC. She was a connoisseur of Asian art and coached me on what to buy. A little over a year ago, she was assigned to Paris. That's when I started seeing your friend, Jane Fabrizi, who introduced us."

"I remember."

Lincoln cleared his throat self-consciously. "Actually, I have a couple more woodblock prints in the bedroom. Would you like to see them? Fair warning. They're fairly erotic."

"Fair warning," Hana responded. "That fits my mood perfectly."

CHAPTER 45

Hana arrived home just after dawn, thoroughly invigorated after a night of lovemaking, despite a scant three hours of sleep. She changed clothes, brushed her hair, and spent a few minutes in the bathroom to remove obvious signs of having spent a romantic evening. Then, she headed next door to retrieve Othello.

Despite Sam's efforts to put on a poker face, Hana knew he'd guessed how she'd actually spent the previous evening. Determined to resume her customary routine, she guided Othello toward the W&OD trail and ran for five miles.

Her thoughts on the trail vacillated between reliving the warm emotions of the date with Lincoln and pondering the next steps in investigating the Ripper case.

After showering and changing clothes, she decided how to proceed. She picked up the phone and dialed Cheryl Livingstone. Annoyed as she had been about Brent's one-night stand with Cheryl, she concluded that was not important in the larger scheme of things.

When the professor answered, she said, "I need your advice. Brent and I have separate theories about the Ripper assassin and the underlying motives and genesis of the killings."

"I'll be happy to help in any way I can," Cheryl said. "What are the theories?"

"Brent is convinced the crimes represent a variation on classic serial killings."

"And your theory?"

"I've come to believe the killer is somehow involved with

China. Perhaps the economic and political conflict the press keeps highlighting around the pro- and anti-China blocs in Congress is linked to the crimes."

Cheryl remained quiet for a moment. "It's possible you're both right. Serial killing is never simple. Contrary to what the FBI's Behavioral Analysis Unit seems to believe, there is no classic model for a serial killer. Each case is unique."

Hana sighed. "Our search for a suspect, as you know, has caused problems. Paradoxically, we've had too many suspects and too few. I've become convinced the killer is someone connected to the China Future Society. Daniel Ming strikes me as the most likely suspect. The problem is he has a seemingly ironclad alibi."

"What's his alibi?"

"He was giving a speech at the Waldorf Astoria before a large group in New York the day of Kathy Wu's murder. He flew back on his private jet to Dulles the next morning, according to the evidence he provided."

Cheryl laughed. "Things are not always what they seem, and rarely so when murder comes to call. I've worked for Ming as a consultant before. He has *two* private jets. Dig deeper."

"I'll do that," Hana said.

CHAPTER 46

Hana eyed the dozen cops seated in the briefing room before desk-sized individual tables. Having arrived a few minutes late for the planning meeting, she was relieved the assembled officers looked ready for action.

"Thanks for volunteering to guard the outer perimeter of Pearl Chen's house," Hana said. "The duty will be entered into your personnel jacket as 'volunteering,' although you'll be paid overtime for your service."

Chief Mahoney let it be known via the grapevine that anyone who passed up the opportunity to "volunteer" would be frowned upon. No one wanted to get on the bad side of Fire Engine Red Mahoney.

She waved to Eva Sanchez, who mouthed "thanks" from the back of the room. Eva filled in for her when needed with the unarmed combat class. She'd been doing so ever since Hana had been designated lead detective on the Ripper case.

Eva was more than a protégé and friend. Hana recalled a couple of years before when the athletic Hispanic had saved her life in an encounter with a Chicano street gang. She was confident Eva, a policewoman at age twenty-six, would make detective in a few years. To add one more star to Eva's resume, Hana arranged to have the young cop included in the group.

"Here's the situation. Jack killed Kathy Wu's two bodyguards before he killed her. We suspect him of killing six people in Fairfax. A similar kill in Philadelphia appears to have been Jack's rehearsal for his killing spree here. Make no mistake. Your life will be at risk. We need to review ways to minimize risk and to organize the specifics of your duty tours. You'll be on four-hour guard shifts. In order to keep Jack guessing, we'll randomly vary the length of the shifts. Some shifts will be as short as three and a half hours, some as long as four and a half. In fairness, the timing will average out. Questions?"

Al Sweeney raised his beefy arm. "Hana, how do we take a bathroom break?"

"You'll be assigned in pairs. Nadine will post the roster of who's on duty and the time of the shifts." Hana pointed to the administrative assistant at the back of the room, who waved to the group.

Walking to a white board at the front of the room, Hana wrote: *PARTNERS STICK TOGETHER.*

Moving to Sweeney's table in the front row, she said, "Bathroom breaks are like everything else. You stick together. When one of you has to go, you alert the bodyguards inside the house, and you go in together."

"Does my partner hold my hand when I go?" Sweeney, ever the wise guy, asked.

"Only if you've forgotten how," she retorted, bringing a chorus of laughs that loosened up the group.

"The first key to your safety is sticking together. You watch my back. I watch your back. When you're at the police cruiser, take turns—one of you stay inside, the other one stay outside the car and keep your eyes open. From time to time, walk around the perimeter of the house. Avoid a regular time for patrol. Don't be predictable."

The message was getting across. With the possible exception of Sweeney, she was encouraged by the reaction.

"A second key to your safety is to stay away from shrubbery."

She scribbled on the white board: *REMAIN IN THE OPEN.*

"Nadine, pictures of the house please."

Using PowerPoint, Nadine displayed digital photos she'd taken outside Pearl's house.

"These are various views of Pearl's house in Oakton," Hana said, pointing to the screen. "The arrow marks the front where you park your cruiser. Before you go into the house, alert the bodyguards. Pearl lives in a big, sprawling McMansion on a two-acre lot, but you just have to worry about routes providing access to the house. There are only a few landscaping plants. No large clumps of bushes where an intruder could hide. Shouldn't pose a problem. Your concern is the outside; Wellerton's bodyguards have the inside."

The visuals completed, Nadine turned off the projector.

Holding up two fingers, Hana turned to the group. "Remember these two points and you'll stay alive: partners stick together and remain in the open."

Sweeney spoke up. "Why won't Jack just use a silenced pistol or a bow and arrow or some other quiet shit to take us out from a distance?"

"Psychology."

"Huh?"

"Psychology. In Jack's way of thinking, he needs to kill within arm's reach. A knife is his weapon of choice. That's how all the murders were done. Knowing how he thinks gives us the edge."

Determined to argue, Sweeney said, "But couldn't Jack rush us and kill one of us with a knife before we could draw our weapon?"

"Sure. But what's the point? Your partner would have time to get off a shot. Even if Jack weren't hit, the bodyguards would be alerted. Backup would be called. No way Jack would have time to get past the protection and reach Pearl. None of the rest of us count in this game. Jack only scores when Pearl Chen is murdered."

Sweeney shut up, having run out of ways to harass Hana.

The briefing over, Hana pulled George Manley aside.

"George, I have a special assignment for you." She described her belief that Daniel Ming was a viable suspect in the killing of Kathy Wu, except for concern about whether his alibi would hold up of being in New York when the murder was committed and not returning to the Washington area until the following morning on his private jet. Given Brent's role in helping protect Pearl, Hana was skeptical he'd have time to follow up checking Ming's alibi.

"I recently learned Ming has two jets, so his alibi may not hold water. I'd like you to check with the Federal Aviation Administration and any other agency that has information on the comings and goings of passengers in private jets. We need to confirm when Ming returned to this area. Once you have the information, give it directly to me."

"I'll take care of it," George said.

On their way out of the meeting, the cops checked Nadine's posted roster.

Brent Sasser and Eva Sanchez caught the first shift. Al Sweeney and Pete Yardley drew the second. Hana Brown and George Manley were paired on the third.

"Al's gonna be trouble," George whispered in Hana's ear.

CHAPTER 47

Al Sweeney drove and Pete Yardley rode shotgun as their police cruiser motored up Hunter Mill Road. A crescent moon peeked through a veil of dark thunderclouds. Uncertain visibility made driving hazardous.

He kept a sharp eye out for deer, prone to dart across the road in this part of Oakton. He'd just missed colliding with a buck that showcased an impressive rack.

Al turned off into a rural neighborhood, once salted with horse farms, now peppered with two-million-dollar homes on two- to five-acre plots. He arrived on time in front of Pearl Chen's house for the beginning of their 10:35 p.m. shift.

On the drive over, the young cop listened as Al related successive complaints about Hana.

"Hana made detective when she'd only been on the force four years. Took me twelve years. To top it off, the brass puts her in charge of the biggest murder case to come down the pike. It's just 'cause she's a woman and Oriental to boot."

"Asian," Pete said.

"Huh?"

"You're supposed to say Asian, not Oriental."

"Whatever," Al said, looking around.

He pulled the cruiser next to the one occupied by Brent Sasser and Eva Sanchez. The tired-looking pair reported "all quiet" on their shift.

"That's the way I like it," Al confided as he watched the taillamps of Brent's Police Interceptor fading in the darkness.

"Time for a patrol," he said, taking the lead role in the duo.

Maglites punched holes in the dark. The two cops circled the house, checking out the perimeter. Al strolled casually, bravado hiding his anxiety. He was openly scornful of Pete's caution, as the young cop scrupulously followed Hana's guidance to "stick together" and "remain in the open."

The arrogant cop grew bored as the night dragged on. A light shower blew through, doing nothing to improve his mood.

Shortly before two, Pete said, "I've got to piss. Let's head inside."

"You go. I'll stay in the cruiser."

"No way. Hana said we should stick together."

"Screw her. She's not gonna tell me when and how I piss," Al said, still annoyed at how adroitly Hana had turned the tables on him for his feeble attempt at bathroom humor.

Pete said he'd hold it till the end of their shift, but his full bladder had other ideas. A few minutes later, he capitulated.

"I'm going in. You coming?"

"No. Go ahead. I'll have a cigarette and hold the fort."

Relaxing in the shotgun seat as Pete was let into the front door by the bodyguards, Al lit up. He emitted a satisfied groan and exhaled a cloud of smoke. The sensation reminded him how he hated the restrictions against smoking in the squad room and felt like a pariah when he went outside for a smoke break in the designated area.

The cigarette, held casually between thumb and forefinger, dangled out the window at the end of his extended arm, glowing like a firefly in the gloom.

A dark figure, almost invisible against the gray backdrop in the feeble illumination provided by the sliver of a moon, moved out of the woods. The figure approached the police car from the cop's blind side, circled around the trunk, and crept to the right front window. The steel blade glinted at the figure's side.

Al lifted his beefy arm to take another drag on the cigarette. Just then, the knife slashed toward his neck. The razor-sharp edge sliced like butter through the hard muscles in his thick wrist, ripping away tendons, and ravaging the bone. The forearm broke with an ugly snap. The artery spouted blood like a miniature fire hose. But the throat was spared.

Just when another thrust was poised to aim at the now unprotected neck, bright lights illuminated the scene.

Hana was determined she and George Manley should arrive early to ease her concerns about Al Sweeney. As the cruiser pulled near Pearl Chen's McMansion, she saw a dark figure stabbing an arm outside the cruiser window.

She hit the siren and flicked on high beams.

"Call for backup and paramedics. I'm chasing Jack."

Flooring the accelerator, she attempted to run down the attacker with the speeding cruiser. But she wasn't fast enough.

The figure raced toward the woods. Hana leaped out of the still rolling vehicle, leaving it to George to slam on the brakes. Drawing her weapon, she started firing as her target slipped into the shelter of the trees. She emptied her magazine. BAMBAMBAMBAMBAM.

She reloaded, switched on her tactical light, and charged into the woods. Stumbling around in the scrub trees and underbrush, she realized further pursuit was hopeless. Heading back, her eye caught a shiny reflection. She stopped near the tree line, dropped to one knee, and pointed her light on a patch of weeds. The sight of blood confirmed she'd winged the son of a bitch.

When she returned to the cruiser, George was applying a tourniquet to Al's arm. The victim was going into shock. Pete stood by with weapon at the ready. Sirens blared in the distance, rapidly drawing near.

Calling dispatch, she said, "Get CSI here ASAP. Pass the word to Dr. Williams and Dr. Edison that we've got the killer's DNA."

Walking toward the two cops rushing toward the action, she yelled, "Take a look in the woods; you may have better luck following the attacker than I did. Watch out for the pool of blood at the edge of the woods."

She watched the two cops searching the area, hoping for the best while believing the chase would prove futile. But the experience would give them a feeling they were part of the action.

Returning to the cruiser, she said to George, "I winged Jack. Probably a flesh wound. Our perp lost some blood. A couple of officers are trying to track him down, not that I'm too optimistic. Once we have a suspect, we can confirm whether or not he's Jack."

CHAPTER 48

Hana called Pearl Chen's perimeter protection team together for a late morning debriefing. She walked to the front of the room and the murmur of voices died down.

"Al Sweeney's in Fairfax Hospital. He'll pull through, but his arm may be permanently messed up. Pete will brief us about last night."

Pete explained the sequence of events leading to his partner's stabbing. He didn't gloss over violation of the "partners stick together" rule.

Hana replayed the instructions of how to stay alive on protection duty, then she dismissed the group. After a pause to consider next steps, she turned to Brent.

"Let's grab some lunch and talk strategy."

Lost in thought, the partners stoically waited their turn in the cafeteria line, paid for their lunch, and moved to a table in a quiet corner.

"We're back to square one," Brent said.

"Right. We've jailed Rambo and Johnston, prime suspects in the serial killing of Chinese American women. Jack's attacks during the times they were incarcerated clears them both—at least of murder. The press is crucifying the department for what they've described as a 'bumbling investigation.' I'm surprised they haven't pointed the finger at me, since I'm heading the so-called Ripper Task Force."

Brent nodded. "Mahoney's acceptance of full responsibility for the debacle got favorable treatment in a *Post* editorial. The paper contrasted her stand-up behavior with that of most public figures who mouth 'accountability,' but don't know the meaning of the word. The best news for the task force was Lincoln Bartlett's column exposing Johnston's bribery to influence legislation. Senator Jimenez is implicated. The blackmail appears to have forced the senator to back off from tipping votes against China in favor of the protectionists. The *Post* assigned a team of investigative reporters, headed by Bartlett, to get to the bottom of the scandal. The protectionist cause is experiencing a severe backlash. So far, there's no mention of what role, if any, Vice President Costello played. You may be right about the political infighting behind these killings."

Without alluding to her date with Lincoln, Hana said, "Let's stay focused." She returned Brent's stare without blinking. "Our job is to catch a killer. The bribery and blackmail may be just a diversion. Except for Executive Director Wang, we're running out of suspects, Daniel Ming looks guilty to me, and we need to double-check his alibi."

She continued to eye her partner to judge his reaction to her next statement: "I think it's time to go back to Professor Livingstone. She may be able to reboot our brains."

Brent reddened, stammering, "No way I'm going to meet with you and Cheryl."

"Why not?" she asked, feigning innocence.

Professor Livingstone welcomed Hana and Brent into her office, carefully studying their body language. She was secretly amused the detectives were so desperate they would ask for her help. She decided to avoid any mention of her telephone conversation with Hana regarding Ming as a suspect.

"Congratulations, Hana. I read in the *Post* you saved Detective Sweeney's life. I assume the attack at Dr. Chen's house rules out Johnston as a murder suspect."

Hana waved her hand dismissively. "We're running out of suspects."

Summarizing the status of their investigation, she highlighted plans to follow up with Wang and Ming, pointing out Ming's shaky alibi regarding his trip to New York.

Cheryl listened, raising her eyebrows at the extensive involvement of the Wellerton investigators in the Ripper case.

Hana apologized for being unable to share information from the official file, citing Mahoney's imposition of the "need to know" rule.

Cheryl shrugged. "I have my own sources of information. Raymond Malik's ex-wife Belinda Raintree Malik has an intriguing background. He married her when she was in her early thirties. They divorced a year later. She couldn't tolerate his womanizing. They split before he became a billionaire, even though he already had millions. Belinda was left extremely well off, despite Malik's best efforts. They hate each other. He's convinced she's transferred her loathing of him to the China Future Society."

Cheryl strode to a filing cabinet, removed a tan envelope, and placed it on her desk. She took out a picture of Belinda. The woman, in an athletic pose on a mountain path, was tall and gorgeous. Except for reddish-brown hair, which contrasted with Cheryl's blond locks, the professor knew she and Belinda looked enough alike to be sisters.

"Belinda's a distinguished writer, with a specialty in mountaineering. She's a part-time professor at Georgetown, where Deborah Chu taught. The two knew each other. Unlike Deborah and Kathy Wu, Belinda Malik avoids the limelight. On the political scale, she's just to the right of Genghis Khan. Her early history is murky. She grew up in East Asia. Caucasian, but speaks flawless Mandarin and other Chinese dialects."

"What's the relevance of Belinda Raintree Malik to the Ripper killings?" Brent asked.

"Raymond Malik contacted me. He believes Belinda is Jack. He's been getting death threats, on parchment, signed 'Jack the Ripper.' At first, he ignored the threats. The more he learned about the killings, the more he took them seriously. He asked me to investigate. Before the attack last night, he was certain he would be the next victim. He was reluctant to go to the police, but he agreed to have me share this information with you. I was about to contact you when you called asking to see me."

"How'd Malik happen to seek your help?" Brent asked.

"I've done a few small services for him in the past, mainly international consulting. The work is more lucrative and far more interesting than domestic work. You'll recall our friends at L'Auberge Chez Francois . . ." Cheryl smiled coquettishly at Brent with the last remark.

He blushed.

Pretending to ignore the byplay and annoyed she had failed to investigate Malik earlier in the light of his prominent position on the board of the China Future Society, Hana said, "How do we get in touch with Belinda Malik?"

"I've prepared a dossier for you." The professor picked up an envelope and handed it to Brent.

CHAPTER 49

A fine mist fell in the twilight dusk. Car lights were glaring. The squeaking swish-swish of windshield wipers complained about pushing too little water.

Hana followed the rush hour pack north into McLean, Brent in the passenger seat. She was too tired to hurry, and there was no need. They would arrive on time for the meeting with China Future Society Executive Director Wang.

Rush hour clogged Route 123 north from Tysons. The time was long past when traffic ran mainly south from the District as commuters headed home. Development and jobs had crept out to the suburbs. Midrise office buildings dotted the once-rural Tysons area, which was now Northern Virginia's central business district: the home to myriad think tanks, consulting firms, lawyers, international entrepreneurs, luxury hotels, and two lavish shopping malls. Commuting routes now ran north and south, sending tired travelers up and down 123, with a similar east-west pattern on Route 7, often leading to gridlock.

Hana turned into the Evans Farm palatial community of multimillion-dollar town homes and individual residences. "Years ago, Evans Farm Inn was located here. The inn was famous throughout the Washington area for Revolutionary War-era food and atmosphere. When I was young, my mom and dad brought me here every Christmas. One of my favorite family outings."

Wang greeted them at the entrance to his single-family home. Their host bowed them through to a spacious, but tasteful and relaxing, living room. Coffee, tea, soft drinks, and light refreshments were set out on a sideboard. "I have something stronger, if you would like," he said, encountering protestations that they were still on duty.

"I apologize for having to reschedule our last appointment," Hana said. "Please fill us in on your relationship with Deborah Chu and Rose Lee."

"What about Kathy Wu?" Wang asked.

"We'll get to her," Hana said. "Right now, focus on Deborah and Rose."

"You've learned of my affairs with both women. I like the ladies. I'm a bachelor. They were unattached. What's the harm?"

He hesitated. His rhetorical question didn't elicit a response. "I saw each of them for a period of several months. Sexual favors were exchanged. Small gifts given as a token of affection. The receipts from Tiffany are around somewhere. I went to their condos for our trysts. Would you like me to describe our sexual encounters?"

She waved her hand to indicate the intimate details were not germane.

Wang continued. "I have no knowledge of the who or why of their assassinations. The mystery surrounding their deaths is bizarre beyond belief. The only clue is their connection to the Society. This suggests the real target was the organization, not them as individuals. To be sure, we have many powerful enemies who see the Society as a surrogate for attacks against China. But, if such was the purpose, why kill Deborah and Rose, neither of whom played a prominent role?"

He stared at the detectives as if seeking an explanation for the bizarre turn of events.

"Did you know the two women were blackmailing Albert Johnston?" Hana asked.

"Deborah and Rose?"

"Yes."

"Why would they do that? Their families are extremely wealthy."

"Maybe they wanted money of their own," Hana said. "Mrs. Lee told me Rose turned down an offer to join the family firm in favor of working for the Society. Deborah Chu may have had the same need to feel independent. Whatever their motives, we know they worked together in the blackmail. They left evidence on their laptops. We found confirming documentation in Rose's safety deposit box."

"So the stories in the press about Johnston's bribery are true," Wang said. "He was an even bigger bastard than we knew."

"Were you conspiring in the blackmail with Deborah and Rose?" Brent asked.

"Me . . . conspiring? Ridiculous. Check out my laptop."

"Thank you," Hana said. "We'll take the computer when we leave, along with the Tiffany receipts. Can you think of anyone else in the Society who might have been in on the blackmail scheme?"

Wang considered the question. "If monetary gain were the motive, that's unlikely. The members of the board range from extremely wealthy—Raymond Malik, Daniel Ming, and Madam Sun—to quite well-to-do—Jin Yang, William Qian, and Mah Ho. Kathy Wu was not rich, but close to it. Pearl Chen is the beneficiary of a trust from her grandmother. Take a look at my home, I have money of my own. Of course, if the motive were political, to gain an advantage for China, anyone associated with the Society could be considered a suspect in the blackmail."

"What was your relationship with Kathy Wu?" Hana asked, shifting gears.

"Your image of my sex life is more exciting than the reality I live with every day. I tried to entice the captivating Kathy into my bed without success. A failure I experienced in common with most of the males who ever met her. My suspicion is she was a lesbian. But I have no firm knowledge she had sex with anyone of either gender. She was the most private celebrity since Greta Garbo."

"What progress have your private investigators made in tracking down Jack?"

"So you heard about the Society's arrangement with Wellerton,"

Wang said, a bit on the defensive. "Little progress. The investigators discovered someone hacked into the Society's computer system. If it were Jack, as we suspect, all our secrets have been revealed. This includes decisions of the board known only to Pearl Chen and me. Wellerton's investigators also uncovered indications Deborah, Rose, Kathy, and Pearl have been surveilled for several months. Their phones were tapped. GPS trackers were hidden in their cars. In Pearl's case, her laptop was hacked. We assume the same was true of the other women, but we were unable to verify the hacking because the police confiscated their computers. The investigators attributed all of this to Jack."

Hana made a mental note to have Edwina double-check the three laptops still in the CSI lab.

After cross-examining Wang for the better part of an hour, without learning much, Hana and Brent departed, taking the laptop and Tiffany receipts.

Brent sighed, as though discouraged at the little they'd learned from the Society's executive director. "Did you believe Wang when he said Kathy Wu was gay?"

"Sexual orientation could explain her close friendship with Pearl Chen. Perhaps they were more than friends. But my hunch is no. Pearl was involved romantically with Wang, and their relationship seemed genuine. Not that Pearl or Kathy would be the first women in history to be bisexual."

Hana paused to deliver her coup de grâce.

"To me, it sounds like a case of sour grapes. 'Kathy turned me down, so she must be a lesbian.' A lot of guys say that about girls who won't have sex with them."

"Where did that come from?" Brent asked. "Personal experience?"

"Yes," she said, recalling her consternation when she first heard from Wilhelmina at Legal Sea Foods she was suspected of being her lesbian partner.

"You're kidding. Right?"

"No. I'm not."

He sat quietly, stunned by Hana's revelation. As they neared the Ritz-Carlton Hotel, he said, "Why don't you come up to my room for a light supper."

"I have to go see my mom. I told her I'd stop by tonight. We talk every day now, just a few minutes by phone. I have a lot to make up for, and I can't start by breaking my word."

CHAPTER 50

Eriko Brown answered the phone on the first ring, delighted to hear Hana was on her way. Homemade sushi was the order of the day. She debated whether to tell her daughter about the delicacy or to surprise her. She decided to wait, to ensure their get-togethers did not slip back into the routine of appearing as choreographed as Kabuki drama.

The vinegary-flavored rice was cooked and cooled. Pulling the fresh fish out of the refrigerator, she set about cutting pieces no bigger than her thumb. On a lacquered tray, she arrayed tiny dishes: special ginger, fiery green wasabi, soy sauce, and takuwan—the pickled radish that was her daughter's favorite condiment.

Testing the rice to be sure it was just right, she shaped it, and completed the process by placing raw fish on top of each piece. She artistically arrayed the sushi on an emerald green plate, which she set on the tray and carried into the living room. She put the tray on a small table in front of the couch, where they would dine, seated side by side. The sushi was showcased to evoke happy memories before the Chinatown tragedy had destroyed the rituals of family togetherness.

Hearing her daughter's Camry pull up outside, she anticipated Hana bounding onto the porch, the same way she did as a teenager in their old house in Vienna.

They chatted as they ate, catching up on news since their last phone conversation. Wiping her mouth with a napkin, Hana said, "The sushi was delicious. Gochisousama."

Her mom bowed her head in acknowledgment.

Eriko retold the story of how she met Mike in Tokyo and fell in love with the husky Marine Embassy Guard, the initial opposition of her tradition-bound parents, and how, in time, they came to adore Mike as a son-in-law.

Brent heard the buzzer. Hoping Hana had fresh information to share, he moved to the door and swung it open. The glow from the room was insufficient to penetrate the murky black of the hall. He stepped out and leaned right.

He sensed movement to his rear, raised his hand defensively, and started to turn around. He felt a garrote slip over his head and grab him around the neck, trapping his hand in a painful vise. Only the bones and muscles below his wrist prevented instant strangulation, and those were at risk of being crushed by excruciating pressure.

Knowing he couldn't resist the encircling ligature for long, Brent threw himself violently backward. He flew against his attacker, propelling both of them into the sitting room. His goal was to reach the SIG SAUER on the desk.

The two figures rammed into the floor lamp, extinguishing the only light. They continued to struggle in the darkness. The detective missed the desk. He slammed his assailant into the wall, but without apparent effect. Struggling bodies staggered into the bedroom. Brent picked up momentum and smashed his adversary against the doorframe, eliciting an audible groan, proving the attacker was human.

The hold on the garrote unexpectedly shifted; one of the attacker's hands grasped both grips where before there had been two hands holding the ligature. Pressure on bones and muscles eased. Brent braced himself for another violent thrust backward.

Without warning, a knife handle hammered Brent's head. Dazed, he lurched, nearly falling to the carpet. Another blow landed, perilously close to his right temple. Consciousness began to trickle away. He made a final lurch, and the impact of two bodies sent the bedroom TV crashing to the floor.

Hana parked her car in the Ritz-Carlton garage and took the elevator to the twelfth floor. The elevator doors swished open. She paused before exiting, wondering why the corridor was pitch-black. She spied the open door to 1207 in the light from the elevator just as she heard the explosion of the television hitting the floor. She drew her pistol and raced into the suite.

"Brent, I'm coming in, ready to fire."

Silence.

Shuffling forward, she detoured left to the kitchenette, and propped the refrigerator open, allowing illumination to leak into the sitting room. Being backlit put her at risk. Against Jack's knife, it was a calculated gamble. But it was safer than blundering ahead in the dark.

Vestiges of a struggle were apparent in the empty sitting room.

She charged into the bedroom and saw the hazy outline of her partner kneeling on the floor. A shaky Brent was trying to claw the garrote from his neck.

She sensed the attack too late to stop the knife from slashing her gun hand. Blood spouted. Her pistol flew across the room. Only lightning reflexes saved her from having her wrist savaged.

When she crouched to pull her backup weapon, a ripped pants leg and an empty holster met her left hand.

Skills honed through years in the dojo triggered an arm thrust that saved her from being gutted. Still, she felt warm blood flowing from her abdomen. Excruciating pain radiated from the wound.

She retreated into the sitting room to gain maneuverability and take advantage of the dim glow of the refrigerator light. Hana was gratified the killer followed her rather than turning on Brent.

Gambling what worked once might work twice, she hustled outside into the unlit hall.

Hana knew she was losing the struggle. Her right hand was virtually useless. The cut on her stomach was more than a flesh wound. Fatigue and blood loss were slowing her reactions.

She remembered the human body has about five quarts of blood. Wondering how much blood she could lose and still function, she fought off panic and determined to end the struggle fast.

Hana landed a strike with her left hand, but with insufficient force to slow her dancing adversary.

Her leg sweep missed.

The knife slashed again—a glancing cut on her shin—which further compromised mobility.

⚊⚊

Beginning to recover from the assassin's attack, Brent staggered into the sitting room and flipped on the TV. A weak beam filtered into the hall.

As he rushed out the door, he yelled, "Hana, duck, I'm shooting at anything moving." He began firing the SIG SAUER.

Shaky, with blurred vision, he shot high, hitting nothing.

He saw the figure dart to the stairwell and disappear. His shots were too wild to threaten the fleeing assassin.

CHAPTER 51

Wilhelmina marched into Fairfax Hospital like she owned the place. In her snow-white coat she was indistinguishable from the other doctors prowling the halls. The physician's uniform gave her instant access, without question, to all areas, even those restricted to outsiders. Her name tag read *Wilhelmina Williams, MD*, with the title *Medical Examiner*. There was no misrepresentation, merely sleight of hand to cut through red tape.

She made her way to the corridor where Hana and Brent's rooms were located side by side. She knew George Manley and Pete Yardley shared guard duty.

George rose from his chair when he saw the ME approach. This was their first meeting without others since George's dating ploy.

She smiled, but her face revealed nothing of Hana's pleading of George's case during their lunch at Tysons. She decided not to discuss with George why she'd resisted his romantic gesture.

"How are Hana and Brent?" Wilhelmina asked.

"In amazingly good shape, considering what went down," George said, his expression guarded to conceal his attraction for the comely physician, now out of dating reach.

"Brent has a concussion—bruises, no breaks. Left hand mangled. The hand will be okay but may need a cast. Neck abraded, most likely a rawhide garrote. Like a bad rope burn. Hana has a nasty wound on her hand. Jack's knife cut her stomach. Slash on her shin, just an annoyance. Docs say she should be out of here in a few days."

Wilhelmina grimaced at the matter-of-fact assessment of what a physician would consider serious wounds. With a wave of thanks to George, she entered Hana's room.

A few moments of light-hearted banter ensued, the detective trying too hard to assert she was okay. Wilhelmina examined her and studied the chart at the end of Hana's bed.

"I'll check your x-rays and other tests later. Looks as though you're in good hands. When we're finished here, I'll look in on Brent."

Wilhelmina grinned broadly. "Before I go, Edwina asked me to pass on some really big news. She received the DNA test results on the blood you found in the woods near Pearl Chen's home. Jack is actually Jill."

"What?" Hana said, struggling to prop herself up in her hospital bed.

"Jack the Ripper is a woman. DNA results were conclusive."

After Wilhelmina left, Hana called George into the room and told him to ignore her directive that he investigate Daniel Ming's alibi. George confessed he'd made no progress, largely due to lack of time because of competing developments.

Hana reached for the bedside phone to call Lieutenant Krause. After confirming he was aware of the killer's gender, she filled him in on the meeting with Professor Livingstone. She emphasized Belinda Raintree Malik must be considered the prime suspect. The lieutenant agreed to have Belinda picked up.

Resisting the effects of the opioids given her for pain management, Hana strained to keep her eyes open. She rang the China Future Society and asked Pearl Chen to pass her through to Dr. Wang.

She filled Wang in on the unexpected DNA results, emphasizing the suspicion Malik's ex-wife might be Jack or Jill. She was losing track of how to think of their killer. She asked for the executive director's help in having the private investigators track down background information on Belinda Malik.

After alerting Wang, Hana relaxed and fell into a drugged slumber.

CHAPTER 52

Chief Erin Mahoney and Captain Carver Washington marched into Hana's hospital room, startling her awake. Mahoney said, "Congratulations are in order for arriving in time to save your partner. I told you and Brent to 'shoot to kill' the next time you encountered our suspect. Too bad Brent missed during the attack."

Carver stood silently by the bed and pressed Hana's hand, a glint of moisture in the eyes of the crusty veteran.

"We were dumbfounded to learn Jack is a woman," Mahoney said. She circled Hana's bed, pulled up a chair, and sat down.

"Belinda Malik has disappeared. When we searched her home, the housekeeper said several pieces of luggage were missing, along with a wardrobe of clothes and personal effects. As best the housekeeper could tell, Belinda has been gone a day or two."

Carver chimed in. "She withdrew a ton of cash from her local bank. She also has funds squirreled away in Swiss banks, the Cayman Islands, and other places known for laundering money. We believe she's fled the country, but there's no record of her traveling under her own name."

"We've alerted Homeland Security, the FBI, and other agencies to be on the lookout for Belinda," Mahoney said. "Through Interpol, we've notified police forces in Asia and worldwide. If she avoids commercial airlines and doesn't use her credit cards, it could take a while to track her down. Lieutenant Krause sent a couple of detectives to question Raymond Malik. He said his best guess is she'll head for China, but he has no hard information about where she might have gone."

After the police higher-ups departed, Hana called Wang to pass on the information about Belinda Raintree Malik. The Society's executive director said he couldn't believe Malik's ex-wife was a suspect. But he agreed to order the Wellerton investigators to intensify efforts to locate her, focusing on China and Europe.

In response to the drugs, Hana again felt the fog of fatigue clouding her eyes. She fell asleep and awoke to see Captain Brian McNab and Lieutenant Walter Krause standing by her bedside.

McNab coughed theatrically. "The Ripper Task Force stays active until we've got proof Belinda is Jack."

Hana pushed the button to raise her bed, allowing her to sit up. "We should continue protection for Pearl Chen."

Nodding agreement, Krause said, "Be aware, you and Brent have a new team of guards. George and Pete were sent home with orders to rest."

"Who's the new team?"

"You're looking at them," McNab said.

"Since when do captains and lieutenants pull guard duty?"

"Since we're dealing with two bullheaded cops who've gotten it into their heads they're the only ones who can protect you. The loo and I told them we've stood more guard duty than they'll ever pull. I said I'd fire their asses if they didn't get the hell home."

"Relax," Krause said. "The captain and I'll make sure you're safe."

Hana grinned.

She recalled her mother's words after relating the story about the day the lieutenant saved her dad. Maybe she would cut Walter a little slack.

CHAPTER 53

Belinda Raintree Malik relaxed in the plush leather seat of the luxury charter jet as the plane climbed to cruising altitude. She had total confidence in the Gulfstream G650 crew's ability to get her to Montreal, the first of many stops she planned to make hopscotching around the globe.

"I'm safe, at least for now," she murmured, pushing aside lingering concerns about the future.

She sipped Dom Pérignon. Raymond, her erstwhile spouse, had instilled an appreciation of fine wine and spirits. A taste for the good life and a fortune totaling tens of millions of dollars were his enduring gifts.

Belinda closed her eyes, relishing the bubbly, satisfied her plan of escape had thus far unfolded successfully. Subterfuge and evasion came readily to her, having learned them early.

Dual citizenship made it easy to mask identity. She carried two passports. One US, in her married name, which she still used professionally in her role as a travel writer and lecturer. And the other, French, in the name of Amélie Lisette Bonnet, kept for emergencies, which she'd known would arise sooner or later. Belinda was convinced no one in the life she'd abandoned in Fairfax, Raymond included, knew her as Amélie. Neither was the name she was given at birth, a fact she tended to forget since deception had become a way of life.

Taking stock of her looks as others might see her, a knack of role playing at which she was quite proficient, she glumly shook her head. Not that Belinda was unattractive. Quite the contrary. Her full figure would have given Scarlett Johansson a run for her money.

Even lounging in the fawn-colored seat, she knew the steward admired her statuesque beauty. She had to accept there was no way to trim more than half a foot off her height to look "average." She could have played varsity on the University of Colorado's basketball team— which, in a moment of weakness, she'd tried out for—had she not chosen to devote as much time as possible to her passion of mountain climbing.

Her reddish-brown locks hung shoulder-length, framing sharply defined cheekbones. An aspiring sculptor in Boulder, fascinated with her bone structure—or so he said—had persuaded her to model, eventually nude. Following some haggling with the artist, she had purchased (using sexual bartering as currency rather than hard cash) the bronze sculpture and, in later years, displayed it prominently in her home in Virginia.

Masking her appearance was virtually impossible. She contemplated several disguises, including wigs and dyeing her ginger hair.

Tiring of these mental gymnastics, she realized such speculation was useless. If any pursuers got that close, impregnating another color wouldn't be enough to throw them off the scent.

Gazing across the aisle at the traveling companion asleep in her seat, Belinda owned up to a more serious problem. Lucy Mao's looks would stand out in a crowd, even in San Francisco's Chinatown, where she was born. Lucy was nearly a head shorter, and slender. As a pair, they made a head-turning couple. Belinda shrugged fatalistically at the possibility height alone, which was not subject to alteration, might give them away.

Belinda hoped no one in the States would learn they were partners.

The women had taken care to be discreet about their relationship. Lucy lived in a condo at the Watergate in the District of Columbia. She was less than a half hour's drive from Belinda's McLean, Virginia residence, which was just down the road from the Central Intelligence Agency.

Their professional collaboration as writers provided further cover, embracing a mutual enthusiasm for mountain climbing, at which they had world-class reputations. Both had conquered K2 and the Eiger, published articles and books about their exploits, and earned handsome fees on the lecture circuit.

Lucy's petite figure appeared fragile, but Belinda had good reason to remember her body was made of tensile steel. A few years earlier, climbing K2 as a pair, the women had gotten into trouble with an unexpected equipment failure. Belinda was left dangling, in imminent danger of a drop into the abyss. Lucy crept down the sheer side of the mountain, maintaining some holds with three fingers, clinging to an outcropping, until finding a foothold where she could secure a belaying rope to rescue her climbing companion.

Prior to their escape from Fairfax, Lucy had assured Belinda she'd left word with friends and colleagues that she was departing on a long-delayed six-week vacation in the Caribbean and would be inaccessible on a friend's yacht. A story that, while untrue, was impossible to check.

Considerable thought had been devoted to their escape via Canada. From Montreal Dorval Airport, they would travel by limo, rented under an assumed name, to Fairmont The Queen Elizabeth Hotel. Bypassing the registration desk, Belinda and Lucy would proceed to the train station below the hotel, catching the express to Toronto. They were skilled at taking advantage of the anonymity of rail travel.

From Toronto, a charter jet would take them to Schiphol Airport in Holland. Once on the Continent, the ploy of transiting to a different city by rail to catch yet another charter jet would be repeated.

Albania was their penultimate destination. They would arrive in Tirana, the capital, and take a train to Durres. Belinda had rented a secluded villa on a beach overlooking the Adriatic Sea, where they would take it easy for a few days and catch their breath. Upon leaving Albania, they would travel to China, their final destination.

Albania was remote and had a reputation for being inhospitable to Westerners. The country maintained close ties with China, a carryover from its former Communist regime, smoothing the process of gaining entry and ensuring a quiet exit. Civil service officials were notably corrupt, and travel records could be easily falsified to erase any sign of their presence in the country. Most important, close friends who were longtime mountain climbers occupied powerful positions in the government and were willing to cut red tape to facilitate their travel and obscure any official record. Neither the Fairfax police nor Interpol would penetrate the web of obscurity clouding their itinerary.

Satisfied with her mental review of the travel plans, Belinda set aside the champagne and lowered her seat. Sleep came quickly.

CHAPTER 54

Carver Washington, accompanied by his wife Fatima, visited Hana and convinced her the safest place for her and Brent to recuperate was their Leesburg farm. After talking it over with Brent, she decided they would keep in touch with the rest of the task force by phone with developments in the investigation.

Prior to her release from the hospital, Lieutenant Krause informed Hana, "I don't want to see either you or Brent around the squad room before Monday of next week."

Assured they had a safe haven and wouldn't require a guard detail, he'd reassigned Officers Manley and Yardley to other duties on the Ripper Task Force.

Clennie Washington came by in his truck to pick up the detectives. The nurses insisted they take the ceremonial wheelchair ride to the exit courtyard, despite protestations they were well enough to walk.

Hana reflected on the colleagues and friends who were looking after Brent and her. Perhaps she was not as much of a loner as she tended to believe.

Driving the truck, Clennie turned his head to look at the detectives. "The Johnston bribery case is turning into a major political scandal. An anonymous tipster mailed Senator Blair incriminating information, which he wants to share with you, off-the-record, before turning it over to federal investigators. Hana, the senator will meet you and Brent at the farm in a day or so."

Hana smiled. More confirmation Lincoln Bartlett was right about the web of political intrigue that entangled the Ripper killings.

"The senator believes this new evidence may help with the Ripper case," Clennie said. "Blair is concerned that once the materials leave his possession, they won't see the light of day for months, at best. At worst, this could be another scandal like the eighteen minutes erased from the Nixon tapes by Rosemary Woods."

The ride to the farm took an hour, including some maneuvers by Clennie in an effort to evade anyone attempting to tail them.

When Hana and Brent arrived at the farm, Fatima met them on the porch. "I stopped by Vienna to visit Sam and inform him about recent developments. I picked up the items you and Brent wanted me to get from your town house and his hotel."

After listening to their thanks, she added with a smile, "Sam talked about an attractive senior citizen who'd just moved into your town house complex. He said Othello was quite taken with the woman's Chocolate Lab. The way he went on about his new neighbor, I had the impression Sam was taken with her and was looking forward to having Othello and her Lab spend time together at the dog park."

Hana listened to Fatima recounting the events, thinking, *I wonder if Sam could be bisexual?*.

Drawn to the kitchen by the enticing smells, Hana and Brent sat down at a table piled high with home-cooked food: pork chops, fried fish, mashed potatoes with gravy, peas, Waldorf salad, and homemade bread.

Brent grinned. "After a stay in the hospital, it's good to see real food."

Fatima busied herself getting drinks. She assigned tasks to Clennie, which, in the way of close families, he was already finishing by the time she spoke. Clennie cleaned his plate and headed out, after promising Hana he'd let her know when the meeting with the senator was firmed up.

After lunch, Fatima showed Hana and Brent to their rooms, upstairs at one end of a long hallway in the rambling, much remodeled structure. The house still bore signs of the Washington's five children, none of whom lived at home anymore.

Hana's bedroom overlooked the pond at the back of the house. She felt at home in a room she'd slept in many times over the years. Brent's bedroom overlooked the front, with the road barely visible in the distance through the trees. Both bedrooms opened to an adjoining bathroom, the kind with doors at either end. When one of the entrances was locked, it created a private bath dedicated to one bedroom. If both doors were open, the effect was a two-bedroom suite, with shared toilet facilities. Both bathroom doors were discreetly closed but unlocked.

Stiff and out of condition from the aftereffects of wounds and hospitalization, Hana suggested, and Brent agreed, a walk would do them good. She led the way on a tour of the farm.

The spring air was crisp and fresh. Warm sunshine and a clear blue sky made it perfect for a hike. A red-tailed hawk flew lazily overhead, searching for its next meal.

Following a path down the hill toward the pond, Hana guided Brent through her familiar haunts, which she hadn't visited since Chinatown. Climbing a small incline heading toward the pond, she said, "I don't know about you, but my body is still reluctant to move after being laid up in the hospital."

He grimaced and nodded agreement.

They circled the pond, striding past beds of yellow daffodils. Ducks cavorted on the water.

She pointed out landmarks that sparked memories from her childhood—spots where the best fish could be caught and the path deer followed on their way to the apple orchard. She called attention to a hollow tree trunk where she'd stumbled across a family of skunks and been sprayed when she was eleven.

"I never knew skunks made homes in tree trunks. When I think about that day, I can still smell the stench. I thought my clothes would never be clean. Mom probably felt the same way. That was the last time I saw those clothes. But Mom never complained about that or any of the other mischief I got into roaming this farm."

Hana told Brent about a hunting trip around the time of her thirteenth birthday, the first of many once she was old enough to join her dad's shooting party at the Washington's farm.

"I was in that tree," she said, indicating a platform more than head high. "Clennie was in a shooting stand in a tree over the next hill. We started so early, I had a hard time staying awake, and wondered if he'd fallen asleep. It was a freezing-cold November day. We'd been waiting for what seemed like forever. From time to time, the sounds of turkeys gobbling could be heard in the distance."

She realized from the way Brent was looking at her, he was seeing a Hana he never knew existed.

"An eight-pointer walked out of the darkness from the direction of Clennie's stand. I'm sure he let it go by to give me the advantage of the first shot. I suffered a classic case of buck fever—blurred vision, rapid breathing, shaking hands. My view was okay, but it seemed impossible to hold the scope steady for a clean shot. The buck got away."

Her moment of disappointment was reflected in her voice.

"Fate gave me a second chance. Two large does came into the clearing heading down the path away from Clennie. One hesitated and looked around. I was mesmerized watching the deer. Would she jump? Would she smell me? Would a turkey spook her? This time all senses were under control. I slowly squeezed the trigger and knew exactly where the crosshairs were when the gun kicked the image of the deer out of my view. The shot knocked the doe off her feet. It was a clean kill. The other doe turned and ran back down the path because she 'knew' it was safe. The deer was moving fast, but Clennie dropped it. He's still a crack shot, especially with a pistol."

Brent explained he was not a hunter. There were no wild animals around the pool tables he'd frequented as a youth. He asked, "How do you feel about killing and eating deer?"

"Why should I feel differently eating venison I've shot, than buying beef at the store that someone unknown and unseen slaughtered?"

Not wanting to overdo it the first day, they cut their walking tour short, looking forward to exploring the farm's total expanse of sixty acres during the week.

Back in the sitting room before the fire, Hana and Brent relaxed and caught up on the news. The Washingtons subscribed to a wide array of newspapers, including the *Washington Post, New York Times,* and *Wall Street Journal.* Hana read coverage of the Ripper case and the Johnston bribery scandal, marveling that she was at the center of a case drawing national attention and wondering what unforeseen developments were yet to surface.

Rumors implicating Senator Jimenez and Vice President Costello were increasingly explicit, accompanied by the ubiquitous leaks from backers seeking to quash the stories and opponents determined to fan the flames. Lincoln Bartlett had written a column explaining how the protectionists had gone too far. Free trade with China was an idea whose time was overdue.

Hana was disappointed at the report Lincoln had provided her, but she realized, as more information trickled out, he would be publishing a column in the *Post.* She was pleased he'd never pressed her to deliver on the promise of exclusive coverage of the Ripper case.

Carver and Fatima returned home and joined Hana and Brent. Chatting amiably in the sitting room, sipping coffee, the foursome agreed the weather, the economy, politics in Washington, and the love life of today's celebrities could all stand improvement.

By nine o'clock, the houseguests pleaded fatigue and retired to their rooms. Hana and Brent took turns using the bathroom—by unspoken consent, closing, but not locking, the entrances to the adjoining bedrooms.

CHAPTER 55

After sunrise, the expedition left base camp in China for Mount Qomolangma, Mother Goddess of the Universe, as the Chinese called her—Mount Everest, as she was known to the rest of the world. The climbers were tackling the dangerous North Col route from China, rather than one of the many approaches from the Nepal side. Forty-eight grueling miles later, more than halfway up the mountain, they arrived at Rongbuk Monastery.

Following a brief rest, they moved on, blessed with good weather as they continued the ascent. The farther they went, the more conditions worsened, starting with a deceptively mild snowfall. The storm eventually hit full force. The party pressed forward, searching for a secure site where they could make camp.

The scream of the wind reminded Belinda of earlier times she'd been caught in winter storms, particularly one time in the Colorado Rockies. Conditions made it difficult to talk and impossible to hear. Visibility was impaired. The climbers tied themselves together in groups of three, communicating by hand signals. Belinda found herself trailing Hans, a German, and Pierre, a Frenchman. She was not worried. Both were experienced mountaineers.

Driving snow striking any bit of exposed skin felt like stinging bees. Ears pained from the frigid cold and the unrelenting shriek. Visibility declined to near zero. Hans, in the lead, advanced by inches, testing the trail ahead at every step. Belinda realized too late—Hans had made a fateful mistake. He'd taken a side route, one seldom used, separating the trio from the main party.

They stumbled forward for hours, until Hans led them to a level area wide enough to pitch two tents. With numbed fingers and a sluggish mind, Belinda painstakingly followed the familiar routine of establishing camp. She anchored her tent with huge rocks to ensure it would not be blown off into space by the gale-force winds.

Belinda forced herself to eat and drink enough to keep up her strength. She crawled into her sleeping bag fully clothed with her boots still on. Content all the essentials were covered, she let her body succumb to exhaustion.

Groping hands shocked her awake as sunshine poured into the tent. *The storm is over* was her first thought. Then, realization took hold: Hans and Pierre were dragging her from her sleeping bag, ripping at her clothes. She fought back viciously. Her mountain-hardened body was strong. But the men were stronger. And there were two of them.

Dazed from repeated blows, she fell back on the bag. Hans held her helpless in a full nelson. "Lucky Pierre. You first."

Pierre tore away her underclothes, brushing aside her feeble kicks. The two ravished her again and again, taking turns holding her down and raping her.

The pain and shame became unbearable. At first, she resolved not to give them the satisfaction of crying or begging. In time, the rape became too much to endure. She couldn't stop whimpering.

Spent and no longer able to perform, the men tied her up. Before retiring to their tent, they promised her a return engagement.

She shivered. Pain racked her body. After an interminable time, the iron resolve that had seen her through past crises asserted itself.

The captive tested her bonds. The ropes were expertly tied and more than strong enough to hold her. Twisting her torso, she found it possible to inch her hands toward her boot. There was enough slack to enable her to loosen her fetters by millimeters.

Twist. Reach. Loosen.

She counted. Reaching one hundred, she stopped. Nothing

remained except grim determination. The number of times she had to try no longer mattered. She would overcome. An eternity later, she was able to touch her boot. Fingers crept into the space between boot and leg. Now leverage could be obtained.

Willing her foot to move closer to groping fingers, she persevered. Hope, at last. The knife, hidden in a special sheath inside the boot top, was within her grasp. Further maneuvering brought it out. Numbed fingers almost dropped it and her heart lurched. At long last, she could touch the release that caused the blade to spring out.

The rest was just a matter of time. The razor-sharp edge sawed through the rope in seconds. Her hands were free. Next, feet.

She readied her mind for what must be done.

With quiet determination, she entered the other tent and found both men asleep.

Lucky Pierre was the first victim. Grabbing his hair and pulling his head back exposed the throat. The sharp blade did its work, nearly taking off the head in one vicious swipe.

Awakened by the commotion, Hans sought to free himself from the entangling sleeping bag. Too slow. The thrust to the heart was followed by a flare in his eyes signaling he knew he was dying. One hand reached toward Belinda, trembled, and fluttered to his side.

Painstakingly, the avenger carved the Chinese characters for rapist on each of the men's foreheads.

Belinda eyed a nearby crevasse and decided it was to be the rapists' tomb. She dragged the bodies over, one by one, and watched them fall, nearly out of sight, to an outcropping of rock. She set aside food, drink, and all the equipment she could manage for the climb down the mountain. The rest followed the bodies into the chasm.

Belinda remembered little of the trek back to Rongbuk Monastery. The monks praised her for being the only person ever to traverse that part of the mountain alone and to survive the experience. Her explanation of what happened to her companions was sufficiently vague to satisfy the authorities who interviewed her at the base of the mountain. They were never anxious to investigate Westerners who brought much needed foreign currency into the region.

Lucy moved to the seat next to Belinda, stroking her hair. She had witnessed the aftermath of her lover's nightmares before, but this one seemed worse. Belinda thrashed in her seat, whimpering, arms flailing. The champagne flute went flying. Her mind, still trapped on Everest, refused to awaken.

Lucy comforted Belinda as she would an infant, with soft words and gentle touches. Moments later, she saw Belinda's eyes fly open and reason return.

"Thank God you're here with me. I felt so alone," Belinda muttered, sweat dripping from her forehead.

"The same dream?" Lucy asked.

"Always. I experience my dream as though I'm reliving the real-life nightmare through one of my articles." She managed a bitter laugh. "Freud's way of sheltering us from the torture of our subconscious, I suppose."

"They were monsters. You had to kill them," Lucy said.

"Yes. At one level, I know that."

Belinda hesitated. "Perhaps I'm a monster too."

CHAPTER 56

By the third day, Hana and Brent settled into a daily ritual at the farm. Arise early, eat a hearty breakfast with the Washington clan, do the dishes (they insisted on this contribution to the household routine at all meals), take an exploratory hike, read the papers, have a light lunch, undertake a longer hike, nap, dinner with the family, chat before the fireplace, and early to bed.

Every morning, Hana called to touch base with her mom. She sensed they were growing closer with each conversation. She also talked with Sam to inquire about Othello's latest antics in visiting Vienna's dog park with the Chocolate Lab, and to pry into Sam's feelings toward the woman who was the dog's owner and their new neighbor. She'd often wondered if Sam's romantic interests were solely stirred by male partners. While she gained new insights into Othello's attractions to the Chocolate Lab, she was unsuccessful in extracting any details from the retired detective.

Her calls to check on the task force were perfunctory. Not much was happening. Of course, if Belinda Malik were Jack, and if she fled the country, nothing would be happening.

Hana looked forward to this evening's meeting with Senator Blair to discuss the connection between the Johnston bribery scandal and the Ripper case. Clennie told her the senator, younger in appearance than his years, had won his spurs in the Civil Rights Movement. Shot and beaten in Mississippi, he still bore a scar on his forehead that blazed white against his black skin.

Blair had come up the hard way from the position of classroom teacher in still segregationist Virginia to principal, assistant superintendent, and ultimately, superintendent. Backed by teachers and PTAs across the Commonwealth, the school system was his launch pad into politics.

He'd advanced in the Senate as a result of a keen intellect, industry, and a pragmatic recognition on both sides of the political aisle of the symbolic value of showcasing an able Black man in a series of prominent roles. He was now a stalwart on the prestigious and powerful Foreign Relations Committee.

He'd locked horns with Senator Jimenez on many occasions, usually concerning trade with China, and he'd heard rumors of questionable fundraising linked to Jimenez's voting record.

In addition to Senator Blair, Hana was told Carver Washington would be present, accompanied by Lieutenant Carlos Martinez, who Carver had brought into FCPD as a recent addition to Financial Crimes. Carver had filled her in on Martinez's background.

Martinez was recruited from the federal Department of Homeland Security. In his midforties, the Hispanic's resume was impressive, spanning a broad range of financial investigations, including counterfeiting, during his time with the Treasury Department.

During his career at Treasury, he became a Secret Service Agent. When training ended, he was assigned to a protective detail for the diplomatic corps. Carlos told Carver his tour of duty was far from his idealized vision of risking his life guarding the president—Clint Eastwood, as portrayed in *In the Line of Fire*.

Tired of the tedium of bodyguard duty for foreign dignitaries and disillusioned at the bureaucratic jockeying in the aftermath of the transition of the Secret Service from Treasury to DHS, he'd jumped at the advancement opportunity when the Fairfax lieutenancy opened up.

John Blair and Clennie Washington arrived, followed soon after by Carlos Martinez.

The senator got right to the point.

"I received several items of evidence from an anonymous informant that link the Johnston bribery and the Ripper case. Included was a flash drive containing telephone conversations and other incriminating information. What I have to share is extremely sensitive. I must have your assurance you'll treat this as background. What you'll learn here will not become available as evidence for months. Once it's in the hands of federal investigators, some of it may never be shared officially."

Blair looked over the group.

"Do I have your word?" Murmurs of assent gratified the senator.

"Clennie, play the recording."

The voices of three men filled the room. The subject was pending legislation, mainly affecting China and other Pacific Rim trading partners of the US. The gist of the conversation was Johnston would solicit bribes from both sides, lobbyists favoring the bill and those opposed. Not just money was sought, but also commitments of political support. No matter who paid or what was promised, the speakers intended to push through a protectionist law to the detriment of the Asians.

"The voices with Johnston are Senator Jimenez and Vice President Costello's chief of staff, Barney Edwards," Blair said. "It would have to be authenticated, but I've known these men for years. Their speech patterns are distinctive."

Carlos spoke up. "The flash drive is not evidence, even assuming confirmation they're the speakers. Recording phone conversations without knowledge and consent is illegal."

Blair nodded. "But the recording is political dynamite that'll explode if the media get wind of it. Overnight, the political landscape will change. Costello can kiss his hopes for the presidency goodbye. Fear of retaliation, and, among responsible journalists, a sense of fair play is muting the story. If this information becomes public, the wolf pack will be unleashed. No one can withstand such intense scrutiny. Other leaks will reveal evidence that can be used in court."

"You said *if* the information comes to light, not *when*," Hana said.

"Precisely," Blair said. "The last generation has given us too many examples of top officials in the FBI, leaders in the Justice Department, and even the president himself obstructing justice. No one can guarantee this won't happen again. My obligation is to pass the material to the proper federal authorities. I'm exercising my discretion to inform you."

Blair held up a khaki envelope nearly an inch thick. "This file includes documentation of Johnston's anti-China bias. His father was a general in the army during the Korean War. The general was a leader in MacArthur's offensive that overwhelmed the North Koreans and pushed them back to the Yalu River. The offensive prompted China to enter the Korean conflict. Chinese hordes forced the Americans to retreat. General Johnston was killed in the fighting. Johnston's hatred of the Chinese stems from childhood trauma of growing up from age one without a real father, who was replaced by the idealized image of a war hero."

Clennie added, "Among the items was information that X, who conspired with Deborah Chu and Rose Lee to blackmail Johnston, was a composite identity. Kathy Wu and Pearl Chen were X. They simulated a single conspirator to confound detection."

"This confirms the four women Jack targeted were Deborah, Rose, Kathy, and Pearl," Hana said. "The killings—in Pearl's case, the attempted killing—are directly related to the blackmail scheme, which strengthens the belief April's killing was a red herring."

CHAPTER 57

Lucy Mao congratulated Belinda Malik on her choice of the villa in Albania, situated on a beautiful stretch of beach on the Adriatic. The remote villa was the ideal location to relax after a nerve-racking series of events that had culminated in the Fairfax police pursuing Belinda as a suspect in the Ripper assassinations.

Lucy rolled over in the king size bed, snuggling deeper into the warmth of the bedclothes. She swung her arm over to the spot next to her and failed to find the comfort of her paramour. Coming awake, she sat up in bed. Glancing at the mirror on the ceiling, last night's scenes of ardor replayed in her mind's eye.

Bending down, she retrieved the terry cloth robe from the floor where it lay from when she bounced into bed the previous evening. She pulled on slippers and swung open the French doors leading onto the veranda.

She took a deep breath of pure air and viewed the sunrise spraying golden light over the ice blue Adriatic. Shore birds swooped toward the waves in an endless symphony of movement. White beach and sea stretched to the horizon.

Lucy spied Belinda jogging on the beach. Strolling toward the water, feeling a chill breeze caressing her robe, she waved and called a greeting. Belinda responded, picked up the pace, and ran toward the villa. They embraced and walked back arm in arm.

The serving girl left breakfast on the table by the window and stole away, having readied the villa for the enjoyment of its occupants. The lovers were barely aware she was around, but somehow food was prepared and served, fragrant flowers decorated the villa, and fresh linens replaced those marked by their nightly romps.

The *International Herald Tribune* and papers in diverse languages had been left on a table inside the living room. Belinda noted that coverage of the political aspects of the bribery scandal was increasing, although, in the absence of sensational developments in the past few days, less attention was devoted to the Ripper murders.

When every tidbit of interest had been extracted, papers were dropped on the floor. The morning ritual of breakfast followed by catching up on the news completed, they moved to the couch to talk and enjoy the magnificent view of sky, sea, and sand.

"You never ask any questions about the incident on Everest," Belinda said.

"There's no need. You've told me the essential facts. Hans and Pierre violated your trust and your body. In raping you, they were no longer human; they turned into animals. You were trapped, alone and helpless. They would have continued to use you as a sex slave, killed you, and left your body in a ravine. You escaped from your bonds and left their bodies to rot on the mountain. Their corpses and equipment had to be hidden. Had they been found while you were on the mountain, you would still be confined in a Chinese jail, assuming you hadn't long since perished. You did what you had to do. What else is there to know?"

"What I've not told you," Belinda said, "is how I felt when the knife cut Pierre's throat and again when it stabbed Hans in the heart. I enjoyed it. More than enjoyment . . . I experienced the apex of sexual ecstasy. If anything, as intense, perhaps more sublime, than when we make love. Can you understand that? Killing makes me come. What kind of monster am I?"

CHAPTER 58

The monitor blinked. *ACCESS DENIED* glowed in the middle of the screen. Mahoney cursed under her breath.

Fire Engine Red Mahoney had tried all her computer tricks, and nothing worked. She could think of no other password. The security of the Wellerton Agency had managed to thwart her best efforts.

Fairfax County's police chief felt no shame about being a closet hacker. In other situations when she ran into a stone wall, Mahoney turned for technical assistance to the loosely organized community of hackers. Hackers were her help network. The confederacy of hackers had been instrumental in feeding her clues to crack the FBI's firewall. Fragments of information had come from different sources, which she had skillfully woven together.

Accessing hackers was a court of last resort, never a first choice. Pride was the primary reason. She enjoyed the thrill of solving these puzzles on her own. For the chief of police to tap into the hotbed of illegality in the subterranean hacker world—crawling through the Dark Web—was risky in the extreme. She shrugged. There was no alternative. Reach out or give up.

Mahoney began to surf the chat rooms that the best hackers were known to frequent. She used the moniker "Cracker Babe" when playing this game. Her fingers flew over the keyboard.

NEED ACCESS TO WELLERTON AGENCY. WILLING TO TRADE SECRETS.

CRACKER BABE

She waited for a response. Nothing. Figuring any workable

answer would take time—there could not be many hackers who'd penetrated Wellerton's firewall—she picked up the *New York Times* and began to do the crossword in ink.

The puzzle was nearly completed when her mailbox beeped to indicate a response marked *EYES ONLY.*

BABE

BEWARE! THESE ARE SCARY DUDES. A BUDDY GOT IN, BUT A COUPLE OF KNUCKLE DRAGGERS SHOWED UP AT HIS HOUSE ONE NIGHT. TRASHED HIS SYSTEM AND BROKE BOTH HIS HANDS. SAID THAT WAS JUST A SAMPLE OF WHAT WOULD HAPPEN IF HE TRIED AGAIN.

HI FLIER

Mahoney pondered an appropriate response. Finally, she settled on macho.

FLIER

I CAN PLAY ROUGH TOO. HOW DO I POKE A STICK IN THEIR HIVE?

BABE

A flurry of messages back and forth proved her hunch paid off—"Hi Flier" was himself the "buddy" who'd been assaulted for his hacker bravado. The motivation to avenge the personal hurt and injured professional pride was sufficient grounds to feed Cracker Babe the information needed to infiltrate the Wellerton system.

Once she had the procedure for penetrating Wellerton's security, with backup suggestions in case they'd made changes or improvements, she thanked Hi Flier and promised she owed him one. Mahoney was aware repaying such a risky debt of honor at some future date might force her to stray across the boundary separating criminals from the technically law abiding. She rationalized the end of catching Jack the Ripper justified the means.

She began the tedious task of setting up a false internet trail, bouncing around the globe like a peripatetic soccer ball. If the goons at Wellerton sought to track her down to retaliate, they would find themselves at a computer address in India.

This was a novel approach to outsourcing a scapegoat. Back when she was a midlevel police official, she had been schooled in the stratagem by a teenage hacker in Philadelphia as a quid pro quo for helping the youth avoid serving hard time. The trick was akin to spreading breadcrumbs on a deceptive trail. Once security was safeguarded, she got down to the serious business of outwitting the systems administrator. A couple more hours of trial and error and eureka—her labors paid off.

She was in.

The list of Wellerton clients scrolled down the screen. The triumphant hacker highlighted the folder marked *CHINA FUTURE SOCIETY* and pressed *enter*. The mother lode was ready for mining. She opened the *BILLING* file and skimmed it. The monthly retainer, plus the amount for expenses, was eye-popping. The Society was committed to a full-court press. Six million dollars had been expended to date, the amounts rising each week.

More relevant to the Ripper case were the findings of the investigation. Had Wellerton made any progress in uncovering Jack's identity? What other evidence had emerged that Hana's task force—Mahoney considered it her task force—could use? When each information tidbit was discovered, she downloaded copies of the pertinent files onto her computer. She would not take the luxury or run the risk of reading any more online. Her goal was to get in and get out as quickly as she could, leaving no footprints.

Dawn sent the first rays of sunshine into her study. An exceptional sunrise painted the sky with a palette of rose hues and brought her back to the world of daily living. Thankful for the diversion, Mahoney stretched and walked to the window. The prism dangling in the east window refracted the beams of light into a kaleidoscope of patterns leaping around the room like a friendly multicolored alien.

Anchored to her desk by driving curiosity—first fixated on the computer monitor, next mesmerized by the hard copy the printer spat out—she'd scarcely budged for hours. She knew it was time to brew a pot of coffee to recharge the depleted batteries in her brain.

The tired hacker started the coffee, poured a glass of orange juice, cut an English muffin, and popped both halves into the toaster. She carried the breakfast to the study and settled into a red leather executive chair that duplicated the one in her office at police headquarters, with the added luxury of a footstool. She leaned back, munched a muffin slathered with butter and bitter orange marmalade, and savored the aroma of coffee. Draining the mug, she got a refill, and took another large swig.

She wondered if the return on investment of a night of hard labor and high risk was worth gambling her future. The answer would be unveiled in time, but at one level she knew the adrenaline thrill of risk was its own reward.

Wellerton's investigations spanned the globe, with the overseas focus on Europe and East Asia. Bribery of foreign officials was among the illegalities recorded in the firm's computer record. Intimidation and violence were not uncommon. She realized Hi Flier had gotten off easy. Others touched by Wellerton fared worse.

The data in Wellerton's files served to confirm her department's task force's discoveries. Deborah Chu and Rose Lee had instigated the blackmail. Their partners in the conspiracy were Kathy Wu and Pearl Chen—the mysterious X. The private eyes accessed Pearl's laptop at home during the time the special assistant was at her office. For a moment, Mahoney was jealous of Wellerton's operatives, who could ignore the need for probable cause. She took comfort knowing, in this instance at least, the fruits of their labors would serve the cause of justice.

Although there was no proof Belinda was Jack the Ripper, Mahoney was impressed with Wellerton's findings on the elusive suspect.

Belinda Raintree Malik's recorded history began in her teens at an exclusive girls' school in France. She transferred there from a prestigious school in Switzerland. The Swiss records were destroyed in a fire. Nothing was known about her early years.

The French school's files indicated her parents were Ralph and Marie Raintree. The father was an engineer, the mother an artist. Wellerton could find no confirmation the parents existed. Officials at the two schools could not recall any visits or correspondence from them or anyone else.

A trust managed by a prominent Swiss bank had paid expenses during Belinda's teenage years and later at undergraduate and graduate studies at the University of Colorado. The bank upheld the country's reputation for discretion about financial matters. Nothing was unearthed about the original source of the funds.

Belinda's academic brilliance and athletic abilities, especially her passion for mountain climbing, were demonstrated early. School vacations were expeditions in the Rockies and the Alps. Her height, climbing skills, and social sophistication enabled her to be taken for an adult and accepted into the tightly knit fellowship of mountaineers.

She breezed through the normal four-year program in three years and achieved her MA and PhD in two more. Apart from the customary coed dalliances and an appetite for sexual experimentation, her love life had been unremarkable until she met Raymond Malik. They had a stormy marriage. The divorce was notably acrimonious, albeit lucrative for Belinda.

Mahoney was surprised to learn of the recent discovery of Hans and Pierre in the mountain crevasse. The monks at Rongbuk Monastery who found the corpses, had pieced together an account of rape, followed by murder. The climbers had been assassinated with a knife and their bodies dumped in a crevasse on Mount Qomolangma. Although Belinda was identified as a person of interest, Chinese authorities had let the matter drop, marking the case as unsolved. Belinda was described in sympathetic terms by the police, monks, and guides. She was praised for her mountaineering virtuosity and fluent command of Chinese.

Lucy Mao—Belinda's partner in climbing, publishing, and lecturing—was believed to be her partner in bed. Lucy fit the description of the petite Asian woman traveling with Belinda when the two women had arrived in Montreal by chartered jet. When the pair vanished under the Fairmont The Queen Elizabeth Hotel, the spooks realized they must have boarded one of the express trains in the station below the hotel. Wellerton's operatives recovered their trail in Holland, where the two women disappeared anew.

Mahoney was aware none of Wellerton's illegally acquired information could be used officially, but it could serve other purposes in the investigation. Her next step was to take action based on what she'd just learned. She phoned Hana Brown and Edwina Edison, asking them to come to her home for a midmorning meeting. The topic of the morning conclave was left somewhat vague. At the time, she was undecided how much to sugarcoat the illegality of how she'd acquired the new information.

CHAPTER 59

On the dot of ten o'clock, the doorbell rang. Mahoney hurried to answer the door. She felt rested and relaxed, despite a scant three hours of sleep. She led the detective and the CSI tech into her study.

"What I have to share with you is likely to take some time. Help yourselves to refreshments." She steered Hana and Edwina to coffee and pastries on a corner table.

"What we discuss today is confidential. The information is for your background use only and not to be shared with anyone else."

"What about Brent?" Hana asked. "I'm uncomfortable keeping anything material from my partner."

"Mr. Straight Arrow . . ." Mahoney snorted, "He's still an FBI special agent. I acquired this information illegally by hacking into the Wellerton Agency's computer system. The department can't use it officially. But it'll be helpful in evaluating data you obtain from legitimate sources and for leads to acquire evidence we *can* use. I stuck my neck out. But I'm not willing to risk implicating myself any more than necessary. This is off-limits to your partner. Besides, we're not doing Brent any favors by making him collude in a criminal act."

Hana shared a look with Edwina. *But it's okay for* us *to be guilty of illicit behavior.* They both nodded in silent acceptance. All too obviously, their hostess had not given a moment's thought to the possibility they might be reluctant to join in the conspiracy.

Mahoney handed out copies of the pertinent files and briefed the two women on the highlights.

Edwina hurriedly skimmed the sheaf of papers. "I've accessed the hidden files on the laptops of the three victims—Deborah, Rose, and Kathy. The facts dovetail with what's set forth in your findings. With this background info from Wellerton, we should gain more insight into the connections among bribery, blackmail, and killings."

Hana said, "The information about Ming is fascinating. Brent and I knew he was lying about something. Now we have confirmation he wanted in on the blackmail of Johnston and Senator Jimenez. He concocted the cock-and-bull story about needing help in writing an article for the Society's journal to throw us off the trail. If we weren't already aware Jack is a woman, Ming would be number one on our hit parade of suspects."

Grumbling, she added, "Besides, the bastard has an alibi."

Edwina tapped the Wellerton papers. "Another indication of Belinda's possible involvement in the Ripper murders is her use of a knife to kill her two fellow climbers on Mount Everest."

"Right," Mahoney said. "But we can't dismiss the possibility coincidence is at work here. A knife and poison are weapons of choice for murderesses worldwide."

Mahoney stood, signaling the meeting was over. "Hana, you and Brent meet with Raymond Malik. See what you can learn that might point to Belinda's whereabouts."

CHAPTER 60

H ana was pleased when her call to Malik was put through without delay. The billionaire told her he preferred to meet for lunch at one thirty that afternoon at his residence in Great Falls, rather than at his office.

Driving Brent to the appointment, it dawned on her the entrepreneur lived across the road from An-Mei Lee, Rose Lee's mom. She pulled into the long driveway that led up to Malik's mansion and motored to the steel gate barring the road.

"I can't believe it. Malik's house is a mirror image of Mrs. Lee's, right down to the security gate, electrified fence, closed circuit cameras, and the exterior architecture of the home. Small world department among the ultrarich." Hana kept up a running commentary on the similarities between the two estates.

At the steel gate guarding the mansion, Hana was buzzed in and cruised to the roofed parking area in front of the mansion. The detectives were met by an imposing Chinese woman in her forties who wore a charcoal gray business suit complete with a mannish white blouse and conservative tie. The woman's haughty attitude made Hana feel she should scrape her feet before crossing the transom.

"I am Mrs. Outerbridge, Mr. Malik's housekeeper," she announced with a clipped British accent. "Welcome to Shanghai West Manor. Mr. Malik is waiting for you in the garden dining room. Follow me, please."

Brent and Hana trailed the woman whose demeanor suggested more a high-level executive assistant than a housekeeper. Hana soon realized the resemblance to the residence across the road stopped at the porte cochere. Mrs. Lee's home radiated a welcoming warmth and charm, with the rooms cozy despite their size. Malik's residence was cold and formal, a feeling not disguised by the expensive furnishings and artwork.

Mrs. Outerbridge led them through the foyer, past the library, across a huge sitting room centered on a massive fireplace, and into a small dining room whose immense windows overlooked a beautiful garden. Hana felt the similarity to Mrs. Lee's Sun Room. In stark contrast to the rest of the mansion, this space felt comfortable and lived-in.

Malik was seated, like a reigning monarch, in a king-sized, ornately carved mahogany chair on one side of a round table designed to seat eight. In the center of the table was a lazy Susan, the top inlaid with mother of pearl. Mrs. Outerbridge directed them to take the seats bracketing their gargantuan host.

"Please forgive me if I don't rise to greet you," Malik said. "I find it easier to remain in the chair once wedged into it. My agility has suffered since eating replaced soccer as my principal hobby."

"We appreciate you meeting us on such short notice," Hana said.

Malik nodded acknowledgment. "Thanks for agreeing to meet over lunch. Mrs. Outerbridge will serve us. My practice is to take meals at home, combining business with pleasure. This is my favorite room. I hope you enjoy the view."

"A spectacular garden," Brent said. "It reminds me of the grand English gardens I saw around London during a too-brief liaison assignment with New Scotland Yard."

Following a few moments of polite banter about the splendor of the garden, Malik got down to business. "You needn't concern yourselves about making choices from the lunch menu; all dishes will be served on the lazy Susan. Please help yourselves."

Mrs. Outerbridge hovered in the background.

"Everything looks delicious," Hana said. She sat at the table nibbling her lunch.

"I met with Mrs. Lee to discuss her daughter Rose's death. I was amazed to learn you live across the road from her."

"And you were even more amazed to discover our estates are carbon copies."

Hana laughed. "True. Most of the estates in this area are quite distinctive."

"The explanation is simple. I bought the firm of architects who designed her place. The good lady has proven to be a gracious neighbor over the years. We became friends once she forgave my crass behavior. 'Imitation is the sincerest form of flattery.'"

Hana recognized the quote from Charles Caleb Colton, an obscure English cleric whose writings were popular in the early nineteenth century—one of many obscure factoids she'd learned from her mom's never-flagging attempts to instill in her a love of literature.

"The architects' assignment was to replicate the house, grounds, and security arrangements. They did so admirably, don't you think?"

"Your home is impressive."

"The interior, of course, is completely different, reflecting the contrast between Mrs. Lee's charm and my somewhat cooler personality. Hers is a classical Chinese garden, modeled on Vancouver's Sun Yat-Sen masterpiece. Mine emulates a formal English garden. 'Tade kuu mushi, mo sukizuki.' You know the quote?" He turned to Hana with the question.

"Everyone in Japan knows that quote, since it's the basis for the title of Junichiro Tanizaki's world-famous novel, *Some Prefer Nettles*."

"How would you translate the title?"

"'Different strokes for different folks' is an idiomatic translation, or perhaps, 'There's no accounting for taste.' The literal translation is 'some insects prefer to eat nettles.'"

Malik clapped his hands. He appeared delighted at the performance of the detective, as though she had passed some obscure test.

"Where did you learn Japanese?" Hana asked.

"In Tokyo."

"What were you doing there?"

"My business was based in China, centered in Shanghai and Beijing. Our goal from day one was to be the dominant firm in what is now known as the Pacific Rim. I recognized Japan would be China's leading competitor for a generation or more. My vision for the future saw the Land of the Rising Sun as a potential partner of the Middle Kingdom. In order to learn as much as possible, I lived in Tokyo off and on for several years. When one knows Chinese, it's no great stretch to master Japanese."

Hana thought, *That would be a revelation to countless students of Asian languages.*

Moving to the substance of their interrogation, she asked, "Where did you meet Belinda Raintree?"

"We met in Paris at the George V. I was there on business. She was attending a conference on mountaineering. I never understood why people who climb mountains need to go to conferences. What is there to talk about anyway, what kind of ice axe to carry?"

"Everyone goes to conferences," Brent said. "That's the main reason for joining organizations. There's always something to talk about. When they run out of things to say, they set up a committee to select new topics."

"I was immediately smitten and canceled my business meetings. She played hooky as a panelist from her assigned session. We scarcely left the bedroom except to extend our sexual repertoire into the bathroom and various locations and innovative positions throughout the suite. She possessed an intimate knowledge of the Kama Sutra, probably not learned in the fashionable girls' school she'd attended in Paris before going to Colorado. We were married within a month."

"Quite a whirlwind romance," Hana said.

"The marriage was more tempestuous than the courtship, and almost as brief. Her passion for argument was comparable to her passion for sexual adventures. We fought, off and on, all day long.

And we made up each night in tumultuous lovemaking that often lasted until dawn."

Hana listened intently, wondering how to steer the conversation toward Belinda's supposed killer instinct.

"We soon came to realize, if we stayed together, one of us would murder the other. The last straw was when she learned of my dalliances with Chinese women on business trips to our home office in Shanghai. At the end of our marriage, the flame of love burned out, leaving the ashes of hate. I came to fear her. Perhaps she came to fear me."

"Why would she fear you?" Hana asked, relieved Malik brought up the topic of the threat within the Malik family.

"Would I have harmed her? I can't say. But no doubt, given the opportunity, she would kill me. I'm convinced she's the killer masquerading as Jack the Ripper."

He interrupted his soliloquy to take third helpings of lobster soufflé. "Belinda spent her youth in China. She has strong and ambivalent feelings about China and the Chinese. Her hatred for me extends to the China Future Society. It's easy to believe she murdered the women affiliated with the Society. That's her way of attacking me vicariously. Her madness has accelerated, and she will no longer settle for surrogates. Make no mistake. She intends to kill me."

"Here's the proof," he concluded melodramatically.

He drew a missive from his breast pocket and handed it to Hana.

She unfolded it, noting the familiar parchment emblazoned with red ink. Positioning it so Brent could see, she read:

Dearly Beloved,

We are gathered together to join this man and the Devil in unholy wedlock. May the fires of hell consume you. Will my knife or Satan's pitchfork impale you first?

Jack the Ripper

An involuntary shudder reminded Hana how Jack was able to instill fear with word imagery. She asked, "How'd the note arrive?"

"FedEx delivered it this morning."

Wearing latex gloves, Mrs. Outerbridge laid the distinctive red and blue envelope on the lazy Susan. Hana noted the New York return address of a generic business shipping firm.

"If Belinda is on the Continent, as we believe, how'd she manage this?" Hana asked.

"Easy enough," Malik said. "She would send a letter to one of her mountaineering confederates. They will do anything for each other. If you're willing to die on K2 or Everest for someone, would you hesitate to forward a letter? The friend would go to the local mail packaging outfit and pass on the message as instructed."

"Where is Mrs. Malik likely to be?" Brent asked.

"Hiding in plain sight somewhere in Eurasia. She has hundreds of friends throughout Europe and Asia who would cover for her. I've long suspected she had multiple identities. Too many missing links in her background. Too many evasions."

"Evasions?"

"She lived simply, even though there was no doubt she had ample funds. I pressed her, eliciting vague references to a family trust. Belinda was able to depart on mountaineering expeditions at a moment's notice. She financed some climbing teams during the period she was a college student. And, of course, once we were divorced, a lot of my wealth stuck to her fingers."

"How was she able to win such a large settlement?" Hana asked.

"My divorce arrangements were generous because she was privy to industrial espionage. She blackmailed me about sensitive business dealings that in some countries—not the United States—might be considered less than legal. Neither the Fairfax police nor Interpol will be able to track her down. Wellerton's investigators might have better luck."

"We're giving this case top priority," Hana said. "If she's responsible for the killings, the Fairfax police will eventually arrest her."

The tycoon interrupted his discourse by pausing to take a bite of pecan pie. Chewing thoughtfully, he said, "Your best bet, I regret to say, is she will sneak back here to kill me. You can apprehend her in the attempt or capture her after the deed is done and I am dancing with the Devil. Needless to say, I wish you early success."

Hana offered police protection which Malik declined.

"Having police in the mansion would interfere with my business. Most important, they would disrupt my repasts."

CHAPTER 61

C arlos Martinez flinched, annoyed at the interruption of the ringing telephone. He was cranking on the computer, writing his summary of the Ripper case to record the salient facts in one place and to clarify his understanding of the chronology.

On a yellow pad, which rested on his desk beside the computer, he'd sketched a diagram, centering the names of the key players. Vice President Bernard Costello, Senator Raphael Jimenez, and the senator's legislative assistant, Albert Johnston, in the bullseye were foremost in his thinking. Political bribery trumped murder in his scheme of values.

The women who were killed— Deborah Chu, Rose Lee, and Kathy Wu—were in a cluster of names at the bottom left of the paper, with Pearl Chen, who was still alive and well guarded, to the right. April Kwan, the George Mason student, was in a small circle at the bottom center of the page, with a question mark next to it.

The narrative in his computer spelled out the story summarized in the diagram. Carlos was a visual person; he used the diagram on the yellow pad to imprint the story deep in his subconscious. He was mildly dyslexic and believed the adage: "A picture is worth a thousand words."

The sound of the phone competed in his consciousness with the productive tapping of keys recording his thoughts on the computer. He debated with himself whether to answer the phone or to let the machine take the message. Inertia won. He opted for the magic of the electronic secretary.

The final ring cued his laconic voice, instructing the caller, "You know what to do after the beep."

"Lieutenant Martinez, I'm Barbara Lacrosse. I need to speak with you urgently concerning the bribery scandal and the Ripper case. I'm in danger. Please call me at—"

Carlos leaped for the phone and grabbed the receiver, cutting off the message. "Hello. This is Lieutenant Martinez. Are you still there?"

"Yes," answered the panicked voice.

"How imminent is the threat? Where are you?"

"I think I'm safe at the moment. I believe I've lost the men who were following me. I'm at Union Station."

"Listen carefully. Take the Metro to Rosslyn, the first stop in Virginia on the Orange Line. Do you know how to do that?"

"Yes."

"We'll meet on the platform in Rosslyn headed in the direction of Vienna. How will I recognize you?"

"I'm five-seven, a hundred and twenty-five pounds, well, maybe a hundred and thirty on a bad day. I'm a brunette, wearing a dark blue jogging outfit. I'll be carrying a tan briefcase, the kind that doubles as a purse."

Carlos wondered what kind of woman corrects her weight when she's in danger. Momentarily distracted, he forced himself to get a grip.

"I'll probably be there by the time you arrive. I'm Hispanic, five-ten, a hundred and seventy pounds. I'm wearing jeans with a red plaid shirt and an unzipped black windbreaker. Go directly to the Metro. Stay in areas with a lot of people. Talk to no one. Avoid the edge of the subway platform. Wait for me at Rosslyn in case I'm delayed. Got that?"

"Yes."

"One more thing. Do you have a cell phone?"

"No. I destroyed it when I was trying to get away from the men tailing me. I've heard a pursuer can use your cell phone's GPS to locate you."

Carlos gave her his cell phone number and repeated the salient instructions, emphasizing she should avoid the edge of the platform. He collected his pistol and jacket and ran to his car.

He drove from his condo in Falls Church toward the Rosslyn station, wondering what the hell was going on. A woman in fear for her life. A high-profile political scandal linked to blackmail and murder. The drawing with the vice president in the bullseye flashed in his mind.

He needed backup, but whom to trust? And who could respond in time to get to Rosslyn before Barbara would arrive? Making a quick decision, he pulled his cell phone off his belt, and dialed.

Hearing the hoped-for response, he said, "Clennie, this is Carlos. I need immediate backup and you're elected. Do you still have a concealed carry permit for your SIG SAUER?"

"Yes . . ." Clennie Washington replied, sounding bewildered, but responsive to the urgency in Carlos's voice.

"How far do you live from the Rosslyn Metro?"

"A five-minute walk."

"I need you to head there right away. I'm driving to Rosslyn and should arrive in less than fifteen minutes. Come armed. We may need to protect a young woman named Barbara Lacrosse. She's meeting me on the Rosslyn platform of the Orange Line going in the direction of Vienna."

"I'll be there before you are. Give me a description."

Carlos repeated Barbara's description and hung up, concentrating on weaving through traffic, using siren and flashing lights.

He cleared the steps of the long Rosslyn escalator two at a time. He jumped over the entry, flashing his badge at the attendant. He ran onto the platform, where Clennie was pacing back and forth.

Clennie, visibly relieved to see Carlos, said, "I called Carver to alert him. You must be desperate to rely on a civilian for backup."

"You're not just any civilian. You're the son of a Fairfax police captain and a terrific marksman. You're one of the few people I trust who are up to speed on the Johnston bribery and the Ripper murders."

Carlos recapped his brief conversation with Barbara, finishing as a train pulled into the station. He noticed a young woman exiting the train.

"Barbara Lacrosse?" Carlos asked.

She nodded, her eyes fearful.

"I'm Carlos Martinez."

"And who's he?" Barbara asked suspiciously, pointing to his unexpected Black companion.

"He's Clennie Washington. His dad is a Fairfax police captain. Clennie's the legislative assistant to Senator Blair. He knows the ins and outs of the Johnston bribery scandal. I didn't know what kind of danger you were in, so I asked Clennie to serve as backup. You can trust him the same way you can me."

"What kind of senator's aide is a police backup?" Barbara asked.

"Let me worry about that. We've got to get you someplace safe where you can brief us on what's going down."

"The farm . . ." Clennie prompted.

Carlos nodded. "Captain Washington has an isolated farm near Leesburg. You'll be safe there. Is that okay with you?"

"I guess I'm out of options. If you're wrong about Clennie and his dad, I'm already as good as dead."

254 MOTIVE FOR MURDER

CHAPTER 62

Carver Washington hurried to the farm and broke the news to Fatima about the imminent arrival of visitors. On his heels, Hana and Brent showed up. Moments later, Clennie brought in Barbara Lacrosse and Carlos Martinez.

Offered food by Fatima, Barbara protested she was too frightened and upset to eat anything, but she soon gave in to hunger. "I haven't eaten since breakfast."

Carver took charge, assembling the group before the fireplace, and introducing everyone to Barbara.

"Barbara," Carver said, "I'm going to put us all on a first name basis, if that's okay with you. Please tell us what's going on."

Hana wondered what revelations Barbara Lacrosse would share.

"I'm a graduate student in economics at Georgetown University, working on my PhD. China trade is my specialty. Deborah Chu was my thesis adviser and a good friend. Since her murder, I've been following the Ripper case and the bribery scandal, which appear to be linked in some way that's never spelled out in the media."

She hesitated, noting her audience's expectant attitude. "My research focuses on recent political events in the United States that affect US-China trade. The protectionists scream, 'Cheap foreign labor is stealing our jobs and ruining America.' The free trade advocates counter, 'American prosperity depends on a strong world economy, and we should promote trade with Asia with no strings attached.' The bullshit truck fills up faster than you can empty it. Proponents on both sides of the issue shovel an equal amount of crap."

Barbara took a sip of coffee.

Hana noted Barbara scanned a practiced eye over her listeners to gauge how her remarks were being received.

"The only way to get the skinny on what's really going down is to analyze legislation in Congress. It's easy. Just read the *Congressional Record* and committee reports. What's hard is figuring out what's happening behind the scenes, where all the real decisions are made. The dirty little secrets between K Street lobbyists and people on the Hill. The backdoor deals engineered between the White House and Capitol Hill. Luckily, the Freedom of Information Act is designed for the purpose of promoting transparency in government. If citizens ask, they can learn a lot of stuff known only to insiders. I became an expert at FOIAing the topic of China trade with State, Commerce, and other agencies."

Except for the crackling of logs burning in the fireplace, the room was quiet. The smell of coffee mingled with the aroma of smoking wood—the cozy atmosphere belying the tension in the room.

Muffling a sob, she said, "While FOIA doesn't apply to Congress, you can still obtain a lot of information if you know how to investigate. My life went to hell when I received the response to my last request from Senator Jimenez's office. What I asked for was routine. What I got exploded like a nuclear weapon. Some asshole had mistakenly accessed secret email files. They were included in the stuff sent to me. The messages were to and from the senator's legislative assistant, Johnston, Jimenez himself, and Barney Edwards—Vice President Costello's chief of staff. I've brought the info with me in my briefcase to hand over to Lieutenant Martinez . . . Carlos, I mean. The emails directly implicate the VP."

Clennie looked over at Hana, silently communicating, "Just as we suspected."

Barbara continued her commentary. "The motives were soliciting funds and shaping votes in Congress. The funds were to be used to bankroll Costello's run for president. The advantage of a hidden cash slush fund is dirty money lacks accountability. 'Follow the money' was what Deep Throat told Woodward and Bernstein during Watergate. I guess things haven't changed much in Washington over the past generation."

Hana blanched. Lincoln Bartlett's tip about the link between domestic politics and the Ripper case was confirmed. Once again, she realized she should have briefed Brent during the trip to Philly about her conversation with Lincoln. She knew guilt over her sexual fantasies about the reporter overrode her belief in sharing everything with her partner. When would she sort out her relations with men, or were they always fated to end in disaster?

"What did you do?" Carlos asked Barbara.

"I didn't know what to do. I was scared shitless. My first thought was to contact the *Washington Post*. We learned during Watergate the media are our best defense against dirty government, right?" She looked at the faces of her audience and resonated to the rapt attention.

"I decided to hand over my evidence to the FBI. My call got bounced around from office to office, moving up the food chain in their bureaucracy. After a runaround, I was told to stay by the phone, and someone would call me back. About ten minutes went by before an unidentified source called. I took it for granted the person on the line was still FBI. My instructions were to wait in my apartment and a special agent would arrive to escort me and the documents to the Hoover Building. Don't ask me why, but I got spooked."

Barbara took a deep breath, appearing to draw on some secret source of strength.

"There's a cleaning closet just down the hall from my apartment. My front entrance is visible from the closet, so I waited in there. Two guys showed up. They drew their weapons, gave a token knock, waited about one second, and broke down my apartment door. Staying inside long enough to conduct a quick search, they left as quickly as they'd come. I snuck out the back way, leaving my car in its parking space."

She stopped talking and shuddered.

"My destination was Union Station. I decided to flee out of town. On the way, my cell phone rang. The voice on the phone sounded like the same guy who'd called me and said to wait in my apartment. He asked my location. He said my life would be in danger if the documents weren't turned over. I hung up and smashed my cell phone. I had no doubt the men pretending to be FBI special agents were following me."

Hana knew notifying the FBI would alert the cabal who showed up at Barbara's apartment. She said, "Any FBI involvement would provide an insurmountable barrier to effective steps being taken by the Fairfax police."

Brent said, "I concur."

Clennie left the room to consult his boss by phone. He came back and said, "Senator Blair believes the only way to protect Barbara and get to the bottom of these crimes is to go public and take the Fibbies out of the game. He wants to see the documents and talk to Barbara before he determines what action to take. He's on his way, and he'll advise us what to do when he gets here."

Senator John Blair arrived and greeted Barbara. He praised the young woman for her courage and patriotism. While taking notes in a small moleskin notebook, he examined the documents she'd received from Senator Jimenez's office.

When finished, he questioned her at length, inquired about the basis for her interest in trade with China, and had her recap her research findings. He probed for inconsistencies in her story about the telephone call to the FBI and its aftermath.

Satisfied with the answers to his questions, he said, "Fairfax can't move on this as long as the FBI is involved. There may be a way to take the FBI players off the board. I'm bringing these documents with me. We'll return a copy to Carver in the morning."

He turned to Clennie. "Let's go to Washington. We've work to do."

Putting a comforting hand on Barbara's shoulder, he said, "You've given us some valuable information. Don't worry. We'll keep you safe."

CHAPTER 63

Wilbur Barnstable "Barney" Edwards glared at the time in the lower right-hand corner of his computer monitor. Christ. It was only five in the morning. He'd always thought the hours working on the family farm in Kansas were bad. Hours were even worse in the White House.

Uncharacteristically nostalgic for a distant youth growing up in the Midwest, he thought back to his fifteenth birthday when his dad had told him he'd be going East to attend a "prep school." He had no idea what a prep school was, or how going East would change his life.

He recalled his dad's remarks.

"Your brothers love working the farm, but all you seem to be interested in is reading. Ma and I agreed. If you're gonna spend time on book learning, you oughta do it right. We talked to some folks at this boarding school in Massachusetts called Andover. Important people, including presidents, have gone there. The headmaster said you look like 'Andover material.' If you make good there, getting in one of those Ivy League Schools should be a snap. He said with a Yale, Harvard, or Princeton education, you can go anywhere."

Dad was right. Andover was Barney's ticket to Yale, which led, indirectly but inevitably, to Washington, DC, and the White House.

Classmates at Andover began calling him Barney, a humorous take on Barnstable, saying he reminded them of Barney Fife, the deputy sheriff on *The Andy Griffith Show*. The nickname stuck, and, in later years, proved useful as an opening to talk about his rural Midwestern roots. Most listeners equated farming with poverty, which amused Barney when he thought of the six-figure investment his brothers had recently made in a single piece of farm equipment for their multimillion-dollar spread.

Barney was an excellent scholar, an accomplishment his family took for granted. Much to everyone's amazement, he also became an outstanding athlete. The reason was simple: he ran faster than anyone else. This was an enormous advantage on the football field, where, despite being built like a beanpole, he excelled.

His principal claim to fame had occurred during his sophomore year at Yale. He was a tight end, perhaps not the tallest or skinniest tight end ever to start in the Ivy League, but certainly the fastest. There was less than a minute to play in the fourth quarter of the Harvard-Yale game. Yale trailed by four points, third down on their twenty-yard line. The quarterback hit Barney on the numbers with a ten-yard pass. He got one block, evaded another tackler, and turned on the afterburners. No Harvard player was within fifteen yards when he crossed the goal line. Fans in Yale Bowl went crazy. The home team held on to win a game that turned out to be the premier win of the season.

From that moment on, Barney had joined the ranks of Big Men on Campus. The ultimate BMOC honor came during his junior year when he was elected to Yale's elite secret society, Skull and Bones. There he would hobnob with those who would hobnob with presidents—past, present, and future. At Skull and Bones he met and became close friends with Bernard Costello.

Their friendship evolved into a highly successful political partnership. Costello was the personification of a politician—charismatic, articulate, seeming to stand for whatever the voters wanted—and Barney was the brains that got him elected. Barney managed Costello's campaigns when he ran for and was elected state legislator, congressman, governor, and senator. Today, Costello was a heartbeat away from the presidency, and Barney was the vice president's chief of staff. Barney was confident his boss would be chosen president in the next election. Barney would help him run the country.

But all of Barney's accomplishments and dreams were turning to dust. Ever since the murders in Fairfax and the bribery scandal, he knew his career was sliding down a slippery slope. The latest slip had occurred when someone in Senator Jimenez's office downloaded secret emails and sent them to Barbara Lacrosse, the graduate student from hell.

Barney cursed quietly, "If Barbara hadn't asked for those documents, I wouldn't have to authorize extreme measures to keep the emails from falling into the wrong hands. She brought this trouble on herself."

Although Barney knew he'd authorized killing Barbara, he hid behind euphemisms even in the privacy of his thoughts. He'd grown callous playing hardball politics over the years, but condoning assassination wasn't something he was willing to own up to. One simply wasn't brought up that way on a farm in Kansas.

Introspection was interrupted when the red phone by his elbow buzzed, indicating the vice president had arrived and wanted to see him.

Barney knew Costello would expect him to be at his post even at this ungodly hour.

"I'll be right there."

As soon as he came into the room, Costello said, "Son, we're in deep shit. Where is she?"

"We don't know. The searchers are confident they'll locate her soon."

"Hell, son . . . I guess it doesn't matter anyway."

He'd started calling Barney "son" upon winning his first term in the House of Representatives, even though they were the same age and had been college classmates. The practice continued, although only when they were alone. Calling him "son" somehow captured the spirit of their relationship, with Barney dependent upon the politician for his future.

Barney addressed his boss as "Mr. Vice President" at all times, figuring it was good practice for when he would be calling him "Mr. President."

Costello went to the credenza by the far wall and opened the concealed bar. He pulled out a bottle of scotch and poured two stiff drinks.

Barney stared at the VP bug-eyed. Dawn hadn't yet broken. He'd never seen Costello touch alcohol before noon, not even when they were in college. And what did he mean by "it doesn't matter?" He kept his bafflement to himself and waited for events to unfold.

"The president called me at home. He woke me up. That's a first. He said to meet him in the Oval Office. I've just come from there. He asked me to resign. No, that's not true. The old fart demanded my resignation before noon today."

Pausing to drain his glass, Costello poured another and one for Barney. "Drink up. You've also got to resign, effective immediately."

"What happened?" Barney grabbed his glass and downed a healthy slug of scotch.

"John Blair led a bipartisan delegation of senators and representatives who met secretly with the president last night. They had compromising emails. They also had records of some of your telephone conversations about China trade, although they're not legally admissible. Blair was very convincing. The president decided to appoint a special prosecutor. He's going to make the FBI turn over Barbara Lacrosse's protection to the Secret Service. The president will hold a press conference at one o'clock."

Barney stared, only half believing what he was hearing.

"I'll be impeached, probably even if I resign. Who the hell knows how that works? Anyway, I'll resign this morning. All of us are destined to end up in prison with that incompetent bastard Jimenez."

He gulped his second drink. Hand shaking, he poured another and put the bottle down.

"Call off the searchers. Rescind whatever orders you've given them concerning Barbara Lacrosse. No need to add gas to a roaring fire. We're in enough trouble already."

He slammed down the half-full glass. A few drops splattered the papers on the desktop.

"Now, get out of here. I have to go home and face my wife. She always said those damn Chinese would bite me in the ass if I didn't leave them alone."

CHAPTER 64

Hana entered Chief Mahoney's office suite, wondering if she was mentally prepared to watch the president's upcoming news conference. Rumors of Vice President Costello's resignation marked the climax of the fast-breaking scandal, now inextricably linked to the Ripper case. The murders were tied more closely to domestic political events than she would have believed, despite what she'd heard from Lincoln Bartlett.

Wilhelmina Williams and Edwina Edison were talking with Brent Sasser at the far end of the conference table. Captain McNab and Lieutenant Krause, to Hana's astonishment, were laughing with Carver Washington and Carlos Martinez across the room.

Hana walked over to join Brent's group.

Edwina leaned close and whispered, "The parchment used in the message you received from Malik is identical to the other notes. So is the ink. The text reads like the Jack we've come to know. If Belinda Malik were the writer, the reference to 'unholy wedlock' would make sense. Of course, the acrimony of their divorce is public knowledge, so anyone could make that up."

"Given Jack's track record, Malik is in mortal danger," Hana said in a normal tone of voice. "He refused our protection."

Joining the conversation, Wilhelmina said, "Malik may have a death wish. His gluttony is one clue. Declining protection is another. My hunch is he knows a great deal more about his ex-wife than he's told us. She could have information about his shady dealings going back years."

When Mahoney turned up the volume on the TV, a hush fell over the room, broken by the solemn introduction, "Ladies and gentlemen, the president of the United States."

The president approached a lectern and began to speak. "My fellow Americans, I come before you today to provide information about a scandal that has shamed our nation. I'll read a brief statement and take your questions.

"You're aware of media reports concerning allegations of bribery to influence legislation related to international trade. This matter initially came to light during investigations conducted by the Fairfax County Police Department into killings of Chinese American women.

"Last night, a bipartisan delegation from Capitol Hill, led by Senator John Blair of Virginia, met with me at the White House. The delegation implicated Vice President Bernard Costello and Senator Raphael Jimenez of California in a conspiracy to rig votes in the Congress in return for cash and political influence.

"Evidence came to light when a graduate student at Georgetown University, Barbara Lacrosse, turned over to Fairfax authorities copies of emails she obtained from Senator Jimenez's office. She acted with great courage after her life was threatened by impostors, pretending to represent the FBI, who were trying to get her to hand over the emails.

"I have asked the Secret Service to assume responsibility for her protection until we can be assured of her long-term safety. The nation owes a debt of gratitude to Barbara Lacrosse and the Fairfax County Police Department for shedding light on these dark deeds.

"Some will say the accused are innocent until proven guilty. I'm making the evidence public so the American people can draw their own conclusions. I'm also requesting the attorney general to appoint a special counsel empowered to analyze this information impartially, obtain any necessary evidence, and take whatever action is required to achieve justice.

"I have asked the vice president for his resignation, and he's complied with my request. His chief of staff Barney Edwards also resigned. Both resignations are effective immediately. I'm confident the Congress and the Justice Department will take swift and certain action with respect to Senator Jimenez and anyone in his office who may be implicated in improper or illegal acts.

"The issue at the heart of this scandal is trade with China—should it be encouraged or restrained. This is a matter about which reasonable people can reasonably disagree. What we cannot condone is improper influence, exercised in the shadows, to shape our policy deliberations.

"There remains little doubt this occurred, and protectionist special interests were behind it. I wish to reassure our friends in China that we will not permit US national interests to be decided by any secret group. Rather, our national interests will be determined in open negotiations in which the gains and losses for all parties affected can be debated in a public forum.

"Thank you. I'm ready for your questions."

The president recognized Lincoln Bartlett.

Mahoney listened to the back and forth a few minutes, then turned off the TV. Gesturing to Carver, she said, "Please tell everyone what happened with Barbara Lacrosse last night."

Upon getting the nod from Carver, Carlos related the events step by step, starting with the initial call to the FBI from the graduate student and concluding with the president's order for the Secret Service to take over Barbara's protection.

"We now have a picture of the blackmail and the bribery schemes," Hana said. "Pearl Chen and Kathy Wu were the mysterious X. They teamed up with Deborah Chu and Rose Lee to blackmail Johnston and, through him, Senator Jimenez and the VP. All four women were affiliated with the China Future Society. Three were killed by Jack, and an attempt was made on Pearl's life."

Encouraged by Mahoney's close attention, she continued.

"Motives behind the crimes need to be reexamined. We've been told the women's killings were a way of attacking the Society and undermining its goal of promoting trade on favorable terms with China. Counselor Pei of the Embassy tried to point us toward an economic and political plot against Asian trade and an overall anti-China policy. Executive Director Wang echoed similar beliefs."

In apparent confusion, Hana said, "If we take that theory seriously, we'd have to conclude Jack failed. The actual outcome is the reverse of Pei and Wang's warnings. In his talk, the president reassured China about US trade policy, and he criticized the protectionists who have sought to torpedo close relations between the US and China."

Edwina interrupted. "This is a classic case of misdirection. I knew Jack was fucking with us. If we assume the objective from the beginning was to ensure the political scandal would come to light as the blackmail plot unraveled, everything falls into place. The murders weren't intended to undermine the Society. Just the opposite. The women were sacrificed to further the Society's goals."

"Let's not get ahead of ourselves," Wilhelmina said. "Before we get too engrossed in the moves on the political chessboard, keep in mind the human element. Whatever else she may be, Jack's a serial killer. Her actions are distinctive in combining elements of control and rage, but I can't believe that scenario is all phony."

"The rage is real," Brent said. "Everything we know about serial killers tells us their motivation comes from deep-seated psychological compulsions. The killer can't help herself. Her inner demons take over."

Hana shook her head. "That's too pat an explanation. Freud tells us behavior has roots in multiple causes. That's the clue to Jack's motivation. The drive to kill comes from the fire of inner compulsion and the ice of cold calculation."

CHAPTER 65

Thirty Years Earlier

Victoria Franklin walked up the dirt road. The lights of the village were ahead and the dwelling's inferno behind. The young girl never looked back. The past was past. She had no choice but to face the future.

The savagery of stabbing her father in a futile attempt to save her twin brother had left her barely aware of what happened. Gradually, the realization penetrated. All her family members were dead. The fire she'd started with the candelabra destroyed her home.

Bare feet stumbled over ruts in the roadbed, which were dimly illuminated by shafts of moonlight tunneling through foreboding clouds. Her torn and bloodied nightgown was stark testimony to the attempted rape and ensuing violence. She was indifferent to the celebration taking place; drumbeats from the village festival resounded as a funeral dirge.

She knew she would find no help at the seaside ceremony where the village elders were congregated. Nor could she expect support from the household staff whom her father had released for a rare night of partying. A plan took shape, infusing her aimless wanderings with purpose. Her steps turned toward her best friend's home.

Victoria had thought of her life as parallel to Kimberly's until a couple of years ago. They both had English mothers and American fathers. The men worked in the mercantile firm owned by Victoria's family—her father was president and Kimberly's father was general manager. Both girls had been brought up in two cultures, with frequent visits back "home" to England and the United States.

Though their education was classically Western in content, they were tutored in Mandarin and could read and speak it fluently.

Each of the girls had lost her parents within the past three years—Victoria a mother from heart failure and a father whom she'd just stabbed to death, and Kimberly a father and mother. Kimberly's situation went to hell two years ago when her father was stricken with cancer and perished. Her widowed mother married a Chinese, Weng Chiang, who took over as general manager of the mercantile firm. Her mother had died recently of influenza.

Chiang was a Chinese traditionalist when it came to family values; he brought concubines into the household with Kimberly's mother. Thus far, since his wife's death, he had not molested his stepdaughter. But Kimberly had confided her fears to Victoria. She was terrified lust would lead to rape.

Upon arriving at Kimberly's home, Victoria rapped on the wooden shutters of her bedroom.

"My God, what happened?" Kimberly asked, horrified at the disheveled apparition entering her room.

In hushed whispers, the story unfolded. The two girls embraced and sobbed, clinging together through the long silence that ensued.

"Tonight, I was certain the same fate would befall me," Kimberly said.

"Chiang sent everyone to the festival, staying home to drink. I came down to get something to eat. The way he looked . . . as though he was starved for sex. He started to rise out of his chair. I thought he was going to rape me because none of his concubines are around. But he was already too drunk. He fell back in his seat. As I ran to my room, he reached for the whiskey bottle and knocked it over. He's still down there. I don't know what to do."

"I do," Victoria said. "Come with me." She led the way to the kitchen.

On a wall rack, neatly arrayed, were the cook's knives. She took the two with the longest blades and handed one to Kimberly.

"No. I couldn't."

"Yes. You can. And you must. I'm going away. You're coming with me. We'll leave nothing behind in Taiwan."

The girls crept through the house until they came to the room where Chiang lay sprawled in the chair where Kimberly had last seen him. The odor of whiskey impregnated the air. Two bottles and a glass littered the floor. The Chinese stepfather was dead to the world. Knives flashing, the girls consigned him to a permanent demise.

They returned to the bedroom and prepared for their journey. Victoria selected items from her friend's wardrobe. Kimberly searched for money she knew Chiang kept hidden. When all was ready, they torched the mansion.

Kimberly followed as Victoria led the way to Xie Tian's house on the outskirts of the village. Xie was Victoria's father's lawyer. She confided to Kimberly she'd only talked with him a few times, but he'd treated her with kindness and respect.

Hiding his wonder at two girls carrying suitcases, arriving at his home in the middle of the night, Xie ushered them into his study and offered them food and drink.

Neither young nor old, Xie bore his diminutive stature with dignity. Clothed in gray flannel trousers and a red silk smoking jacket, he mimicked the garb of a Western aristocrat.

Once satisfied the social amenities were observed, he got down to business. "To what do I owe the honor of this visit?"

"We need your help," Victoria said. "Tragedy has struck our village." She described the night's drama at the two households. Kimberly chimed in with details. They left nothing out—the aborted rapes, the murders, the arson, their culpability.

The lawyer listened without interrupting. He nodded gravely, not reacting to stories of adult lust, death, and terror.

"What would you have me do?" Xie asked.

"We must leave Taiwan," Victoria said. "We require money, a place to live, means to complete our education."

"Is that all?" he asked.

Clearly confused by his calm reaction, Victoria's body language communicated it was quite enough.

"Arrangements will be made. Victoria, you are the sole survivor of your father's considerable estate. You are a rich woman. Kimberly, I'm afraid, my dear, you are penniless. Chiang's son at university in Taipei inherits everything."

"Kimberly and I'll share equally," Victoria said.

"Of course," the lawyer said, as though that were a foregone conclusion.

"There's the small matter of three bodies, not to mention the two mansions, which, by your accounts, have burned to the ground. I'll speak to the village elders, and they'll intercede with the proper authorities. Neither of your parents was a sympathetic figure. The concern of the elders will be the financial consequences of their deaths to the village. We can assure them an orderly transition to new ownership and management without the problems they've endured in recent years. The village will prosper. Everyone will be better off. The official record will show these were tragic accidents."

"What about us?" Kimberly asked.

"You'll be taken care of. I shall arrange everything. Tonight I'll have you driven to Taipei. From there, you'll fly to Switzerland. The Swiss are the best with money. And their schooling is said to be satisfactory for young people. The Franklin family business will be sold. The earnings put into a trust. Two trusts would be best, which each of you will control when you are older."

"How can we ever repay you?" Victoria asked.

"You'll pay enough," Xie said, smiling. He explained the percentage of their fortunes he would draw down for himself every year during his lifetime.

CHAPTER 66

Arriving home after digesting the implications of the president's television address outing Vice President Costello and Senator Jimenez in the unraveling of the blackmail scheme, Hana was puzzled when she received a telephone call from Hazel Jackson. She hadn't heard from the chairwoman of the Fairfax County Board of Supervisors since meeting her in Fairfax Hospital to reassure Hazel her daughter Lizzie hadn't suffered any lasting damage from being kidnapped.

"Hana, I need to talk with you, in private. Could you come to my home tonight after ten o'clock?"

"Yes. I'll park my Camry on the next block and walk over. Just in case any nosy neighbors, cops, or reporters are sniffing around."

Seconds after the doorbell rang, Hazel opened her front door. She ignored Hana's outstretched hand and pulled her close in a welcoming hug.

Even at home in the evening, Hazel managed to look elegant. Her brown hair was styled in a French twist. Native American turquoise jewelry dangled from her ears. A matching turquoise beaded necklace hung against the backdrop of a simple gray Princeton sweatshirt. Although her eyes were barely even with Hana's chin, somehow she seemed taller, almost queenly.

"Every day, I think of you and that moment when you told me

Lizzie was safe. I'll be forever grateful." She took Hana by the arm and led her toward seating in the living room.

"I was just doing my job," Hana said. "As I mentioned at the time, the one really responsible for the rescue was my confidential informant when I was working gangs. She led me to the warehouse where Lizzie was being held. I'm glad we could meet tonight. I've never had an opportunity to thank you for exerting influence behind the scenes that got me upgraded to detective."

Hazel shook her head. "No thanks are necessary. Chief Field agreed that, even apart from rescuing Lizzie, your record merited the promotion. He delivered on his commitment just before he retired and was replaced by Chief Mahoney."

The chairwoman waved her hand to underscore her next comments.

"Enough talk about the past. I called you tonight out of concern for recent developments. The president's denunciation of Costello and Jimenez over the China trade bribery highlighted what appears to be the underlying issue in the Ripper killings. As is often the case in my life, the issue has a direct impact on politics."

"National politics, you mean," Hana said.

"And local politics, here in Fairfax, which is key to how Virginia votes, with a ripple effect nationally. To put it bluntly, the protectionists who back Costello have mobilized to attack me. They're using the Ripper case as a pretext. They accuse me of supporting the Fairfax County Police Department on the issue, which is true as far as it goes. My support has been primarily based on your role leading the Ripper Task Force. I have complete confidence in you, and I'm giving the department the benefit of the doubt."

"What doubt? The president gave FCPD kudos, along with Barbara Lacrosse, for uncovering the basis for the blackmail plot."

Hazel stood and began pacing the room nervously, staying silent for a few moments. Finally, she pivoted and pointed a finger at the policewoman.

"While it hasn't surfaced publicly, I've received documents claiming the Ripper investigation is a fraud, orchestrated by the China Future Society, to undermine Vice President Costello's crowd."

Hana jumped to her feet. "That's utter nonsense. There's not a shred of evidence to support such a claim. The documents must be forged."

Hazel's face turned grim. "My political future hinges on how I handle this issue. Can you give me your personal pledge that this accusation is baseless?"

"Yes. I'm absolutely certain. I don't doubt the killings by Jack the Ripper might have some link to the blackmail scheme. But I'm satisfied the Society itself is not the prime mover. Moreover, the department's investigation, from its inception, has been focused on solving the murders of the Chinese American women who were killed. There's no fraud, except for your political opponents trying to manipulate the issue."

The chairman crossed the room and once more hugged Hana. Holding her close, she said, "Your pledge is good enough for me. I'm ready to gamble my future on you."

CHAPTER 67

"Mom, this is Brent," Hana said, when Eriko Brown met them at the front door with a welcoming smile.

"So good to finally meet you, Brent," she said, bowing him into the living room. Uncharacteristically, Eriko hugged him.

She reached out and squeezed her daughter's hand. "For dinner, we're having sukiyaki."

"What's that?" he asked.

"Let's move into the kitchen," Eriko said. "I'll explain while we're getting ready to cook."

She led the way down a short hallway into an immense room at the rear of the house. Through the floor to ceiling windows, the view looked onto a wood fronted with towering Virginia pine trees.

Eriko talked as she moved about the kitchen.

"Sukiyaki is a traditional Japanese dish that is prepared and served in Asian hot pot style, from which everyone shares the food. In Japan, we cooked it in a wok. Now, I use an electric frying pan. Some modern conveniences are better for achieving old-fashioned ends."

She pulled the frying pan out of the cupboard.

"The main ingredient is thinly sliced beef, which is cooked at the table. The beef is simmered in a hearty broth of soy sauce, rice wine, and sugar. We add tofu and vegetables, including shiitake mushrooms, scallions, and Chinese cabbage. A jelly-like thin shirataki noodle adds a unique chewy texture. The cooked meat is dipped in a flavored sauce, next dipped into beaten raw egg, and eaten with rice."

Seeing Brent flinch at the mention of the raw egg, she added, "Enjoying raw egg with sukiyaki is an acquired taste. Trust me, it's better than it sounds."

The fixings for sukiyaki were arranged on a large tray on the table. Hana plugged in the electric frying pan, the center of the action. When the pan was heated, the cooking began.

Hana poured *sencha* into delicate Japanese teacups.

Seated at the large farm table sipping tea, Brent relaxed and chatted. "Dr. Brown, how'd you become a professor at George Mason University?"

The mother waved away the formality. "Call me Eriko."

She stared out the window at the pine trees, as though evoking the past.

"My father was an English professor at Tokyo University, so I was steeped in the best of American and British writing almost from birth. Acquiring the academic background was easy for me. I was fluent in English when Mike and I arrived in Virginia, but I spoke with a noticeable accent. Worse yet, I discovered no one in the States speaks the language the way it's written. I realized the importance of speaking like Eriko Brown, not Jane Austen or Elizabeth Barrett Browning."

"How'd you manage? Your accent is flawless."

"I became addicted to movies and TV. I watched everything. I'm a natural-born mimic with a good ear. In time, I was captivated by the entertainment industry and chose to make that my specialty. Someone in Hollywood heard about my PhD thesis and called me out there to consult."

Brent's apparent fascination with the account encouraged her to continue.

"The movie and TV gurus thought I could show them how to broaden their appeal to Asian audiences here and abroad. I won my spurs as a so-called expert on the Asian niche market. From then on, the moguls sought my advice on mainstream audiences. Today, my most popular class is 'TV and Movies—Windows to the American

Mind.' Universities gloat when their professors are esteemed by the business community. The institution shines with reflected glory, and that inspires dreams of hefty endowments."

Turning the conversation back to Brent, Eriko said. "Tell us some of your experiences with the FBI. I read your book and found the inside story about what the Bureau did and didn't do leading up to 9/11 fascinating."

"I don't often talk about my work, but for Hana's mom I'll make an exception. A special agent's life is organized around cases. We had a series of bank robberies in the Boston suburbs. The gang would break into the home of the bank manager and threaten his family. Two gang members would stay in the house with the wife and children. The other two would accompany the official to the bank, where he would be forced to give them the money so the gang wouldn't harm his loved ones."

"What a cruel way to steal," Eriko said.

"I got involved in a case where the wife and sixteen-year-old daughter were taken hostage. One of the gang members stayed downstairs guarding the mother. The other hustled the girl upstairs and handcuffed her to the head of her brass bed. The crook wasn't much older than his captive. The daughter could see he was growing sexually excited by the situation. She pretended to be attracted to him and suggested he use her camera to take pictures of her lying helpless. She talked him into switching places in order to snap his photo. Once she got the cuffs on him, she gagged him and bound his legs using her pantyhose."

Brent paused to assess how the anecdote was being received. Encouraged, he continued.

"The girl left him on the bed and slipped out the bedroom window, climbing down a nearby tree. From a neighbor's house, she called 911. Police and FBI nabbed the crooks when they came out of the bank with the loot. They easily apprehended the one holding the wife. The moral of the story is, never underestimate teenage girls."

Laughing, Eriko and Hana joked about the discomfiture of the bank robbers.

"What about your teenage years, Hana?" he asked. "You must've been a handful."

"I suppose I was a 'handful' for my grandparents during frequent visits to Tokyo. Like many gifted athletes, I was full of myself. Performing at the highest level in sports takes a lot of ego. That's hard for adolescents to keep under control. I was no exception. My granddad was wise and patient, but I finally pushed him to the limit."

"What happened?" Eriko asked.

"One summer day, granddad took me to see Watanabe sensei at his training camp in the countryside near Tokyo. In itself, that was not unusual. He was always exposing me to different schools of martial arts. What was out of the ordinary was Watanabe sensei was a kendo master and only trained students in Japanese fencing. I was experienced, and, even at the time, was highly ranked in most types of martial arts—judo, karate, taekwon-do, aikido—but I'd never been exposed to kendo."

Eriko leaned forward, not having heard the story before.

"Granddad left me at the training camp. I was cocky. Knowing little of kendo, I reasoned, 'How hard can it be?' The next day, I found out. Sensei observed the training drill. I tried to keep up with the other trainees, all of whom were younger than me since I'd been placed in the lowest group. My performance was dismal. Nothing worked. At every turn, I was beaten unmercifully with a bamboo sword. That night I was so exhausted I could barely crawl into my futon. But sleep wouldn't come. My body pained too much. The next day, the other trainees showed me no mercy. Sensei watched but never said a word. None of my skills seemed to transfer to kendo."

Hana interrupted her reminisces to take a few bites of sukiyaki and to check out how Brent was reacting to the evening. By all appearances, he was relishing the meal and was mesmerized by her anecdote.

"This went on for the first week. The second week, I improved somewhat and only occasionally got whacked. The third week, sensei moved me to the next higher group, and the torture started all over. During the summer, my skills improved, little by little, but the challenges increased. Always a day late and a dollar short. Eventually, I was moved to the highest group and paired with the most skillful teenage girl. I lost the match but escaped being beaten as badly as before."

She was gratified to see Brent smile.

"For the first time, Watanabe sensei spoke to me after practice. He said, 'Today, I was not ashamed to be your sensei.' Never before or since have I felt more pride at anything I've been told by a coach. From that day on, my performance improved."

Tears streaming down her cheeks, Eriko said, "Why didn't you ever tell me about grandad exposing you to kendo?"

"Because I was too embarrassed about the adolescent behavior grandad found a unique way to punish. When granddad came to pick me up at the end of training camp, I wept tears of joy. The hard lesson of humility he'd felt I needed had been pounded into me by a thousand blows with a kendo sword."

CHAPTER 68

Belinda Malik gazed out the window of Shanghai's St. Regis Hotel. The hurry-skurry of small boats on the Huangpu River and the frenetic construction in the mushrooming Pudong District mirrored the confusion of her thoughts.

For hours, she'd been mulling over a problem. At last, she sighed and squared her shoulders. Like a pilot flying past the point of no return, she knew she'd arrived at an irrevocable decision.

She strode into the bedroom and confronted Lucy Mao lying on the bed reading.

Her lover reacted with alarm at her grim expression. "What's wrong?"

"Nothing. Everything. I can't explain. The upshot is I've gotta return to Fairfax."

"You . . . what? Are you crazy? The police are looking for you. They've got this foolish notion you're Jack the Ripper. Raymond is threatening to kill you. In Shanghai, your friends can protect you. Back in the States, you're vulnerable."

"None of that matters. I have to go."

Lucy looked incredulous.

"Why?"

"I can't explain. You have to trust me. If I can, I'll return. We'll move into our condo and have our own view of the river. If not, I'll send for you."

"No way." Lucy's inner turmoil fractured her face in a thousand wrinkles. "Fine. I'm going with you."

"No. You can't." Belinda held out both hands as though pleading with Lucy to stay safe in Shanghai. "I'm going. If you don't want me in Fairfax, I'll stay in New York. I have friends who'll put me up, no questions asked. No one will know I'm back in the States. I'm not going to let half a world come between us."

CHAPTER 69

Lights flashing and siren blaring, Hana pushed the gas pedal to the floor. Racing through Tysons, headed for Great Falls, the gray Camry snaked through traffic. She steered north on Route 123, swinging left onto Old Dominion Drive in the direction of Great Falls National Park.

"You know what we're going to find when we get there," Brent said, putting into words what Hana was thinking.

She grimaced. Frustration overrode logic. She knew arriving a few minutes earlier or later wouldn't matter. Nothing would change the facts. Raymond Malik would still be dead. The killer—Belinda Malik or whoever—would be long gone.

Police cars were positioned on either side of the driveway leading to the billionaire's estate. Light bars illuminated the dark country road like a squad of colored ghosts standing guard.

George Manley was waiting for them outside the wide-open steel entryway.

"Pete's inside. When we got the call, we were just coming back from perimeter duty at Pearl Chen's."

He shook his head, gesturing toward the mansion. "Another bad scene. Two guards were taken outside—one with his throat cut, the other with a knife thrust to the heart. Housekeeper stabbed by the fireplace. Malik gutted in a dining room overlooking the garden. His body mutilated. The chef alerted 911."

"What about the perp?" Hana asked.

"No sign of Jack. We've kept everyone out till you and CSI

arrived. Dr. Williams is on the way."

"Was the gate open when you got here?"

"Gate and front entrance; the whole place was wide open. My guess is Jack somehow fucked the security system. There's no other way to account for the bodyguards being taken by surprise."

The CSI team rolled to a stop outside the gate. Edwina Edison, famous for staying in her beloved lab rather than traveling to crime scenes, jumped down from the shotgun seat of the Ford Expedition and strode over.

Hana hid her shock at seeing the CSI tech in the first group to arrive. "Edwina, we're trying to figure out how the killer got in without raising an alarm. Get some techies from the security company over here. Have them see if there's any CCTV record of what went down."

Edwina hurried off. Hana and Brent shared George's observations with the other CSI techies. Once assignments were made, the detectives moved toward the mansion to size things up for themselves.

Hana tapped Brent on the shoulder, "Start with the grounds. I'll begin inside. We'll compare notes when we join up."

She headed in. Everything appeared to be in order until she reached the sitting room. Mrs. Outerbridge, lying on a blood-spattered rug, was sprawled in front of the massive fireplace. Her white blouse was ripped open, and bloody red crosses decorated her exposed breasts.

Out of the corner of her eye, she saw movement in the library and went in. Pete was quietly talking to the chef, a petite Chinese woman in her thirties who looked about to lapse into hysterics.

Hana motioned to Pete, indicating she would take his place. She slipped into his chair and began speaking to the woman seated in a matching club chair across from her.

"I'm Detective Brown. I know you're upset by what happened."

The anticipated resurgence of sobs continued until the chef, visibly relieved to be able to share her feelings with another woman, regained some of her composure.

Seeking to establish rapport more than to acquire information, Hana asked, "What's your name?" She gave Pete a look not to volunteer what he'd already learned.

"Mary Teng. I am the chef de cuisine."

"Tell me what happened."

A gentle tone and accepting demeanor guided the chef through talking about the horrific events. Mary Teng told her there were three others in the house whom she'd directed to stay in the kitchen. Hana asked Pete to begin taking statements from the staff.

Apart from confirming she'd dialed 911 upon discovering the housekeeper's body, Mary Teng was unable to shed much light on events. The chef was unaware of the deaths outside. She'd not seen the attacker or any stranger on the premises prior to arrival of the police.

Glimpsing the ME and CSI crew enter, Hana called to Wilhelmina Williams to indicate she would return. She escorted Teng to the kitchen to join the rest of the household complement.

When she came back to the sitting room, Wilhelmina was finishing her preliminary examination of Mrs. Outerbridge.

"Judging from the defensive wounds, the victim knew she would be attacked and tried to protect herself."

Wilhelmina pointed to blood saturating a large area of the rug in front of the fireplace.

"The struggle—if we can use the term for such a one-sided assault—took place here. The victim was struck down but would have had time to cry out."

"The chef told me she heard screams," Hana said. "She instructed the other staff to stay in the kitchen and hurried to the scene where she found the housekeeper. She was too terrified to go into the other room to look for Malik."

Wilhelmina turned to Hana. "We'll do a full exam when the bodies get to the morgue. CSI can finish here."

The ME followed Hana to the garden dining room. Malik's corpse was sprawled on his back near the outside exit, which was wide open. His oversized chair lay on its side.

"It must have been knocked over when he tried to extricate his bulk from the throne on which he held court," Hana said.

A crown roast of lamb was growing cold on the lazy Susan. The remains of a dinner feast were a grisly reminder of the entrepreneur's last supper.

Jack's trademark bloody grin was starkly visible below Malik's chin. Slashes across his hands and arms indicated a futile effort at self-defense. His eyes were gouged out. There were numerous stab wounds in the chest. The front of the trousers was cut away, revealing a bloody abdomen and groin pockmarked with deep wounds. The genital area had born the brunt of the savagery.

After a quick perusal, Wilhelmina said, "Help me roll him over."

There were no additional gashes on the back. Lying on the tile, however, was the telltale parchment. Picking up the note with her gloves, Wilhelmina unfolded it.

The message in red portrayed its authorship:

Dear Hana,

It's the kiss-off. A final kiss to say goodbye. You won't have Jack to kick around anymore.

Jack the Ripper

"This one was addressed to you, Hana. Personalizing the note's a switch. Do you think Jack meant this was her last killing in a dramatic swan song?"

"Could be. But we'll need to get Edwina's take. She's the one with the uncanny ability to read Jack's mind."

As though conjured up by the missive, the CSI tech made an appearance.

"Take a look at Jack's latest," Wilhelmina said, holding out the parchment.

Edwina fished her glasses out of her hair and examined the message.

"Jack's through fucking with us."

Pointing to Hana, she said, "It was personal, Jack and you. Right from the beginning—the note she left in your Camry . . ." Mindful of the slip—Hana had been insistent no one must know about the note—Edwina glanced at Wilhelmina to gauge her reaction. The ME raised her eyebrows but said nothing.

The CSI tech cleared her throat. "The rest of us were bit players. Jack challenged you, mano a mano. There's no doubt Jack feels victorious. But there's affection, even nostalgia. The comment about not having Jack 'to kick around anymore' is an obvious take on Nixon's bitter announcement to the media when he implied he was through with public life. Jack may be doing more grandstanding, comparing herself to a former president. But we know Nixon stuck around, until Watergate finished him off. I wonder if this is Jack's way of hedging her bets in case she gets the urge to make a comeback. I hope to God we're through with her. She scares the hell out of me."

"Me too," Hana said, waving at her partner who had just entered.

Edwina held up Jack's message for Brent to read, recapping her interpretation.

He nodded, shifting his attention to Malik whom Wilhelmina had turned over to his original position. Emitting a low whistle, he shook his head in denial. "I won't say I haven't seen worse, but this one will be hard to delete from my memory bank."

One of the CSI crew came to get Edwina. "The guys from the security company are here."

"Don't expect too much. Looks like Jack destroyed the system," a departing Edwina called over her shoulder.

When Edwina returned, she told the group the killer had bypassed the system to the outside gate and front entrance. "Presumably, after killing Malik, she trashed the system and removed all video evidence."

Hana motioned to Brent. "Let's wrap it up. Get Pete or George to take you over to Wang's home. Maybe he has real-time information from Wellerton about the whereabouts of Belinda Malik. If we can verify she's in Shanghai, she's in the clear. If not, she's still at the top of our suspect list."

He nodded.

"I'm off to pay a call on Malik's neighbor, Mrs. Lee, to see if she has the same security system."

CHAPTER 70

Responding to the chime, Cheryl Livingstone opened her front door. Facing the barrel of a gun, she said calmly, "Good evening, Kimberly. You're late."

Cheryl—Victoria, in her youth—showed no surprise at seeing her childhood friend from Taiwan threatening her with a weapon.

Belinda Malik pushed inside. "No one has called me Kimberly in thirty years, Victoria. Why play the *Seems Like Old Times* theme song now? More to the point, why did you insist I return to Fairfax from Shanghai only to walk into a trap? Raymond was killed earlier today. Quite a coincidence, his murder happening just when I'm in town."

"Not a coincidence. I planned it that way."

"You did it. The murders in Fairfax. Jack the Ripper—that's you!"

Cheryl smiled and nodded confirmation.

"I wondered . . . but I dismissed it as too far-fetched. Now I know why the cops have been searching for me."

Majestic in a white cashmere pantsuit with a creamy turtleneck, Belinda looked like an avenging angel. She aimed the pistol squarely at Cheryl's heart. "You put them on to me from the beginning."

"Of course I did. Our destinies are intertwined. They always have been. We're closer than sisters."

"What sister would betray a sibling? You've put me in the hands of the police."

"Nonsense. They don't know you're here. At least, not right *here*. They'll soon find out you've left Shanghai—the Wellertons have been sharing their information with FCPD. But there's no way they can prove you're in Fairfax. You haven't been near a video camera have you? . . . No. I'm sure you've been careful in public places. At the moment, they have no physical evidence to place you at Raymond's estate. How could they? You weren't there. You didn't kill him. You're in the clear."

Reflecting on Cheryl's wording, Belinda did a double take, jerking the pistol.

"Careful," Cheryl said, betraying nervousness for the first time. "That model Beretta has a hair trigger. The safety's off. You could accidentally shoot me."

"If I shoot you . . . I'm tempted to say *when* I shoot you . . . it won't be by accident. You said the police have no physical evidence *at the moment* . . ." She gave the phrase an ominous ring. The dawn of memory lit Belinda's face.

"A few weeks ago, my boot knife disappeared. I thought the cleaning lady must have stolen the knife and some other items, so I dismissed her. My initials are on the handle."

"Your fingerprints too, Belinda."

"You used my knife to kill Raymond."

"And a neat job, if I do say so. You kept the blade honed razor sharp. You've taken good care of the knife ever since you used it to kill your rapists on Everest."

Belinda glanced around the room. "You wouldn't keep such damning evidence here," she said, thinking out loud. "Stored someplace safe. There's no human being you'd trust with something so explosive. If I kill you . . . I've got it. A dead man's switch. You die and my knife is sent to Hana Brown. How'd you manage?"

"Bravo." Cheryl clapped her hands in mock applause. "I thought I might have to explain the trap. Your knife, covered in Raymond's blood, is safely packaged. Your fingerprints and initials will place you at the crime scene. I send an email message every day to a special address. If the email arrives, the package stays put. No email, the package is sent to the Fairfax police. Simplicity itself. A classic dead man's brake. Relax. You're as safe as I am."

"Why?"

"Why frame you, Belinda? Or, why the killings?"

"Why the killings?"

"Many reasons. The women were whores, concubines. Remember the concubines in the houses of our youth in Taiwan? Feeding the desires of the men. Keeping my father's lust burning for the night he came to rape me."

Belinda shook her head. "Jack the Ripper's victims bore no responsibility for what happened to us when we were thirteen." Her placid demeanor gave way to growing emotional turmoil as her face broadcast recall of the horrors, abuse, and psychological damage experienced as a teenager.

"Maybe you're right," Cheryl said. "Perhaps thinking of the women as concubines was just an excuse for executing them. Slaughter takes on a life of its own. I've found I have a taste for butchery. Perhaps you do too. When you stabbed Pierre and Hans on Everest, did you feel the thrill, the power?"

The anguish in Belinda's face told a compelling story.

"Of course. The sex. The knife. You thrust it in. The orgasm comes."

Belinda gasped for air on hearing the replay of her worst moments on Everest. She lowered the muzzle of her weapon and collapsed into a chair. Shaken by the thought she too had become a monster in response to childhood trauma.

Catching her breath, she said, "There's a difference. I stopped."

"Touché. The violence virus hasn't infected you as much as me." Cheryl brushed off her culpability as though shooing an imaginary fly.

She crossed the room, removed a bottle of wine from a small refrigerator, and filled two goblets. She handed one goblet to her visitor and set the bottle on the table between them.

Quickly draining her glass, Belinda poured another, the Beretta forgotten.

Cheryl knew the threat was over. She sat down opposite her visitor. "Regarding other motives, the sensation of power was primary. What an aphrodisiac. To manipulate the political system, bringing down a venal senator and a vice president corrupted by his desire to sit in the Oval Office. To tilt the balance of foreign policy from wrongheaded protectionism toward pragmatic acceptance of free trade."

"Just power?" Belinda asked.

"Those of us, like you and me, who are invested in Asian markets will benefit financially, both in the immediate future and over the long-term."

"You killed them to make us rich?"

"Don't be so high and mighty, Belinda. We both stand to make millions. You think the Robber Barons of the past got wealthy without blood on their hands? But no . . . the money was incidental. You're already rich. I have enough to live in luxury thanks to my trust fund and a recent financial windfall."

Cheryl smiled, delighted at Belinda's discomfiture.

"I committed the crimes because it was the right thing to do. America's national interest was at stake. I had the power to set things right."

"Bullshit," Belinda said. "Now I know why they say, 'patriotism is the last refuge of a scoundrel.'"

"Well, truth be told, I couldn't resist the adrenaline rush of beating the system. Also, the challenge was personal. Hana Brown was my star pupil. From the beginning, everything focused on competition with Hana. I saw a way to place her at the center of the investigation, jerking the Fairfax police around like a puppet master. We were both champion athletes. We missed our chance to win a gold at the Olympics. Murder is another field of competition. Would she catch Jack the Ripper and be a hero? Or would I commit the perfect crime?"

"There's more to your competition with Hana, isn't there?" Belinda said.

Cheryl chuckled. "I could never fool you, Belinda. Yes. There's more. December of last year, Lizzie Jackson was kidnapped—"

"You were behind the kidnapping," Belinda interrupted. "You're Mr. Big, the one the kidnappers claimed masterminded the crime."

"Guilty as charged. I'm Mr. Big."

"You avoided capture and got off scot-free with a five-million-dollar payday."

Cheryl shook her head and took a sip of the wine. "Not quite. Only four and a half million."

Belinda raised her eyebrows.

"The lawyers for the defense of Kun and his girl Friday, who took on the case as pro bono work, received a five hundred-thousand-dollar anonymous contribution."

"You subsidized the defense?"

"Kun and Grace were promised ten percent of the ransom for their role in the kidnapping. Funding their lawyers to ensure the best possible defense seemed the only just thing to do." To Cheryl's mind, honoring her commitment to the kidnappers was the honorable act. She was indifferent to the ignominy of the kidnapping itself.

"What motivated the kidnapping in the first place?" Belinda asked. "Lizzie testified she overheard Kun and Grace discussing killing her instead of setting her free. You must have really hated Hazel Jackson."

Taking a long drink of wine, Cheryl said, "Politics is a dirty business. Politicians must be held accountable for their actions." She clenched her fist, barely realizing she'd done so. "I developed a plan to create a Murder Prevention Institute in Fairfax County. The Institute would have provided employment to thirty experts in the field and would have reduced the incidence of murder and related crimes nationwide. The Institute would have been the crowning achievement of my career. Hazel Jackson used her influence to kill the plan. I vowed she would pay."

Belinda nodded. "I can piece the whole puzzle together now. The real reason you saw Hana as your bête noire was she rescued Lizzie and thwarted what you doubtless believed was the ultimate revenge."

"You always could see through me," Cheryl said. "Hana was a formidable opponent. I had to test her in the ultimate competition. I manipulated the Fairfax police, using her expertise on Asian gangs to ensure she would be chosen lead detective in what was thought to be a simple killing of a gangbanger, but became the celebrated Ripper case. Everything about the case was personal."

"Speaking of personal, why'd you frame me?"

CHAPTER 71

"I had to frame someone," Cheryl said.

"I couldn't very well let the police pin the murders on me. My plan was to keep the authorities off-balance with red herrings and false leads. The shell game was to confuse them about motive and perpetrator. Everyone connected with the Society cried 'Jack the Ripper is out to subvert our institution as a way of attacking China.' In fact, pretending to attack China was a simple case of misdirection. The end game was strongly to China's advantage."

Cheryl continued. "The cops Rambo and Johnston were hung out to dry as suspects. April Kwan was sacrificed to muddy the waters and implicate Rambo. She was a prostitute wannabe but didn't really deserve to die. I feel a twinge of remorse at robbing the world of the best-sellers she would have authored."

"You can write about regrets in your memoirs, assuming you really feel any. It doesn't address the question. Why me?"

"You always were my hole card, Belinda. Once Hana winged me outside Pearl Chen's, DNA alerted the police Jack was a woman. You were the ideal patsy. Raymond's ex-spouse, you two hated each other; antipathy toward the Society, which I exaggerated somewhat in my conversation with the police; expertise regarding China; a mysterious past; violence in your background, culminating in the killings of Hans and Pierre on Everest."

Cheryl ignored the cloud of anger suffusing Belinda's face.

"I fed disinformation about you to Raymond when I helped him with his Asian business dealings. Convincing him you and your former spouse were mortal enemies was child's play. Intense hate is the flip side of intense love. Once Hana Brown involved me in the case as a consultant, poisoning the well was easy."

"You bitch," Belinda said. "You killed Raymond just to pin suspicion on me. More of your shell game. I loved him once, and, even if our love died, I never would have wished him dead. You'll get me charged with his murder."

"Not a chance. The police may suspect you, but they have zero evidence. No probable cause. I was sincere when I said you're in the clear. Even if they pick you up, all they can do is question and release you. Above all, they don't have enough to require you to give them a DNA sample."

"I'll turn myself in and volunteer my DNA. Modern forensics will clear me."

"If you turn yourself in, the package will show up in Hana's mailbox. Police and juries love physical evidence they can understand—like a bloody knife, initials, and fingerprints. Contradictory DNA would get dismissed as pseudoscience mumbo jumbo."

"We have a Mexican standoff," Belinda said.

"No. We have a win-win. The beauty is no one gets hurt. You return to Shanghai with Lucy and enjoy what you two enjoy doing. The Fairfax police will have their suspicions, but nothing they can act on. No one in China will bother you. You'll drop off the police radar, and you can go back to climbing mountains in the Alps. I'll not come under suspicion. There'll be no more Jack the Ripper murders in Fairfax. Everything calms down."

She reached out and touched her childhood friend on the arm.

"I would never have involved you if there were any risk you would come to harm. You're the only person in this world I truly care for, Belinda."

Amazed by the revelation of Cheryl's feelings and relieved at not being under threat of arrest, Belinda relaxed. The tension gripping her body loosened like a tightly coiled spring. She took a nervous gulp of wine.

The doorbell chimed, breaking the silence.

"Quick," Cheryl whispered. "Grab your glass and pistol and hide in the next room."

CHAPTER 72

Standing on the stoop, Hana saw Cheryl blink as she opened her front door. The professor quickly recovered her equanimity.

"Come in, Hana. I wasn't expecting you. Where's your stalwart partner, my favorite special agent?"

"Brent will be along." Hanna felt her cheeks flame. Her professor could still get a rise out of her with the taunt about Cheryl's one-night stand with Brent.

Hana projected confidence, but she had no way of knowing when her partner would pick up the voice mail message asking him to meet her at Cheryl's home. If he failed to show, she had no backup.

Waving Hana into a chair, Cheryl said, "How about a glass of wine?" When her visitor declined the drink, the hostess set her goblet next to the wine bottle on a side table.

"Why this late-night visit, Hana?"

"There've been some developments in the Ripper case."

"Developments?"

Hana realized she couldn't stall until Brent arrived—if he was coming. She shifted in her chair to make her pistol more accessible for a fast draw, watching Cheryl narrow her eyes at the movement.

"Raymond Malik was assassinated today. The killer got in by sabotaging the security system at his estate."

"Malik? I knew his ex-wife hated him, but I never believed she'd resort to murder. Were any clues left at the scene?"

"Not at the scene, no. Just the usual parchment note from Jack."

"The way you word that makes me think there were other clues."

"An-Mei Lee's estate is across from Malik's," Hana said. "He bought the architectural firm who designed her mansion to ensure his was a carbon copy of her place. I visited Mrs. Lee tonight. She confirmed the security network was duplicated. I asked her how she came to select that particular system. She told me you had recommended the security firm and even supervised the installation."

"Of course, I did. According to Mrs. Lee's requirements, that was the best system to do the job."

"You failed to mention you knew the family when Brent and I met with you about Rose Lee's death."

"My connection with the family didn't seem relevant to Rose's killing. I consult with a diverse clientele, with priority given to foreign clients—including a lot of Asians. Rich Asians utilize my services the most. I've dealt with a great many people connected with the case. Those connections mean nothing."

"Maybe not," Hana said. "But knowing Mrs. Lee's setup means you knew Malik's. You had access to the crime scene. That gave you opportunity." She gestured at the display wall. "You're an expert with edged weapons; there's no question about means. We'll have to see about motive. I have to take you in for questioning. Handcuffs are mandatory."

Removing the handcuffs from the holster on her belt, Hana said "Turn around."

Holding the cuffs, she spied movement out of the corner of her eye. Hana whirled toward the rear of the room to see Belinda targeting her with a pistol. Hana leaped to the side, drawing and shooting. She knew she'd hit Belinda but was horrified to discover she'd been shot in turn. The shock wave of a bullet striking her triggered a flashback to Chinatown. Pain flamed in her side. She fired again at Belinda, who staggered toward her.

Cheryl grabbed the wine bottle from the side table and struck the detective on the back of the head. Hana crumpled, sprawling like a discarded Raggedy Ann.

Cheryl kicked the SIG SAUER out of reach, picked up the handcuffs off the rug, and locked Hana's wrists behind her. She probed for the key to the cuffs and pocketed it. She extracted the .38 snub-nose revolver from the detective's ankle holster. Once she confirmed Hana was out cold, disarmed, and secured, she rushed to Belinda and knelt beside her.

"Why'd you come out, Belinda? You could've waited till we left and escaped. I'd never let you be caught. The package . . . was all a ploy."

Belinda displayed a tortured grin. With each labored breath, a red froth dribbled onto the alabaster turtleneck. "You were done for . . . if the police brought you in. I had . . . to prevent that. You see . . . Cheryl . . . I lo . . ."

Noting the light of reason fading from her childhood companion's eyes, Cheryl remembered better times, growing up as teens, in particular a spring afternoon hike when Belinda held her hand and coaxed her ever higher toward a sunset in the Swiss mountains.

CHAPTER 73

Hana heard Cheryl's voice as if in a dream.

"Aha. You're awake at last. I was beginning to think a stimulant might be needed to bring you around. How do you feel? . . . Never mind. We're past the point where that matters."

Hana stirred and, after a brief pause, came fully alert. When she tried to move her arms, she felt the restraints. Her eyes blinked open to a bizarre scene.

Cheryl was framed like a woodblock print, wielding a Japanese Samurai sword. The deadly katana was poised in the air, ready to strike.

"Do you intend to assassinate me with the katana? Rather more knife than Jack the Ripper needed for her other victims."

Cheryl laughed and lowered the katana.

"Ever the cool one, Hana. No. I don't plan to assassinate you at all. We're going to have a fair competition. A duel to the death. Champion against champion."

"How is that fair? Your expertise is the sword. Mine is unarmed combat."

"I'm prepared to grant you an advantage. Rather than fighting unarmed, you can choose any weapon on that wall."

"Do I have the additional advantage of handcuffs?" the prone captive asked sarcastically.

In response, the key was tossed, landing at her feet.

Hana twisted around, groped for the handcuff key, and took her time unlocking the cuffs, mulling the life-threatening predicament.

There was no doubt Cheryl was serious about thinking of this as a fair fight by her rules. A one-of-a-kind Olympic event. Her only chance to survive was to get past the katana and strike within arm's reach.

"Quit stalling, Hana. You could unlock four pair of cuffs in the time you're taking." The fencer pointed to the display. "Pick your sword. Or I'll gut you where you sit."

The captive rose to her feet and stretched, relieved to discover all body parts seemed to be working.

An angry ache in her side was the only reminder of the wound inflicted by Belinda. "You bandaged my gunshot," she said, racking her brain to think how to survive this crisis.

"A trivial flesh wound, but it bled like crazy. Now you'll have two scars on that side. Don't concern yourself about infection. Everything was properly sterilized. Not that you'll live long enough to die of some unpronounceable pathogen."

"What about Belinda? Did she survive?" Hana brainstormed ways to stall for time and prolong the life-or-death encounter.

"No. Your marksmanship was most impressive. I didn't think shooting while flying through the air was possible, except in the movies."

"What was her role in the killings?"

"None at all. She was another red herring dragged across the path to distract you from my trail. We grew up together in Taiwan. In a misguided gesture of friendship and love, she tried to protect me by shooting you."

Cheryl raised the katana.

"We're wasting time. Select a blade now."

Making a quick decision, Hana pulled down the kendo sword.

"Bamboo against steel? You're trying to write a new chapter in Japanese fencing."

One evening at Watanabe sensei's training camp, the master told the story of Miyamoto Musashi, the legendary Japanese "Sword Saint" of the sixteenth century. Hana remembered how sensei explained Musashi was so skilled, he would take on one or more katana-wielding challengers armed only with wooden sticks or a bamboo sword. She uttered a silent prayer to the spirit of Musashi to endow her kendo sword with similar finesse.

Shaking her head, Cheryl reached for the cavalry saber. "Take this instead. At least that way we'd have a contest."

"This is my weapon of choice," Hana asserted.

"It's your funeral. I mean that literally."

The katana sliced the air without warning. A faint humming marked its swift passage through the air.

Anticipating the thrust, Hana moved away in time. She hurled an end table, impeding her attacker's movement toward the right flank.

The long blade swung downward, missing Hana, but cleaving open the back of the chair in which she'd been sitting when she first came into the room.

Attack and retreat, thrust and parry, slash and dodge—the ballet continued. Furnishings in the room were systematically sliced and diced. Each item was offered as a sacrifice to the awesome power of the katana.

Hana was fully alert, her body recovered. But the clock was ticking until she could no longer frustrate Cheryl's superior swordsmanship.

Hana grasped the fencer's strategy as it unfolded.

Cheryl was jockeying for position, to force Hana step by step to the far corner of the room. Once there, with no more options for her to evade the attack, the battle would be joined. The ultimate outcome was preordained. Once cornered, she'd be finished. Steel triumphs over bamboo. She had to gamble while she still had room to maneuver.

It dawned on Hana that Cheryl's stance emulated the classic Western fencer. Her right leg was thrust forward, and she shifted direction with gliding movements.

Hana recalled Cheryl talking about the skiing accident that had weakened her right leg twenty years earlier. Noting the hitch in the fencer's gait, Hana speculated she must have shot Cheryl in the leg when the assassin was fleeing through the woods from Pearl Chen's house.

Despite injury and age, Cheryl moved with authority and poise. But a Japanese fencer would have her left leg forward to balance the two-handed hold on the long katana. Cheryl was off-balance and didn't realize she was compensating.

Acting on that premise, with a quick head fake, Hana feinted right, and dodged left inside the katana's deadly stroke. The bamboo struck Cheryl's right kneecap with a thunderous WHACK.

The excruciating anguish of a blown knee made Cheryl scream, stagger, and almost fall. Rallying quickly, the riposte to Hana's follow-up attack slashed open a gash in the detective's shoulder muscle.

Both wounded, the combatants warily circled each other.

Taking advantage of the lull in Cheryl's aggressiveness, Hana oriented to the center of the room. The benefits of that position were devalued somewhat because the furnishings used for defensive purposes were badly decimated.

With her right leg a near useless appendage, Cheryl had no choice but to lead with the left leg. She shifted the Samurai sword to match the altered approach.

She dragged the wounded right leg behind for some semblance of balance. Her aggressive glide now had the look of a geriatric shuffle. But the katana's edge was as sharp as ever.

Faking right in an echo of the earlier successful feint, Hana darted right. A momentary hesitation in her opponent's thrust was all it took. The kendo sword struck Cheryl's left forearm, shattering the ulna.

Cheryl shrieked from the excruciating pain in her forearm from which the largest bone protruded. But, like a true champion, she shifted her grip to take the full weight of the sword in her powerful right arm. An oblique blow to Hana's thigh drew blood but missed the artery.

Off-balance, Cheryl stumbled and almost fell.

Ignoring the pain in her thigh, Hana saw the opening, pounced, and seized the wrist holding the katana. Pivot and twist. The sword went flying.

Cheryl's right arm fractured under the ferocious assault. Hana threw the fencer on her back.

Hanna's knee slammed into Cheryl's solar plexus and knocked the wind out of her as the fencer's diaphragm convulsed. Air burst out of her lungs like from a child's balloon just released to jet across the room.

Cheryl lay prone and defenseless, breathing in ragged gasps.

An earsplitting crash prompted Hana to swivel in alarm as the front door imploded. Spent from exhaustion and bloodletting, she was not up to another crisis.

George Manley powered into the room, followed by Brent Sasser and Pete Yardley, weapons drawn.

Hana rolled onto her back, gasping for air almost as pitifully as Cheryl who was choking on every breath.

"She's Jack . . . cuff her . . . Mirandize . . ." Feeling consciousness slipping away, Hana racked her brain for something vital she'd forgotten. "Belinda . . . dead . . . innocent."

She mumbled the last words and crawled into a cocoon of hazy delirium.

CHAPTER 74

Completing a meticulous rereading of Hana's medical chart and a cursory exam, Wilhelmina Williams sat near the window and gazed at the patient who looked up bleary-eyed from her hospital bed to stare at the ME.

In her best bedside manner, which her customary clients were unable to appreciate, Wilhelmina said, "You'll live. The staff here have done an excellent job."

"Thanks Hook, for taking care of me. I feel fine . . . a little lightheaded from the painkillers. Otherwise, no problems. The bullet wound in my side is not an issue, thanks to Cheryl's prompt treatment. But I'll have to endure physical therapy for the shoulder and the thigh. The docs tell me there should be no aftereffects once I've done the prescribed therapy."

"You'll be out of here in a few days. Take the painkillers your doctor prescribes. Give yourself time to heal properly before performing any strenuous exercise. You'll be a hundred percent in a few months."

"How's Cheryl?"

"Jack's pretty banged up," the ME said. "One arm has a compound fracture; the larger bone in her forearm was virtually destroyed. A couple of cracked ribs. The real problem is her knee. She'll require extensive surgery, no doubt a full replacement. Not that any of us are going to shed tears over her suffering. She may be in a wheelchair during her trial for multiple murders. The prosecutor's going to ask for the death penalty."

Wilhelmina shifted a glass of ice chips closer to Hana.

"Edwina searched Cheryl's laptop and was able to decode an encrypted file with a complete record of the homicides, including Philadelphia and her early history. The violence stretches back to her childhood. She executed her father in self-defense when he attempted to rape her. Her father killed her twin brother who was trying to protect her. Cheryl and Belinda—Victoria and Kimberly, as they were known in those days—together knifed to death Kimberly's Chinese stepfather, another child abuser. The seeds of the murders in Fairfax were planted a generation ago in a little village in Taiwan."

Still a bit foggy, Hana struggled to take in what Wilhelmina was saying.

"Other motives came into play, primarily her competition with you. Champion serial killer versus champion detective, going for the gold."

Wilhelmina gestured toward the door. "Brent and Lincoln Bartlett are waiting outside. Your mom was here for the past twenty-four hours, but she went home to get some sleep once she heard you were doing okay. Other visitor wannabes are in the waiting room. I'm going to send them all away for now. After you've seen Brent and Lincoln, you should rest. I'll be back tonight to check on you."

Brent entered the room, walked over to the bed, and kissed Hana gently on her cheek.

"You looked on the brink of death when we broke into Cheryl's house. I've been worried. But Wilhelmina tells me you're going to recover fully."

"Where were you anyway? As I was leaving Mrs. Lee's, I tried to call you on your cell and left a message for you to meet me at Cheryl's."

"My phone battery died. When we left Dr. Wang's, I used George's phone. We couldn't reach you. Cheryl turned off your cell and removed the battery. We got concerned and thought it best to retrace your steps. Mrs. Lee told us you took off like a cat with a singed tail when you heard Cheryl did the consulting on the security systems." Brent shook his head in disbelief. "What were you thinking? Going in without backup."

"World-class stupid. The realization came to me when I was standing on Cheryl's front stoop. By then, it was too late."

"Thank God you're all right." He hugged her enthusiastically.

"Ouch. Take it easy, Kong. I'm not up to close encounters of any kind right now. I'm just happy to be alive."

Brent raised his hands in the air to dramatize his intention to handle his partner with care.

"Maybe it's time to share some news. I got a call this morning from Harry Peters, an old friend at the FBI. There's been a shake-up at the Bureau in reaction to the bribery scandal and the fiasco with Barbara Lacrosse. Harry's been moved to assistant FBI director. He's asked me to come back. I've agreed on the condition I be assigned to this area—DC or Quantico. He promised to pull strings and make it happen."

"You won't be working with me any longer," Hana said. "I'll miss you." Her supportive words masked the fact that she was relieved to be rid of the tension from having to deal with a partner who almost always disagreed about important issues.

When Brent left, Lincoln entered the room. He took a couple of steps, hesitated, then stared at Hana, unsure what her feelings were toward him. Was he there as a friend, a onetime date, or a lover in a relationship with a future?

Hana opened her arms to welcome him. Encouraged by the gesture, he crossed to the bed, leaned over, and gently kissed her on the lips.

When the kiss was passionately returned, he exhaled, realizing he'd been holding his breath in anticipation.

"Wilhelmina tells me you're going to recover completely, but you'll need a couple of months to convalesce."

Hana smiled coquettishly. "I have a plan for recovery."

"What's that? Extended therapy?"

"Physical therapy will be involved, but that's not the most important part of the plan."

Intrigued, Lincoln took the bait. "What is most important?"

"According to the cliché of real estate magnates: location, location, location."

Puzzled, Lincoln kept silent, waiting for the punch line.

"I plan to spend two to three weeks at the start of my convalescence in Hawaii—Waikiki to be specific. I'd like you to accompany me. We can swim, walk on the beach, eat at the best restaurants, see the sights, maybe even climb Diamond Head."

Once again, Lincoln held his breath. He knew his next action would shape their relationship, perhaps forever. Facing a career-bending series of deadlines on fast-breaking stories, he was mindful of the risks if he asked his editor Chad Mclanahan to be away at a time the *Post* regarded as pivotal, if not historic.

"I can't think of anything I'd rather do than accompany you. The *Post* owes me an overdue vacation. Waikiki sounds perfect."

Hana laughed, her relief showing through her apparent self-assurance.

"If Hawaii works out, perhaps we can plan a trip to Tokyo. I'd love to show you my grandparents' home when I was growing up."

ACKNOWLEDGMENTS

The author is only one of a huge and largely invisible team that creates a published book. Much of the task is done after the manuscript is written.

I would like to thank John Koehler and his talented team. My editor Becky Hilliker deserves special mention for working with the draft of my manuscript and turning it into a finished novel. This is my second thriller to be published (after *The General's Briefcase*) and I've gained a better appreciation for the skills and hard work involved in the process.

Danielle Koehler was the leader of the effort to create the book cover and has done an outstanding job in designing and improving the author's website. My daughter Nori Jones has played an invaluable role in many aspects of the book's development and marketing. My wife Betty Ann and children (Ann, Jim, and Susan) have been an invaluable cheering section, as have other friends and relatives.

While the principal setting for *Motive for Murder* is the United States, the story has deep roots in Asia. My thanks to friends and colleagues who have enhanced my understanding of China, Japan, Korea, and Asia as a whole.   •

Printed in the USA
CPSIA information can be obtained
at www.ICGtesting.com
LVHW051622080124
768326LV00011B/159

9 798888 241653